Praise for *Blood of the Father*

"Highly recommended"

Blood of the Father is a legal thriller filled with rare, vibrant descriptions that will especially resonate with readers already familiar with the legal system.

Few authors are in a position to as realistically portray the challenges of being a lawyer as lawyer/author Donald E. McInnis.

The story adds to the A.J. Hawke, Attorney at Law legal thriller series, but also stands alone as an outstanding story that blends political, legal, and crime scenarios in an atmospheric and compelling series of twists and turns that challenge Hawke in unique ways.

Readers who enjoy thrillers that examine legal proceedings such as defense-killing strategies and maneuvers will find the in-court and out-of-court descriptions engrossing and the unexpected developments satisfyingly unpredictable.

— Midwest Book Review

A.J. Hawke Legal Thrillers
by Donald E. McInnis

The Sphynx Murder Case

McInnis infuses the intrigue of ongoing investigations with the suspense of courtroom proceedings. Lawyer A.J. Hawke is clever and crafty in the courtroom as he exposes police interrogation tactics.

—Publisher's Weekly Booklife Report

Return of the Sphynx

Editor's Choice: Nail-biting legal thriller. In this second book of the series, scrappy lawyer A.J. Hawke must use sophisticated science, and his fists, to aid a client accused of murder. Great for fans of Scott Turow, Phillip Margolin.

—Publisher's Weekly Booklife Reviews

Nonfiction by Donald E. McInnis

She's So Cold: The Stephanie Crowe Murder Case—A Defense Attorney's Inside Story

In this true-crime account, Donald E. McInnis unveils the truth behind the coerced confessions that nearly sent three innocent 14-year-old boys to prison for a crime they did not commit.

> *A powerful read. . . . Donald E. McInnis does an outstanding job of pinpointing the problems of juvenile prosecution methods. . . . No reader of true crime or juvenile rights should be without this outstanding book. . . . Law professors will find* She's So Cold [second edition] *holds much fodder for classroom discussion and debate.*
>
> —Midwest Book Review

Reader reviews:

> *It was never going to be rated anything BUT five stars! . . . An absolutely fantastic read. Up there with* In Cold Blood *by Truman Capote. I enjoyed it THAT much.*
>
> —Yassemin T, NetGalley

> *If you enjoy mysteries, you will love this. If you want to see why we need more people like Donald McInnis working for us, you will enjoy this. . . . Mr. McInnis does a wonderful job of laying out the facts without prejudice. He simply states what happened. Fascinating read!*
>
> —Maria's Space

> She So Cold *is one of the most harrowing stories I have read. . . . This is a gripping tale of law enforcement gone lawless.*
>
> —English Plus Blog

Blood of the Father

AN A.J. HAWKE LEGAL THRILLER

DONALD E. MCINNIS

J&E Publications
San Diego, California

Published by
J&E Publications
www.donaldmcinnis.com

ISBN-13: 979-8-9865516-3-0

Library of Congress Control Number: 2023915137

Cover design by Timothy W. Brittain

Printed in the United States of America

ACKNOWLEDGEMENTS

In writing this latest A.J. Hawke novel, I had to think back to the many challenges I faced as a young lawyer. Law school does not teach you how the letter of the law should be applied to life's many different predicaments—the kind of situations which lawyers face every day. Drew Hawke faces such real-life circumstances in this latest book in the legal thriller series A.J. Hawke, Attorney at Law.

Thanks to my editor, Larry M. Edwards of Polishing Your Prose—an award-winning author in his own right—for his assistance. He made this manuscript a reality. Through his help not only did he improve the technical aspects of my writing, but he also helped me to convey the true realities a young lawyer faces when dealing with clients and the power politics of the law.

Once again, I thank Timothy Brittain for his excellent text layout and a cover design that is not only intriguing, but also sets the scene of where the reader will go as one reads this novel.

Thank you, M.L. Meurs, for helping me accurately portray the words of a priest communicating with a parishioner during a confession.

As usual, I could not present the interesting and revealing evidence of how Hawke intends to defend his client without the medical expertise of Doctor William Devor, MD. Thank you, doctor, for all your assistance in making this book a true murder mystery.

Blood of the Father

An A.J. Hawke Legal Thriller

CHAPTER ONE

Four O'Clock Monday Afternoon

THE SOUND OF FOOTSTEPS softly echoed off the barren concrete walls of the dimly lit hallway as two men walked from the elevator toward the underground Sanctum. Their features at first barely discernable due to the flickering fluorescent lights. The Sanctum, as it was called by the few who knew of it, was the secret meeting place for the five most influential people in San Diego.

Once at the door, the taller, heavy-set man pulled the twelve-inch-thick, Soviet-era bomb shelter door open and the two entered. Seated at the head of a long narrow conference table was the Presiding Judge of San Diego's Superior Court, Brian O'Shea. To the judge's right sat San Diego Chief of Police James Shaughnessy, and to the chief's right, Morgan Mayfield, the wealthiest man in San Diego.

"Sorry we're late," said Sam Sandleson, the diminutive San Diego mayor. "Bill and I got tied up in a Zoom conference call with the governor. He just called out of the blue." The mayor had no way to tell the others, since the bunker was impervious to cell phones or any other form of electronics.

"Have a seat," directed the judge, pointing to the chairs to his left. "Now, why the urgent meeting?"

The mayor turned to Bill Brodsly, his political advisor and chief strategist. "Fill them in."

The advisor took a deep breath and began. "San Diego County Supervisor Katherine Pansky, wife of United States Senator Nevan Pansky, is rumored to be running for San Diego mayor next year."

"Judge, it's no rumor. It's fact," Mayor Sandleson said. "Two board members tell me she asked for their endorsement for her candidacy. She's definitely running against me. She already has several wealthy backers. The news just hasn't leaked yet."

Brodsly resumed. "Now, I've run three separate polls. One surveyed name recognition of the mayor versus Supervisor Pansky. The second asked how favorably they viewed Mrs. Pansky and Sam. Not only was her name more recognizable than Sam's, but she was favored over Sam by nearly two to one."

"Did your survey specifically say Sam was the sitting mayor?" asked O'Shea.

"Yes, judge. We also asked why they favored or disliked each person. The mayor's name was associated with the Sphynx rapes and trials. They disliked the mayor and the police chief he appointed because the police couldn't capture the serial rapist, and the fact that the rapes were hidden from the public."

"It was an unprecedented situation," interrupted the mayor.

"The point is," replied Morgan Mayfield, "people want a mayor of action just like Mayor John Bacon who took on the most powerful man in San Diego history, John D. Spreckels, the sugar baron. Everybody knows what happened. When Spreckels started tearing up the trolley tracks for his electric railway, Bacon order Spreckels' railway boss arrested."

"But that was a hundred years ago," complained Sandleson.

"It may have been," cautioned the judge, "but the story was recently a two-part series in the *San Diego Herald*. And the local TV stations ran several programs on the man. Just last month KPBX had an hour special entitled 'The Great Leaders of San Diego.' CBMS aired a program last week entitled 'Mayor Bacon: The Man Who Changed San Diego History.' "

O'Shea's rebuke caused the mayor to slump in his chair.

Turning to Brodsly, Judge O'Shea asked, "Did your surveys indicate anything else?"

"Yes, sir. A surprisingly large number, forty percent, blamed the mayor for the prosecution of an innocent college student for the rapes."

"None of this makes sense," spoke up Chief Shaughnessy. "The district attorney chose to prosecute the kid."

"But your officers failed to protect college co-eds at the beaches and arrested the wrong man," countered Mayfield.

Sensing he was the scapegoat, Chief Shaughnessy continued. "That damn Hawke keeps the whole Sphynx mess front-page news. His latest theatrical antic was the MMA cage fight at the Sheraton Hotel."

Judge O'Shea smiled. "I'll say this much, Hawke put on a spectacular show. He's quite the fighter."

With a surprised look, Mayor Sandleson asked, "Brian, did you go to the fight?"

"Sure did." With seeming admiration he went on. "Hawke was indeed the main attraction at last month's fight. The press and TV cameras focused on him the moment he entered the hall. I snuck out the back after he won as everyone rushed to interview or congratulate him."

"If Hawke keeps going the way he is, he'll be the next mayor," snapped Brodsly, putting a damper on the judge's praise for the young lawyer.

"The fact is, gentlemen, the Sphynx rapes are a stain on our police department for which I am held accountable," lamented the mayor.

The Sphynx rapes, were so named because the rapist had shaved off all of his body hair, akin to the hairless Sphynx cat. Not only had the notorious Andrew J. Hawke successfully defended a dead girl's boyfriend, who police said had raped and murdered her, but he also helped identify the actual Sphynx rapist. Hawke had hogged the headlines for weeks, thus embarrassing both the police department and the office of the district attorney.

Before Chief Shaughnessy could defend himself further, the judge looked to Brodsly, "What was Mrs. Pansky's name associated with?"

"That was the subject of my third survey. Her name was associated with the powerful Senator Nevan Pansky, and the fact she has been a very productive county supervisor. Almost every one surveyed thought highly of her and her husband. In other words, the Pansky name is a great asset."

"Gentlemen, unless something drastic occurs, I will lose in a head-to-head race against her," complained the mayor.

"Brodsly, did your surveys ask about any other possible candidates for mayor?"

"Yes, judge, three other well-known possible candidates."

"The results?"

"At this time, none come close to beating Sam. However, with Mrs. Pansky out of the race, there would be some bleed of her supporters to other candidates. Still, Sam seems to be the strongest candidate."

"Judge, what are we going to do? I and the chief kept the lid on the whole rape situation in order to protect our tourism industry. If Pansky gets in, Shaughnessy will be out and where will we be then? Next thing you know, we'll all be investigated," conjectured the mayor.

"Worse than that, gentleman!" Mayfield added. "A new mayor and police chief may discover the projects I've built and which you helped push through city hall. Hell, they may even discover the money we've hidden in the Caymans."

"Let's not panic, guys. The answer is simple. We get rid of Mrs. Pansky."

The four looked at the judge, who stared back at them, his eyes wide with a blaze of conviction.

"You, Brodsly," commanded the presiding judge. The political strategist immediately sat straight in his seat, as if called to attention. "You're the man to do it."

"Do it? No way. If it has to be done, you get someone who knows how. I sure'n hell don't."

The judge stared at the trembling political strategist and smiled. "Calm down, Brodsly. As usual I have to do everything. I'll take care it."

"If you don't mind, judge, how are you going to 'take care of it,' " asked the mayor, "Or should I ask?"

"It's simple. Every man has a weakness. Expose that weakness and you discredit the man and his reputation. In our situation, it is the senator's unsatiable sex drive. You, chief, should know about such things."

A sheepish look came over Shaughnessy, who looked down. But the rest gave a noticeable sigh of relief, especially Brodsly.

"But, Brian," persisted Sandleson, "how do you know about . . . that?"

"Sam, I know about the indiscretions of every powerful person in this state. I make a point of it. That's how I maintain control. Need we go further?"

"No, sir."

"In the meantime, Brodsly, here's what I want you to do,"

O'Shea continued. "You're going to review every single public statement by Katherine Pansky, and every vote she has taken since being elected to the County Board of Supervisors. You know the routine. Gather a team together and turn them loose. Second, you need to hire a group of private investigators to follow her day and night. Even back to Washington, DC, when she travels to be with her husband. Take hundreds of pictures. You never know who we may catch her with. Do the same for the senator. Hire a PI in the District of Columbia."

Turning to the others, the judge said, "Gentlemen, everybody has a skeleton or two lurking in their closet. People of influence are not saints. They always have sullied hands. Power is power, and no one gets power by being a nice guy. Find the dirt and you've got leverage."

The four powerful men at the table looked at each other, and then to O'Shea, who had a smirk on his face.

Finally, Sandleson broke the awkward silence. "Judge, all this is going to be super expensive."

"Sam, you are going to pay for it out of your campaign war chest," responded the judge. "Further, all of us will contribute when it becomes necessary."

Noticing Mayfield's reaction, the judge turned and glared at the man. "Don't give me that look, Morgan. You of all people should be worried. I can see the headlines now: 'Wealthy developer bribes city and county officials. Morgan Mayfield sentenced to fifteen years.' So get with the plan."

Turning to the other three, the judge continued. "We are in the fight of our lives. The five of us have come a long way and made fortunes running this city. We are not going to lose any of it now, much less our grip on the levers of power."

The other four appeared to be overwhelmed. Chief Shaughnessy leaned forward, saying, "I'll contact a buddy of mine who runs the crime units for the DC police department. He may have some dirt on the senator. You never know. If so, we could use it to tarnish the Pansky name."

"Good. That's the spirit," answered O'Shea.

"Judge, I already have a skeleton campaign staff in place for next year. I'll call them together and determine who we need to add to the team and get them started."

"Thatta way, Brodsly." The judge then scanned the faces of the others, one by one, as if he were a coach heading into a championship final. "Men, we've had troubles before and come through unscathed. This situation will be no different. Now let's call it a day. We'll meet here in few days. By then, each of you will have come up with further ideas on how to scuttle Katherine Pansky, if she indeed runs for mayor."

"Yes, sir!" came the resounding reply.

Judge O'Shea stood and gestured for all to leave except Sam Sandleson. As the mayor stood, the judge grabbed his hand. The diminutive mayor stopped and glanced up with a questioning look at the imposing man.

"Shut the door, Sam," the judge ordered as the last of the other men walked out. After Sandleson closed and locked the door, the judge continued. "As soon as the ship starts to sink, this group of loyal comrades will run for the lifeboats. Mayfield, and even Brodsly, will probably go to the district attorney or the Feds and spill all in an effort to strike a deal."

The mayor started to speak but the judge raised a finger to his lips. In a low voice, O'Shea continued. "I've got an attorney in the Caymans to whom I gave my power of attorney. I have instructed him to take certain actions in order to protect our secret bank accounts. If any of the gang tries to withdraw money, he is to transfer all accounts to another bank in the Seychelles, where I am the only signatory."

Shock creased the mayor's face. "Do what? How did you arrange—"

The judge interrupted. "Sam, I set up the accounts, remember? The important thing is no one will run if they don't have the money." The mayor relaxed slightly as comprehension sank in. "So you get my drift. The current situation will be the closest we've come to losing control. If we do, the public will want blood. The only way we come out of this is if we stay together and fight as a team."

Sandleson nodded in agreement. Then O'Shea added, thumping his fingers against the mayor's chest, "You, Sam. If she runs for mayor, you are the key for us getting through this situation. Once we discredit Katherine Pansky, you'll be re-elected. There's got to be something hidden we can find that will ruin the Pansky reputation, whether it's her or the husband. It may take us a while to find it. Remember, I know how to wield power and ruin lives. In the meantime, you have to organize an aggressive campaign and be the backbone for the five of us. If you stay strong and confident, the rats will not get nervous. Got it?"

"I understand, Brian. As usual you have thought this out well and planned ahead."

"Don't try to flatter me, Sam. The facts are what they are. We will deal with the consequences as they come. I will tell you when to throw the towel in. There are millions stashed away. Enough to ensure we all keep our mouths shut. Without an informant, it is virtually impossible for any new mayor or prosecutor to prove anything. We've covered our asses well by making the city council approve everything and through rulings on questionable issues by judges. Judges I control. There is no way collusion can be proven unless someone opens their damn mouth."

"You're right, Brian. Mayfield is the weak link. I'll keep his confidence up and, if necessary, threaten his ass if he begins to faulter."

"Careful, Sam. Remember, he has more money than us. But Morgan's a greedy son-of-a-bitch and won't want to lose any of the cash stashed away in the Caymans. Talk to me first before you do anything. I have other contingency plans in place to ensure he and the others keep their mouths shut. It's not over until I say it's over. Understand?"

"Yes, Brian. All I ask is you handle this in such a way that my reputation stays intact. I have children."

"You've got my word."

CHAPTER TWO

One Week Later

SANTA ANA WINDS GENTLY MIXED with cool ocean breezes, attracting thousands of tourists to the coast. Once again America's Finest City offered up its best weather with temperatures fluctuating between the mid-sixties at night to the low eighties during the day.

This Monday morning a light offshore breeze blew against the ocean's rising swells, helping to create four- to seven-foot wave conditions. The locals were ecstatic. All they could talk about was the size of the long corduroy swells forming fifty to a hundred yards off Mission Beach and Pacific Beach. As the surf rolled toward shore, the rising sea floor created a glassy barrel for the men and women playing hooky from school and work. Yells of joy could be heard from the surfers as they rode, crouching within the 'greenroom' of long, perfectly breaking waves.

"Man, not a crumbly or dumpy wave. Just off the hook," said one young man lying exhausted on the sand. Andrew J. Hawke, carrying his surfboard and dripping wet, acknowledged the teen's enthusiasm with a broad smile and a *shaka* as he trudged through the warm sand toward the Pacific Beach boardwalk.

Later, in the Gaslamp Quarter, Drew sat in his law office at the George J. Keating Building. After surfing, he had a late breakfast and took a few minutes to catch up on the news. With his feet propped up on the desk, the young man perused a special edition of the *San Diego Herald*. The frontpage screamed in large boldfaced letters:

U.S. CONGRESSMAN DEAD

SAN DIEGO—Paramedics declared a U.S. senator dead at the scene in a La Jolla residence last night after responding to a 911 call.

The medical response team found California Senator Nevan Pansky lying on the floor of the den of his home with a head injury, unconscious and unresponsive to their attempts to revive him.

Senator Pansky was elected to Congress in 1994 and served on the Senate Foreign Relations Committee. The Senate Majority Leader could not be reached for comment.

After calling emergency services, Senator Pansky's wife, San Diego County Supervisor Katherine Pansky, had attempted to revive her husband before the paramedics arrived, according to a San Diego Police Department spokesperson.

Supervisor Pansky, upon hearing that her husband was dead, became hysterical and flung herself onto her husband's body. As police officers struggled to pull the woman off her husband, she fainted and struck her head, the spokesperson added.

A second team of paramedics took the woman to Sharp Memorial Hospital for treatment. Her injury was described as "not life threatening."

Hawke read tribute after tribute to the senator, grandson of the fabled U.S. Senator Theodore Pansky. The *Herald* traced the history of the Pansky family and its long line of public service in the United States Congress. The paper noted Nevan Pansky's great contributions to his beloved San Diego. The San Diego Chamber of Commerce president praised how Nevan Pansky had ensured San Diego remained the Navy's command center for the United States Pacific Fleet. Millions of dollars annually poured into San Diego as a result. The economy flourished due to the hundreds of thousands of military personnel who made the city their home. The once dying ship construction and repair industry boomed in the South Bay due to Senator Pansky snagging tens of millions of dollars in naval contracts for the city. Local corporations were awarded millions more in weapons development, stealth technology, military satellites, and telecommunications research and development. The San Diego area unemployment levels were at record lows.

Environmentalists lauded Pansky for his foresight and leadership regarding pollution, the congressman's support for coastal fish farms to replenish the ocean's salmon and other endangered fish. His stand on climate change was unrivaled.

Drew marveled at the accomplishments of the man and mumbled, "No wonder Pansky was projected to become the next Senate Majority Leader." As Hawke read further, the reality of the senator's death became clearer—death by gunshot to the head. An apparent suicide.

Suddenly, the intercom to Hawke's phone buzzed. He picked up the receiver. "Yes, Debbie."

"Drew, a Mrs. Katherine Pansky is here to see you."

"The woman who just lost her husband?"

"Yes, Drew. The one and the same."

"I'll be right out."

As Drew opened his office door, a woman in her early fifties, dressed in a black suit with a cream-colored blouse, rose to meet the lawyer.

"Mrs. Pansky?"

"Yes, Mr. Hawke."

"Good morning. What can I do for you?"

"I need to talk to you . . . in private."

"Absolutely. This way." The lawyer gestured to the conference room to her right.

Drew went to the head of table and pointed to one of the chairs to his left, "Please, have a seat." Once they were seated, the young attorney spoke in a consoling voice, "I'm sorry to hear of your husband's passing."

To Drew's surprise the woman responded, "I'm not."

Hawke was taken back by her curt and seemingly uncaring remark.

Before he could inquire further, she added, "I'm here to retain your legal services." She handed the astounded attorney a cashier's check for $200,000 made out to Andrew Jackson Hawke. At the bottom left, in the notation area, it read in hand print "Legal services."

The attorney leaned back in his chair. "Mrs. Pansky, I don't understand."

"Are you going to be my attorney or not, Mr. Hawke?"

"If you need legal assistance with your husband's estate, I can refer you to an estate attorney. I specialize in criminal law."

"I'm here, Mr. Hawke, because I need a criminal attorney and I believe you are the best."

Hawke placed the check on the table in front of him and leaned forward, putting his arms on either side of the check.

"Mrs. Pansky, attorney-client privilege attached the moment you came in here. Do you mind if we start over?"

The woman had a slight tremor to her hands and she appeared quite distressed. The skin underneath her eyes seemed to be darkening. Then Mrs. Pansky pulled a tissue from her purse and wiped her sweaty forehead, then nodded in agreement.

Drew rose, walked to the conference room door, and closed it. "I think we can now talk candidly Mrs. Pansky. Why do you need an attorney?"

In the outer office, the hallway door opened suddenly and a well-built, twenty-something man dressed in a pair of jeans and a tight, muscle-revealing T-shirt, hurriedly stepped in.

"Can I help you?" questioned Debbie McCaleb, the office manager.

The man looked around, then headed toward the conference room, opening the door before Debbie could say anything. "Mom, you alright?"

"Yes, Nat. Mr. Hawke this is . . ."

"What do you want?" demanded Drew as he rose from his chair.

"It's okay, he's my son, Nathan," interrupted Katherine.

Without recognizing the attorney, Nathan pulled out a chair next to his mother and sat down.

Drew, still not amused by the man's rash action, looked to Mrs. Pansky. "I'm sorry, Katherine, this is not how I do business. Your son will have to leave. Nathan, please have a seat in the lobby."

Drew turned to Debbie, who stood at the conference room door. "Please show this young man where to wait."

"It's okay, Mr. Hawke," the youthful man said. "I'm a law

student and I'm here to help my mother." He then took up his mother's hand and squeezed.

"Congratulations, Nathan. What year?"

"I start my second year this fall."

"Great. Then you know about attorney-client privilege. Since I will not represent you, please have a seat outside so your mother and I can have a private consultation."

"I know a non-client, third-party presence will jeopardize that privilege. But you will be representing both of us."

"Sorry, kid, I don't work that way. Please step outside," Drew responded as he pointed toward the door.

Before Nathan could protest Katherine spoke up. "That's okay, son. Wait outside. I will talk with Mr. Hawke about that."

The boy shook his head. "Mom that's not what we planned."

"I know, but go ahead and wait."

As Nathan walked out he turned and said, "Don't forget what I said. Stick to our . . ." the man caught himself as his mother shook her head.

"Nathan, please pull the door closed," added Drew.

Once the door closed, Drew turned to Katherine and asked, "What is all this about?"

"I'm sorry, Mr. Hawke, he is just being very protective of me."

"He seems to be more involved than just protective."

"If I can explain, things will be much clearer."

"Okay, but no more surprises. Is anyone else coming in?"

"I understand, Mr. Hawke. I apologize for all this. But I really do need your help."

"Then . . . I believe my question to you before he interrupted was, why do you need a criminal attorney?"

"Yes . . ." The woman paused and looked down as if summing

up courage, then stated, "You see, I killed my husband. I need you to arrange for my surrender to the police and help me through what happens after that."

A silence hung over the room as her words penetrated.

"Why do you believe you killed your husband?"

"I shot him."

The young attorney, still somewhat overwhelmed by the bluntness of the revelation, asked, "Why did you shoot him?"

"He once again raped our daughter, Lydia. I told him four years ago I would kill him if he attacked my girl again."

"When did your husband first have sex with your daughter?"

"I found out about my husband when Lydia was sixteen. I was talking to her about where she wanted to go to college. Lydia said she wanted to go to Saint Mary's University for women in Los Angeles or to a college in Australia. I asked why Saint Mary's. She said the nuns would protect her. When I asked why Australia, Lydia said it was far away. That's when I knew something was very wrong. So I kept asking questions."

"Excuse me, Mrs. Pansky. I know this is difficult for you, but I have to ask, is this when you learned about the incest?"

"Yes. After about thirty minutes or so she broke down in tears. When I asked if Daddy had done something wrong that's when she told me."

"Were there any signs your husband may have been sexually abusing your daughter before this or were you totally clueless?"

"Surprised? Hell no!" Raising her voice, she added, "That man has been a cheating son-of-bitch ever since I've known him. When we met in college, he had a reputation for seducing anyone he could. Women were always an object of conquest to my husband. I don't know why I married him."

"Did Lydia say when it all started?"

"Yes, around thirteen. After she began having periods. I should have known then when she kept asking me about birth control. I just . . . I just . . . oh, God." Tears ran down her checks as she lost her composure.

Between sobs she choked out, "Sorry . . . this is . . . this is all very difficult . . . I told myself I would be strong when I came here . . . my apologies."

It took a few minutes for Mrs. Pansky to compose herself. Drew walked over to the conference room credenza for water and tissue. As he turned to offer her the box of tissue and a Perrier, he noticed Nathan staring intently. Drew resumed his seat and said nothing.

"I blame myself . . . for all this, Mr. Hawke . . ." she said between sips of water to clear her throat, "I should have done something earlier."

She went on to explain that Nevan has always been a sexual monster. She filed for divorce several times because of his extramarital affairs, but stayed for Nathan and Lydia's sake. After she confronted him about Lydia, he promised he would never touch her again.

"Did he?"

"Nevan lived part-time in Washington, DC, and when he was home, everything appeared okay. But predators never change. Every time I was in Washington, his staff quietly informed me about his relationships with young interns. Or should I say, ambitious whores."

Drew nodded as if knowing how deeply the woman was hurting. Her venomous words exposed how long she had kept such strong feelings bottled up.

"Like Nat said," she continued, "my son just completed his first year of law school at the University of San Diego.

I'm so proud of him. Lydia is an undergraduate at USD and lives near campus with him. I thought she would be safe with Nat. I never believed Nevan would have the balls to attack his own daughter again, especially in our house. Obviously, I was wrong about the bastard."

A perplexed look encased the attorney's face. He settled back into his chair and looked away from Mrs. Pansky while he slowly raised his right index finger up and down on the arm of his chair. After a moment, he spoke.

"Mrs. Pansky, the newspaper said your husband took his own life. The police found him on the floor slumped against his den desk with a gun in his right hand."

She looked coldly at the lawyer without responding. Then, in a very determined and calm voice, the woman asked, "Do you want the case or not, Mr. Hawke?"

The two sat there in deep eye contact, neither saying a word. Attorney Hawke finally broke the silence. "I will represent you, but there are two conditions."

A totally surprised look came over her face. "Conditions?"

"First, I'm not accustomed to rolling over and pleading a client out, especially to prison. So . . ." He paused, knowing she was distraught and had a need to cleanse her conscience. "When people commit a serious crime, like you, many need to confess what they did. I understand that. But if I am to do my job, I need to know all the facts so I can best advise what to do."

The woman had a look of consternation on her face. Drew knew she didn't like what he just said, but he continued.

"When you tell me all the circumstances surrounding your husband's death, I can then construct a scenario or defense that might mitigate the consequences of your act. By mitigate I mean get you an acquittal or a vastly reduced punishment."

As the attorney tried to explain what he would do, he noticed Mrs. Pansky sat listening, but her arms were folded, a physical reaction Hawke had seen dozens of times when talking to jurors. The meaning? Not buying what was being said.

"Mrs. Pansky, maybe I could say things another way. May I?"

She answered with a slow nod.

"It's the difference between a preplanned murder with a sentence of twenty-five years to life, or say an act of defense of yourself or your daughter, which could result in an acquittal. Another possibility is you acted out of an understandable anger provoked by your husband's actions. This could result in a charge of manslaughter; again there would be a vastly reduced sentence."

"But, Mr. Hawke, I came here for your assistance to plead guilty. That is what I want to do."

The attorney responded, "To what? A life sentence or a lesser offense that allows you at some point to get out of prison and be with your children and even your grandchildren before you die."

The woman's face softened as she unfolded her arms. "Go on."

"I totally understand, ma'am, how much pain you are in, but to be frank, I have to sleep at night. I can't do that if I willy-nilly go about pleading people guilty without understanding the full story. So why don't you let me do what I am trained to do. Allow me to know all the facts of your marriage and how things culminated Sunday night when you shot your husband. Then I can tell you what your choices are and what you will probably face as punishment."

"And the second condition . . . if . . . if I agree?"

"You have to move out of your home immediately. We will say you can't live in the house where your husband died."

Drew explained that he had several safe houses around the county that he had rented for clients while he investigated their cases. Homes outside of the city so the paparazzi couldn't find them. It would give him time to see and evaluate what physical evidence the police had found so far.

"One other thing," he continued. During your seclusion I will decide what the public should be told about your actions. Public opinion is an important factor in how jurors and judges prejudge a case. All this is part of my job. But I assure you the final decision on everything I do is always yours."

"I also need you to represent my son, Nathan."

"That's an impossibility. I can only represent one client at a time. I will represent you for the murder of your husband. I can't represent your son also, even if he were involved. He will have to get his own attorney. Is he involved in the murder?"

A shocked look came over her face. "Oh, no! No, Nathan and my daughter are not to be involved in this in any way. I forbid you to even talk to them. They can't be traumatized any further."

"If they can help in your defense, I will need their assistance."

"No. No." Tears began to run down her cheeks as the woman shook her head. "If you insist, I will just turn myself in and do this on my own."

"I see." *Best I wait on this issue until I know more,* the attorney thought. "Mrs. Pansky, I will try to keep your children out of this mess. But, they should get their own attorneys. We can discuss how to do this later. For now, how about my terms. Do you agree to allow me to investigate this matter so I can best advise you on how to proceed? I know you love your children, but being locked away from them as they grow up is a punishment no mother should willingly agree to if there is another way."

The woman cast her eyes down and then, looking straight at Drew said, "Alright, Mr. Hawke, I agree to your terms. But I am afraid it is too late to put off my statement to the media."

"What statement?"

"I had my secretary call the press and TV stations and inform them I caused my husband's death and wished to make a statement at one p.m. I'm sure the vultures await now. So you see? I really do need your help."

"How could you do such a stupid thing, Mrs. Pansky?"

"I told you I needed your services. Now you know why. Thank you for accepting my case. It is a great relief to know you will be by my side."

"I did not agree to this."

"You said there are two conditions, which I accepted. You can decide later if I plead or stand trial. That decision I leave to you."

"Katherine, anything you tell the media will be used against you at trial. There is no way I can beat that."

"Mr. Hawke, I can't turn back now. If you find a defense which justifies or mitigates my killing the bastard, then I give you full permission to do whatever you can. If you need more money, I will gladly pay. Please, sir, just do your thing. All I ask is you be thorough and creative."

"Money is not the question, Mrs. Pansky. You have basically sealed your fate and deprived me of any chance of defending you."

"Mr. Hawke, an attorney does more than defend. He also stands by his client while justice is meted out. I will need someone to stand by me and give me the courage to meet my fate with dignity. I beg you . . . do not desert me now."

As Drew looked into her determined face, he thought, *My God, this woman is one magnificent creature. She is about to ruin her life and what could have been a wonderful career of public service, all so she can be held accountable for her terrible act.* Drew tried one more time, "Katherine, you needn't do it this way."

"It's too late, Mr. Hawke. I believe they are outside your building right now. Please give me your strength and help me through this."

"Alright."

Drew got up, opened the conference room door, and walked up to her son. "Nathan, I am representing your mother."

The man grabbed Drew's hand in a very firm grip and shook it vigorously. "Thank you so much. My father deserved everything that happened to him. She has put up with too much too long. Please protect her."

"I will do my best, Nathan. But for now you have to leave. Your mother said that the media is coming here."

"Yes, I know. They were setting up their cameras when I came in."

"Then you need to get out of here. I don't want you making any statements to anyone about the murder, your mother, or anyone. You hear?"

"Yes, sir. How do I get out without them seeing me?"

"Debbie, tell Nathan how to use the back entrance. Katherine and I will be in my office. I don't want to be disturbed."

"Yes, Mr. Hawke," Debbie responded in a business-like voice, as if the situation was one the office manager was used to resolving.

CHAPTER THREE

1:43 p.m.

DREW HAWKE AND KATHERINE PANSKY were still talking when the intercom on his phone buzzed.

"Yes, Debbie?"

"There's a horde of rude reporters in the office asking for Mrs. Pansky. They won't leave. Should I call the cops?"

"No, Debbie. Tell them Mrs. Pansky and I will be right down to make an announcement. Make sure they leave the office and go downstairs."

"I'll try my best."

"And, Debbie, send in Matt." Drew then faced Katherine again. "You're going to do what we've talked about, right?"

"Yes. I just read the statement you've written and say nothing more."

"Nothing more, Katherine, you hear me? Nothing more! And, you will answer no questions. And don't smile. If you need to cry, it is perfectly okay. Tears at this point are natural, if not expected. After you read your brief statement, I will take over and answer a few questions and then send them on their way."

The emotionally drained woman nodded.

There came a knock at Drew's door.

"Yes?"

"Boss, it's me."

"Come in, Matt."

"Has the media left?"

"Oh, yes. Debbie shooed them away."

The two talked briefly and Matt left. Drew and Katherine waited a few minutes, then walked out of the office. When they got to the end of the hallway, two photographers waited. Drew paused to allow them to take photographs, then directed them to proceed ahead.

As attorney Andrew J. Hawke and Supervisor Katherine Pansky approached the glass doors of the Keating Building entrance, Mrs. Pansky grabbed Drew's right bicep and squeezed it tightly. She suddenly stopped and laid her head against the young attorney's shoulder. Drew motioned the two photographers who were still taking pictures to go outside. He then wrapped his arm around the woman's waist.

"Steady, Katherine. Take deep breaths. Tell me when you're ready."

The two stood there as television camera lights clicked on, shinning a blinding light through the glass doors. Mrs. Pansky took several deep breaths, straightened her posture, and adjusted her suit coat.

"Do I look alright?" she asked as she brushed back a loose hair.

"You look wonderful."

"Now, Mr. Hawke . . ."

Drew pulled open the door and they walked out to the glare of lights and a throng of reporters. The crowd spilled out onto F Street amongst four TV remote broadcast trucks with their elevated satellite antennas. Drew stepped up next to his brave client and asked for quiet.

"My apologies for being late in coming down. Mrs. Pansky has a brief statement to make."

Raising a sheet of paper, she began, "I am here today . . ." She cleared her throat. "I am here today to tell you that I am the cause of my husband's death." A murmur rose amongst the reporters. But the crowd silenced one another. It was so quiet that those in front could hear Mrs. Pansky's deep breaths. She continued.

"I stayed in a troubled marriage far too long. Things became nearly impossible after I learned Nevan was molesting my daughter. When I confronted him, he promised never to touch her again."

She paused as she choked up. Her eyes welled with tears. She took another deep breath and looked at Drew, who nodded in support. The crowd of reporters stood in stunned silence.

"I stayed, hoping to keep the family together and, at my insistences, safe. This Sunday I caught Nevan sexually attacking my precious child. That is why he is dead." She cleared her throat once more as she tried to gain control of her emotions.

With tears running down her cheeks, she was barely audible as she continued. "I have retained the services of Mr. Hawke to arrange for my surrender to the police. I ask . . . I ask that you respect the privacy of my children and in particular that of my daughter. She is truly the victim here and should be treated with all due respect. Thank you."

A flurry of questions came from the reporters. Drew stepped forward. He pointed to Jack Zane, the reporter for the *San Diego Herald*.

"Yes, Jack?"

"Mrs. Pansky, did you shoot the senator?"

Drew responded, "I have instructed my client not to answer any questions at this time. Jack, I hope you and the rest of the reporters here understand why and will accept what has been told to you today as just the beginning of a long dialogue, which I intend to keep you well informed on. There will be plenty of time for all the facts of this tragic event to come out. Obviously, at this time, Mrs. Pansky can't say anything further. Thank you for coming. I will be talking to you shortly."

Jack Zane hurriedly asked, "Drew, please! I have a question for you."

"Yes, Jack."

"I believe you have an ex parte hearing this afternoon before Judge Brown. Is it about this case?"

"Well, Jack, I'm surprised you know about that. Yes, I do. I also assume you know that it is about the autopsy of Nevan Pansky."

"Does that mean you also represent the estate of the dead senator?"

"No. Attorney Randall Wright has agreed to represent the estate, and he will also be present at the ex parte hearing. I have also notified county counsel and the district attorney's office about the hearing."

Jack persisted. "Are you going to observe the autopsy?"

"Obviously, whenever a person dies under questionable circumstances that involve a client of mine, I want to be present and even have an expert present at the forensic autopsy."

Drew, are you saying someone other than your client killed the senator?"

Without answering the reporter's question or the volley of other shouted questions, Drew turned and escorted Mrs.

Pansky back into the building, but not upstairs. The two walked down a hallway until they were out of sight and exited the back of the building to an old VW bus with a beach scene mural painted on its side.

Drew slid open the side door. "Watch your step, Katherine."

Drew then stepped in and pulled the door closed. "Matt, drive slowly so as not to attract attention."

ooooo

5:30 p.m., Aboard the Artful Dodger

"Ahoy, there!"

"Pat?"

"Permission to come aboard the Titanic, captain?"

Drew took three steps up the companionway leading from the below deck cabin to the cockpit of his sailboat. There he welcomed Pat De Luca, his longtime friend and valued private investigator, who had responded to Drew's request for an urgent meeting at the Harbor Island marina.

"Pat, why do you always act like this boat is some luxurious ill-fated yacht?"

"Hey, enjoy my exaggerated praise for this old barge."

"Now that's being a little critical of the Artful Dodger."

"Let's face it, even Fagin would pass up this forty-year-old Columbia sloop."

"Ouch. Now my feelings are hurt. Come on down," Drew added with a smile.

The two laughed and hugged as Drew gestured for him to sit at the cabin's dining table.

"So what's the rush to meet? Is it about your spectacular news conference with Katherine Pansky?"

"So you've seen her brief statement."

"That's all there is on the news. The stations even interrupted normal broadcasting to show it. What in the world have you gotten yourself into?"

"Not sure, Pat. I think she's not telling me the whole story. Katherine claims she shot her husband. Yet the newspapers say it was a suicide."

"As you know, Drew, initial appearances of a crime scenes don't always tell the full story. That's where the crime-scene experts come in."

"I know. But things just don't add up."

"How so?"

"She hired me to help turn herself in. The reason she gives for killing her husband, though understandable, doesn't match her emotional state when the police found her frantically trying to save the man."

Drew wondered aloud why would she stay with Pansky when she knows he maintains sexual relations with his young Washington, DC, interns. Worse yet, why stay married after she learned he sexually assaulted her teenage daughter for years?

"Think what that does mentally to a child, knowing the man who molested her was still living in the same house. No mother would put her child through that," he added.

"She told you all this?"

"Yes."

"And that's why I'm here?"

"Correct. I need you to poke around and find out what surrounds the death and if the police suspect it's not a suicide. Before the autopsy happens, I would like to know what the police know and what they've told the county medical examiner about the case. Can you help me on this?"

"Sure. The coroner owes me a few favors. I'll also check with my old police partner, Sergeant MacNeal, and see what the police are thinking."

"Great. I was hoping you'd say that."

"Where is Mrs. Pansky now?"

"Matt took the woman to Liz's apartment for the night. To-morrow, Liz and Matt will take Katherine to a safe house in Poway. I will hide her there until I find out what the police are going to do."

"Who is going to look after Mrs. Pansky?"

"Liz will. She will check in on her every day."

"Who do you have watching the safe house?"

"Ah, what do you mean?"

"Until we understand how and why the senator died, I think it best to have her under close surveillance."

"Really."

"Yes. With your permission I'll have some PI friends set up a twenty-four-hour watch."

"I guess it's a good idea."

Drew wrote down the address on a notepad, tore off the top sheet of paper, and handed it to De Luca. "Should I tell Katherine you will arrange security for her?"

"No, don't. I think it best she not know. Let's see what she does and if she meets anyone."

"Wow. This is getting complicated. What if she becomes suspicious?"

"If she sees the PIs, just tell her they are there to keep the paparazzi away. Okay?"

"Sure."

The two talked further about the PIs, then Drew changed the subject.

"Ah-h, on a personal note. I met this woman a few weeks back. I don't think she's a local. She has long black hair, silky, tanned skin, stands about five-nine or -ten. Very self-asserting but in an attractive way. Last time I saw her, she was wearing a skin-tight red dress. She's not the normal San Diego Pacific Beach woman. You know the type, overly flashy with dyed blonde hair and always self-absorbed with their looks. This lady had a different air about her. Have you heard of anybody new coming to town that might fit that description," Drew asked in a nonchalant way.

"Absolutely. How about a couple thousand tourists," Pat replied with a big smile.

"I knew I shouldn't have asked."

Pat got serious. "Where did you see this lady and what's her name?"

"I don't know her name. I met her at the fight almost a month ago. A fight, by the way, you did not attend."

"I've told you a thousand times your brain is too valuable to be fighting some young punk who is trying to prove himself."

"I hear you, but this Chris guy was easy."

"They all are until you get tagged. Hear me once again—it only takes one lucky punch to put you down."

"You're right, Pat. How about we put a cap on this. How's Lauren?"

"She's fine. But when I told her about the cage fight, she demanded I not encourage you by going to it."

"Oh, I see. Just tell her I'm fine."

"She won't believe me until she sees you in person. You know how she worries about you."

"I know."

"Drew, I don't think you do know. You can't raise a teenage boy without worrying night and day about him. I got all sorts of grief when I sent you off to Thailand. Lauren now blames me for all your fights. She didn't sleep for months after your concussion from fighting the Sphynx."

Pat didn't have to remind Drew that he and his wife, Lauren, had basically adopted him after the death of his mother, who had never revealed to her son the identify of his father.

"You know I love the two of you," Drew said.

"We know you love us, but every time you step into that cage for a fight I get a world of shit."

"I'll come to dinner soon and smooth things over."

"When you do, don't talk about the fight. And be prepared for a grilling about your love life."

"What! Is Debbie talking behind my back again?"

"They talk all the time."

"Christ. I told her to keep her big yap shut."

"It's a woman thing. When you love a child, you worry about them all the time, less so when they get married. It's like passing the worry baton to another woman who now loves you equally."

Desperate to change the subject, Drew asked, "Pat, how about a beer?"

As the two pulled the tabs on their beers and had the first sip of the ice-cold brew, Drew changed the conversation.

"I read your report which staff attached to a memo on the SMA Construct v. C.T.I. case. How did you find out Mayor Sandleson and Morgan Mayfield are part of a corporation that owns C.T.I.?"

"While I was in the Caymans, I got lucky," Pat replied. "I found signed affidavits certifying Sandleson and Mayfield as the principal officers of the New Jersey parent company."

"That means the mayor and Mayfield are in bed together!"

"Exactly. It also means Mayfield's Citi construction company probably launders money through the Cayman corporation."

"That's a rather big leap," Drew said.

"How else do you hide money other than under your mattress?" Pat asked. "It's the oldest trick in the world. Send money through a series of corporations until it ends up offshore in a tax haven like the Caymans."

"Hmm. What have we got here?"

"I think we may have discovered a backdoor that might expose city officials in bed with the wealthiest businessman in the county. Frankly, it may be the opening link to a huge corruption scheme. Remember, Mayfield does a lot of construction projects for the city and county. And, all his civilian construction business has to go through the government permitting offices."

"Pat, any way you can learn more about this company and its connections to San Diego without raising suspicions or the mayor and Mayfield finding out?

"Sure. But I'll have to make another trip to the Caymans, and I should stop off in New Jersey to see what I can learn about the owners."

"Let's do it."

CHAPTER FOUR

Two Days Later

ATTORNEYS A.J. HAWKE AND RANDALL WRIGHT stood patiently in the lobby of the San Diego County Medical Examiner's Office located in the County Operation Center on Overland Avenue. The two were waiting for the chief medical examiner to collect them and take them to a briefing on the autopsy of Nevan Pansky.

"Drew, I'm impressed you got an order for us to be briefed on the M.E.'s preliminary findings. That's quite the feat."

"I just told the judge I needed to know how the senator died. If Pansky's death wasn't suicide as the papers say, I was fearful for my client and her children. The senator was a very powerful man and powerful people make enemies."

A side door opened and Aidan Cole emerged. "Drew, nice to see you again."

"Likewise, Aidan. Sorry it always has to involve a death."

The chief medical examiner laughed. "That is the business I'm in, Drew. Maybe next time we will try your office."

"Corpse and all—I hope not, doc."

Both smiled and enjoyed the light-hearted exchange. "And your friend is attorney Wright?"

"Yes, doctor," answered Randy, putting his hand out to shake. "I represent the deceased senator's children and estate. Drew represents Mrs. Pansky."

Griping Wright's hand tightly. the M.E. said, "You know, Mr. Wright, one should be careful whose hand you shake in this building. You never know where it's been."

Randy sheepishly smiled as they shook hands, not knowing if Aidan Cole was still joking or serious.

The M.E. turned to Drew. "So, you also got the judge to let my old boss Dr. Wu Tang attend our briefing."

"Yes, sir. How else can I interpret the nuances of what you tell us?"

"I see. You do realize my findings are non-partisan. I just call it like it is."

"Yes, sir. Your reputation is untouchable. I just need someone I can privately confer with so I know what to do next."

The M.E. smiled. "Okay, follow me. We'll take a shortcut through the loading dock." The three exited through a side door.

"This is a big loading area, doctor," Randy said. "You could fit nearly ten big rigs here."

The chief medical examiner explained that the Kearney Mesa complex is a designated command center for the southernmost quadrant of California. Its communication center is connected to all emergency agencies, including military, police, and fire throughout the state and nationally.

"Most of San Diego County's headquarters are here," the M.E. said, "and my department is the primary location where all the county's dead must be processed. Those two big rigs at the far end of the dock are temporary refrigerated morgue trucks in case we need additional storage for the deceased during an emergency."

"I see."

The doctor paused, swiped his security ID card past a reader, and opened a door, motioning with his head for the attorneys to enter. Randy glanced at Drew and wrinkled his nose. Drew nodded.

Noticing the two attorneys' reactions, the doctor spoke up. "What you're smelling is our biosafety air ventilation system with a negative pressure airflow. The air constantly circulates and disinfects the room."

Attorney Wright stared at the cavernous room and the numerous examination tables before him. Four of the tables had people dressed in white bio-hazard suits with waterproof sleeves, gloves, plastic disposable aprons, caps, breathing apparatus, eye shields, and shoe coverings.

"What you are seeing is a mock practice session for a deadly infectious disease emergency."

"But, Dr. Cole, those people are working on real bodies."

"Yes, Drew. It adds to the reality of an epidemic outbreak. The cadavers are donated to us by various entities for such training purposes. Don't worry, the bodies carry no diseases."

The M.E. led them through double doors and down a short hallway. Once again, the doctor used his magnetic entry card and the three entered a conference room, where three people were seated at a large table.

"Folks, attorneys Andrew Hawke and Randy Wright have arrived," the M.E. said, then turned to Drew and Randy. "Let me introduce you to our gathered crowd."

Drew was already looking intently at a tall woman with black hair.

"Drew, this is Lieutenant Maria Alvarez-Steele of the United States Capitol Police," the M.E. said.

Drew's expression showed surprise as he continued to

stare. Catching himself, he stepped forward and shook her hand. "May I call you Ms. Steele?"

"Lieutenant Steele, if you don't mind," she replied with a stern expression.

The M.E. continued his introductions. "I believe you know Assistant District Attorney Jack Farrat, and this gentleman is Special Agent Kiefer Mancini of the Federal Bureau of Investigation."

"Hi, Jack . . . Special Agent," Drew acknowledged and gripped the latter man's hand, then stepped back so Randy could continue his greetings. Drew looked the FBI agent up and down. *He must be with U.S. Attorney General Wyland's office.* But the young attorney's eyes drifted back to Lieutenant Steele, who directed her glance away from Drew toward Dr. Cole. Drew again caught himself staring when he realized Dr. Cole was watching him.

"Mr. Hawke, do you know Lieutenant Steele?"

"We may have met before. My apologies, lieutenant, but you are quite striking for a police officer."

"Really, Mr. Hawke, I might say the same of you. I don't know many young attorneys with such an outsized reputation like your own."

Randy had to look down to keep from smiling at the cutting retort.

Damn, Drew thought. *I deserve that.*

At that moment a man dressed in blue scrubs entered the room.

The medical examiner spoke up. "Folks, let me introduce Dr. Wu Tang, our distinguished retired chief medical examiner. Dr. Tang was chief examiner of this facility for twenty-three years, and I believe, Drew, you retained his services as an expert?"

Drew nodded. "Good morning, Dr. Tang, I really appreciate you attending."

"My privilege, Drew. And Dr. Cole has been a most gracious host."

"Everyone, please be seated. Dr. Tang, will you join me at the head of the table so we can share our thoughts with these guests."

After all were seated, the medical examiner began his presentation, saying that he and Dr. Tang had completed the final stage of the physical examination of Senator Nevan Pansky a little after eight o'clock that morning. "I will have a final report which I will release in four to six days. Do any of you have any questions?"

Special Agent Mancini spoke up, "Have you determined the cause of death?"

"Yes. But first let me emphasize my findings are only preliminary. As a courtesy to you folks, I agreed to this briefing due to the great interest surrounding the death of a very important public servant. With that said, my preliminary opinions are: The senator died from multiple causes. All of which are temporarily classified as homicide. These findings will be made final depending upon a further review of my exam notes, laboratory work, radiographs, and the pictures I took during the autopsy."

Lieutenant Steele asked, "You said multiple causes. What are they, doctor?"

The M.E. described how he and Dr. Tang found the neck of the deceased had been forcibly twisted to his right, dislocating the spine where it connects to the neck and severing the spinal cord. He also suffered a very strong blow from a hard object about two to four inches wide to the lower back of the head in the area where the spinal cord was severed. A second blow to the right side of his head was observed, shattering the right tem-poromandibular joint and jawbone. There were numerous other facial fractures. None of the facial injuries were life threatening.

Dr. Cole concluded by saying, "In addition, Nevan Pansky suffered a gunshot to the brain."

Lieutenant Steele leaned forward and asked, "Are you say-ing the senator may have died from blows to the spinal cord?"

"I believe you are asking if the man died from the spinal cord injury or the gunshot wound," M.E. replied. "That is a fi-nal determination I have not made at this time. I will have to review the photographs and computed tomography taken dur-ing the autopsy to answer that question. The official cause of death is either a catastrophic severing of the spinal cord with associated causes of physical trauma to the neck and head by blunt-force blows, or possibly by a bullet that passed through the brain and exited the back of the skull."

Lieutenant Steele and Kiefer Mancini glanced at each other, shaking their heads.

"Medical Examiner Cole, what further work do you need in order to categorically tell us what exactly killed the man?" Steele asked.

"I may never be able to exactly say which one of the life-ending events killed him. Both the gunshot and the spinal cord injuries would have killed the man. I am of the preliminary opinion the trauma to the spinal cord would have produced a quick death. The man probably could have lived some minutes after being shot."

"Regardless of which caused his death," Steele said, he was, in your opinion, brutally murdered."

"If you are asking if the senator committed suicide as re-ported in the news, the answer is no. This was a homicide."

Lieutenant Steele rose from her chair. "Dr. Cole, you will

cease working on the death of the senator. Nevan Pansky's body, and any evidence you have in your possession, is now the property of the United States Congresses Capitol Police and its Protective Services Bureau. This murder is no longer a local matter."

"Wait a minute, Ms. Steele," interrupted ADA Farrat, now standing, "The murder occurred in this county, and any decisions about the body and this case will be made by my office."

"Thank you, Mr. Farrat, but under 18 United States Code, section 351(f), the United States government now asserts federal investigative and prosecutive jurisdiction over the death of Senator Nevan Pansky. As such, all local and state actions in this matter are suspended by federal law. My office will be contacting your boss shortly with instructions. In the meantime, no one is to do anything with the body."

She turned to face the M.E. "Dr. Cole, you will keep the body refrigerated until it is picked up by us." Looking back to the assistant district attorney, she added, "That also includes any evidence collected by the police or in your possession, Mr. Farrat."

Jack Farrat stood with his mouth agape.

Special Agent Mancini rose. "Lieutenant Steele is correct. This is now a federal murder case. The FBI will take control of all evidence, including the murder scene, and coordinate the investigation with the U.S. Capitol Police from here on. It is a matter of national security. I'm sure you understand. Other government leaders may also be at risk."

With that, Special Agent Mancini and U.S.C.P. Lieutenant Steele exited the room.

"Hawke, is she always like this?" Farrat inquired.

"Jack, I believe my encounter with Ms. Steele was more enjoyable than the one you are about to have."

Drew turned to Dr. Tang. "Doctor, would you meet with me for a brief moment?"

Dr. Tang, Randy Wright, and Drew exited the conference room and huddled in the hallway.

"Wu, I strongly urge you to tell Dr. Cole to finish his work and keep a copy of everything he has, including all notes, radiographs, test results, and pictures. Have him file everything somewhere in his computer system as a matter of routine practice so he can later say, 'Oh, I forgot about those.' These Feds are going to run this thing the way they want and decide what happened in a manner that suits them."

"But Drew . . ."

Drew politely insisted. "Tell Cole preserving the file will be a guarantee they don't try to make him look incompetent. If you can get a copy for us, I would greatly appreciate that as my client will probably be blamed for the murder of her husband. She has already made a statement to that effect. Remember, the Feds have a very restrictive discovery practice. They decide when and what evidence they should turn over to the defense and what they want to make public. The federal government does not abide by California's open discovery laws."

"But Ms. Steele said Aidan Cole was to stop working on the death of the senator," stated Wu.

"Correct. But, until someone in County Administration so orders, or Cole receives a court order, Steele's word doesn't matter. Cole should request a written order from someone in authority, local or national."

"I don't know if Aidan will do that."

"It is his decision, Wu. Just tell him the Feds might view him as an impediment to their needs. As such, they will do what they want with him and his work."

"I understand. But I must be diplomatic. I am no longer his

boss." Drew nodded as Dr. Wu changed the subject. "Drew, I don't think Mrs. Pansky, or any woman in her fifties, would have the strength to snap a man's neck, at least not the way Pansky's spinal cord was so severely traumatized. The senator's death had to have been done by a very strong man, one who knew exactly how to grab a head and violently twist it to the right, tearing apart the spinal cord."

"Really!"

"Further, the evidence I've seen points to Mr. Pansky being dead when the bullet pierced the brain. Cole was just being cautious about his preliminary findings. We both noted the same things. There just wasn't enough blood spatter from the shot. And, the brain already had evidence of post-death changes due to the heart not pumping blood. Further, the area of the brain the bullet exploded through would not have terminated life immediately. I also noted excess pooling of blood in different areas of his body. This would explain why there was so little blood spatter as the heart had stopped circulating blood long before he was shot. Taking all this into consideration, I think he was dead when shot."

"Are you sure about this?"

"I need to work with Dr. Cole further and examine the photographs of his physical examination and microscopic studies to be sure, but right now that's what it looks like."

"So when he died is as important as to how he died?"

"You are correct."

"That's even more reason why I need the autopsy evidence preserved, doctor."

"I'll talk to him, Drew. The last thing Aidan needs as a new M.E. is a scandal."

CHAPTER FIVE

Thursday, 8:30 a.m.

THE INTERCOM on Drew's phone buzzed.

"Yes, Debbie?"

"There's a bunch of folks out here demanding to see you and Mrs. Pansky. What do I do?"

"Tell them I'll be right out."

When Drew opened the door to his office, he was confronted by three well-dressed individuals, two of whom he recognized.

"I thought you might come. What may I do for you?"

"Mr. Hawke, I am Assistant U.S. Attorney Liberty Jala, and I believe you've met Special Agent Kiefer Mancini of the FBI, and, of course, Lieutenant Maria Alvarez-Steele of the United States Capitol Police."

"Thank you, Ms. Jala, and welcome to you all. Especially Ms. Steele."

"It's Lieutenant Steele, if you don't mind."

"What can I do for you folks?"

"Mr. Hawke, where is Katherine Pansky?" Liberty Jala asked.

"Ms. Jala, that information is part of my attorney-client privilege. If she wants to meet with you, then I will be most happy to tell you. But—"

Lieutenant Steele interrupted. "You tell us, Hawke, or I will arrest you for being an accessory-after-the-fact."

"Still the demanding one. You haven't changed since we first met, Ms. Steele."

"Don't be an asshole, Hawke! This is serious business."

"I believe that is what you called me that night, or was it in the morning after? You were wrong then, as you are now."

"How dare you, you arrogant pig."

"Yes, you also called me that, too, and it was in the morning as I now remember."

"Now cool down, you two," Jala ordered. "You obviously have some personal issues to resolve. But not here. Mr. Hawke, I only want to interview your client about the death of her husband and the statement she made to the media."

"I would be most happy to arrange an interview, Ms. Jala. But I have to tell you she will be invoking her Fifth Amendment right to be silent."

"That's a little hard to do, counselor, given the fact that she has already made statements to the public."

"Normally, one might think so, but given the autopsy results she will not be speaking to anyone about the death of her husband. I will even produce my client for her arrest if you think you have sufficient evidence to prosecute."

Drew paused and then asserted forcibly, "Be advised . . . you are not to ask her any questions unless I am present." Again he emphasized, "I am her attorney, and I will not allow any questioning if I am not present."

"Hawke," Steele shouted, her anger at a boiling point. "The murder of my client is of national interest, and I view your actions as obstructing that investigation. So where is she?"

"Ms. Steele, I know you are upset about losing someone you were charged with protecting. It just doesn't look good for you. But that doesn't give you the right to violate the law or my client's rights."

Lieutenant Steele's mouth opened, but before she could explode, Hawke turned to Assistant U.S. Attorney Jala. "When and where do you want to meet with my client? In my office?"

FBI Agent Mancini responded, "It will be in my office, and immediately, if you please."

"How about one o'clock this afternoon?" Drew suggested. "I'm sure Katherine will want to be dressed appropriately."

Steele turned to the other two federal agents. "You're not going to let this guy get away with such a delay are you?"

"Lieutenant Steele, Mr. Hawke is an attorney admitted to practice before the United States Federal District and Federal Appellate Courts," Liberty Jala said. "As such, he is an officer of those courts and I am sure he wouldn't risk being held in contempt by a federal judge for failing to perform his sworn duties."

Turning to Drew, she added, "As such, Mr. Hawke, we will see you with your client at Agent Mancini's office in Sorrento Valley at one o'clock this afternoon."

"Thank you, Ms. Jala. See you then."

The group of federal agents turned to leave as Drew opened the office door. Once they had left, he closed the door and turned to Debbie. "Get De Luca on the phone immediately."

When the call came, Drew said, "Pat, thanks for the quick response. The Feds want to interview Katherine this afternoon. I need you to contact the PIs you have watching the Poway home and have them bring Mrs. Pansky to my office immediately. Have Mrs. Pansky dress in some sort of business attire. But get her here by eleven."

"Anything I should know or have them tell her?"

"No. After we hang up I will call her myself. If she asks any questions, tell the PIs to say they don't know what's going on. Oh, and have them bring her in the backdoor to the building. Cover her up with something so no one can recognize her. I also need you to figure out a way to get her back to Poway without the Feds following her."

"On it. Consider it done."

ooooo

FBI Field Office

"REMEMBER, KATHERINE, you answer no questions without looking to me first," Drew instructed. "If I nod yes, you then answer the question. If I say nothing, you invoke your right to remain silent. If you wish to talk to me in private, just say so and I will take you outside where we can talk freely. Any questions?"

"No, but it appears you want me to answer none of their questions or only a very few questions. Is that right?"

"You have it. We are not here to say anything except your name, occupation, and the fact you were married to Nevan and have two children."

"Okay, Mr. Hawke, I'm ready to go."

The two walked up to and through the doors to the FBI building only to find Assistant U.S. Attorney Jala and FBI Agent Mancini waiting in the lobby, along with another man.

Drew slowly looked over the new man. He appeared to be stocky, if not muscular, nearly six feet tall, and in his late thirties. *Who comes to an FBI interview dressed in an expensive suit? And look at those shoes with no socks, no less. Who is this guy?*

The man did not introduce himself, and the five took an elevator to the third floor. They exited to the right and entered a medium-size conference room, where a stenographer sat behind a small transcribing machine.

"Mrs. Pansky, please have a seat next to the lady who will take down everything that is said. Mr. Hawke, please be seated next to your client. We will be right back," instructed Mancini.

The three agents left the room. Hawke immediately looked at the mirror facing them. He touched Katherine's arm and quietly whispered, "There's a two-way mirror in front of us." Leaning close to his client he added, "The new guy must be Mancini's boss?"

"Drew, I've seen him before."

"Where?"

"At some of the social functions Nevan and I have attended."

"What's his name?"

"I don't think I've ever been introduced to him."

At that moment Agent Mancini opened the door and took a seat across from Drew and Katherine.

"Kiefer, who is the gentleman with you? You never introduced us."

"That is Finnigan MacIntosh, a federal agent."

Before Drew could question further, Mancini interjected, "Mrs. Pansky your testimony today will be taken down by this court reporter and also recorded audibly for accuracy. Is that alright with you?"

Mrs. Pansky turned slightly and looked to Drew, who nodded yes.

"I need a verbal response from you, Mrs. Pansky."

"Yes, sir."

"Then please state your full name and address."

Katherine looked to Drew, who said, "State your full name and the address where you and your husband lived."

"My name is Katherine Margaret Pansky. My address is 7000 Hillside, La Jolla."

"Where do you currently reside?"

Katherine again looked to Drew, who had no reply.

"I invoke my Fifth Amendment right and the other rights afforded to me by the federal and state constitutions and refuse to answer that question."

"Are you avoiding the authorities by not telling us where you currently live?"

Drew again remained stone-faced.

"I refuse to answer that question under the Fifth Amendment and my constitutional rights."

"Mrs. Pansky, did your husband rape or maintain sexual relations with your daughter Lydia or any other women that you know of?"

Drew again had no reaction.

"I refuse to answer that question and invoke my Fifth Amendment right to remain silent."

On and on went the questioning for over three hours. Each time Katherine invoked her Fifth Amendment right to remain silent. Only once did she and Hawke step outside to discuss something.

Finally, Agent Mancini asked, "Do you have a passport of any kind?"

Drew nodded.

"Yes, I have a United States passport."

"Do you have it with you now?"

"No. It is at my home."

Drew spoke up. "I will be happy, Agent Mancini, to provide Katherine's United States passport to you if that's where this is going."

"That is exactly where I'm going. She will have to turn it over to us. Can you get it to me tomorrow morning?"

"Yes. But her passport is at the murder scene. I will need you to authorize entrance to the Pansky home for me and a member of my staff."

"Who would that be?"

"Either my associate Elizabeth Bernquist, my expert witness, Mr. Wu Tang, or my private investigator, Pat De Luca. Say eleven a.m.?"

"Why not just you?"

"Two witnesses are better than one. The extra one can attest to what I do while in the house."

"Very well. One of my agents will accompany you. Give the passport to him."

Drew agreed.

Turning to Katherine, Mancini said, "Mrs. Pansky, you are not to leave San Diego County or the United States. If you wish to go somewhere, please have Mr. Hawke contact us for permission. My office will retain your passport."

"Are you sure you want to restrict the freedom of my client? That is tantamount to house arrest."

"Absolutely. You're lucky I don't arrest her right now and, once before a judge, demand no bail."

"Mr. Mancini, we intend to cooperate fully. She will willingly self-surrender, if necessary. Just contact me and we will be here within the hour."

Without agreeing, Mancini said, "I appreciate the offer, Mr. Hawke. That concludes our interview. Please follow me to the lobby."

CHAPTER SIX

Friday

FRIDAYS ARE ALWAYS BUSY DAYS for the law. It's the day of the week where judges, attorneys, and court staff attend to administrative legal issues. All trials, civil and criminal, usually have the day off, unless a jury is deliberating or the trial is behind schedule for completion. However, Fridays are not a day for relaxing.

Early in the morning, Drew attended two criminal video arraignments in San Diego Superior Court. The afternoon was no less busy with three settlement conferences before Superior Court Judge Brown, and later Judge Montgomery, where the judges pressured the district attorney and defense counsels to agree to bargains in an effort to clear the court's busy trial calendar.

At four o'clock, attorney Drew Hawke treated himself to a visit to his outdoor office at the Bareleymash Café and Bar on the corner of 5th Avenue and Market Street. The café's garage-style windows opened up to outside seating and an unmatched experience of the hustle and bustle of the Gaslamp Quarter.

Drew sat at a sidewalk table, feet propped up on a chair while he perused another report from Matt on the SMA v C.T.I. case. *That young man is a bulldog. Once Matt gets his hands on an issue, there is no stopping the kid. Matt Van Dryden III, attorney at law! This college student just might become the great lawyer I always thought he could be.*

"But enough about Matt," Drew softly murmured. The attorney turned his attention back to the research his young aide had supporting Pat De Luca's findings on the true owners of a series of corporations with ties to Mayor Sandleson and Morgan Mayfield.

After a moment, a waitperson stopped at his table. "Hey, Drew, the usual Jack Daniels?"

"Oh, hi, Eva. You're looking exceptionally beautiful. Watch out for those hound-dog college students tonight."

"I don't know how you can make such suggestive comments and not be offensive. You're the one who's dangerous."

Drew blushed. "Believe me, I was sincere. But you are more radiant than usual."

"Alright, you hound dog, what's your poison?"

"You know, it's been a very successful day. I'll splurge and have a Teeling Single Grain Whiskey. Make it neat."

"It must have been a good day. I'll be right back."

She soon returned with the 92-proof whiskey. "So, tell me what's the occasion for the celebration. Something big about the Pansky case?"

"Actually, no. I just had a lot of little legal matters to wrap up today."

"If you don't mind my asking, how is Mrs. Pansky?"

"Not good. On top of losing her husband, she continues to be the topic of speculation by every news outlet, not to mention—"

At that moment a tall, handsome, young man walked up. Eva turned and smiled as she admired his radiant ebony face and obviously fit body. "I'll come back later," she said, excusing herself.

"Mr. Hawke, you got a moment?" the man asked.

Drew looked up and immediately stood. "Chris Sykes, you looking for a rematch?"

"Nah, you beat me fair and square. In fact, I learned a lot."

"Still training?"

"Yes. But I've been working more kicks into my fighting technique as a balance to my grappling. I can now kick well above six feet, like you."

"Have a seat, Chris."

"No thanks, but . . ."

The man seemed to be suddenly at a loss for words. He just stared at Drew as if frozen. Finally, he stammered, "I just want to tell you . . . your client, ah . . . Mrs. Pansky . . . she's innocent. She would never hurt anyone. So do your best to protect her."

An astonished look came over the lawyer's face. He turned to Eva and without Drew saying a word she spoke up, "I'd better get back to work. Enjoy your drink, Drew."

Turing back to Chris, he asked, "How do you know Mrs. Pansky?"

"Ah . . . that doesn't matter. I just wanted to tell you she didn't murder her husband. She was elsewhere that night."

"Who said he was murdered?"

The man's eyes began to well up with tears. "Mr. Hawke, I've got to go."

"Wait, Chris."

The young man turned and ran off.

"Chris, come back." But the man turned right at Market and disappeared. Before Drew could collect his composure there came a familiar voice. "What was that all about?"

Drew turned to find Pat De Luca standing next to him.

"That was Chris, the kid I fought a month ago. He just told me Mrs. Pansky didn't kill the senator."

"What?"

"Yeah. When I asked him how he knew the senator was killed, he just ran off."

"Interesting."

"Doesn't make sense, Pat. Only Randy Wright, myself, and the Feds know it was murder."

"That's why I'm here," added Pat.

"What do you mean?"

"What do you know about Christopher Sykes?"

"Nothing much other than I fought him."

"His father is, or rather was, Senator Nevan Pansky."

"What!"

"Actually, he is the illegitimate son of the senator."

"How do you know that?"

"Sergeant MacNeal. San Diego's Chief of Police has a contact in the Washington, DC, Police Department. Way back, Mr. Pansky got a Black prostitute in DC pregnant and she bore him a son, Christopher. Apparently, the senator has maintained two families over the years—one here in San Diego, and Chris and his mother in Virginia."

"Holy shit. That man really was a son-of-bitch. Mrs. Pansky told me he chased after every skirt he saw."

"Drew, think about it. If the cops know about the Sykeses, they would now have a motive for why Mrs. Pansky killed her husband."

"That's not good. Do you know why Chris is in San Diego?"

"According to MacNeal, Chris is a student at the University of San Diego. MacNeal has been assigned to get some private investigator in Washington to interview Mrs. Sykes on the QT. It looks like the police are trying to determine if Chris and his mother are somehow involved in the death of the senator or if they are the reason Mrs. Pansky killed her husband."

"Damn. What a mess."

"Here's what I suggest, Drew. Let me follow up on this."

"Okay . . . hey, wait a minute. Chris said Mrs. Pansky was elsewhere the night of the murder."

"I'll look into that, too. But since you've asked me to go to New Jersey and the Caymans to look into Sandleson to Mayfield, I can also check out the Sykes while I'm back east. Remember, I leave this Monday."

"Smart. As soon as you finish talking to Mrs. Sykes, call me. I need to know what's going on before our police and, for that matter, the FBI, find out something."

"What's this about the FBI? MacNeal told me the Feds kicked the San Diego PD off the case. In fact, he said not to tell anyone about their PI in DC. The police seem pissed the Feds have taken over."

"Yeah, the U.S. attorney and the FBI are really pushy assholes. In fact, I think they are watching my office and probably following me."

"In that case, you better watch your drinking and carousing."

"Funny you should say that. Remember that woman in red I asked about?"

"What about her?"

"She's a lieutenant in the United States Capitol Police. You know, the agency Congress formed to protect the Capitol and its members. Her name is Maria Alvarez-Steele, and she was assigned to provide security for Senator Pansky. That woman is a real bitch. She wanted to arrest me Thursday when I wouldn't say where Katherine was staying."

Pat looked at Drew with a slight smile. "I see. It appears you really know how to pick 'em."

"Pick 'em! In hindsight, I think she hustled me."

"Isn't that how it always is? We men think we are the boss

and do the choosing. But in reality, they are the ones running the show."

"Now that's an ego deflating thought. How about you join me for a drink?"

"Can't. Got to get home and break the news to Lauren about us going to the Capitol on the way to the Caymans. How about you join us for dinner."

"I think I'll spend the night on the Artful Dodger. But maybe another time. You know how I like Lauren's cooking."

"You know Lauren would love to see you before we go. How about Saturday evening?"

"That sounds great, Pat. I could do with a home-cooked meal."

The two men talked a little longer, then Drew sat alone with his thoughts. The 92-proof whiskey had its desired effect as the young lawyer began to unwind.

"Drew, another Teeling?" asked Eva with a warm smile.

"Nah, I'm going to get a good night's sleep. The one did the trick."

ooooo

Drew found himself tossing and turning in the normally comfortable master cabin. *It's just too hot.* He kicked the covers off. Even the gentle rocking of the boat wasn't putting him to sleep. Every time his eyes closed, he faded off into a sleepy remembrance of his fight with the kid. The brutal blows they exchanged and then Chris's head violently snapping to the right as Drew powered a roundhouse kick through his opponent's defenses, forcing the young man to stagger to his right and collapse to his knees, falling face down onto the mat.

The sound was unmistakable. Bone on bone as my foot struck the man's jaw, followed by the crackling of vertebrae and stressed tendons and muscles. Drew remembered the sounds as if it were yesterday. *I've heard those sounds a hundred times, and I've seen the results. Could this be how Pansky died?*

Once again awake, the lawyer said out loud, "It's a good thing Chris was young and his neck flexible enough to absorb the blow. I could have severed his spinal cord."

He rolled over onto his side, pulling the pillow underneath his head in an effort to sleep.

Maybe Pat is right. I'm getting older. With age, no matter how much muscle you develop, the neck just doesn't flex enough when kicked the way I hit Chris. An older person would suffer either a broken jaw, a painful neck whiplash, or worse. Wow. Or worse, like the senator.

Half asleep, Drew sat up in a startled gasp for air as if he had stopped breathing.

"Chris just lay there," Drew said softly as he vividly recalled the vision of himself pouncing and viciously pounding on the wounded man's head with blows so hard Drew's hands couldn't touch a computer keyboard for days.

How could I be so violent to such a nice young guy?

"It's cage fighting. It was him or me," Drew said forcefully. *Listen to yourself. That's always your excuse.*

He lay back down, still trying to justify his killer instincts and how he fought.

There's no retreat. No running away in a cage. What else could I have done?

The still agitated lawyer got out of bed and walked up the steps to the Dodger's cockpit. Once out into the warm evening air, Drew grabbed two of the seat cushions and lay down on the boat's foredeck, where he continued to think about how strong the animal instinct is to survive.

"Man," he murmured, "the adrenaline rush is unbelievable.

The greater the threat, the higher the rush. I'm sorry to say, better than cocaine."

I can see how beating a man to the death could be such an exhilarating rush—one you have to live with, justified or not.

"We are a horrible species," he said as he slipped into a deep sleep.

CHAPTER SEVEN

THE WARM AUGUST NIGHTS usually meant a hot day ahead. This Saturday morning was no different as Drew slowly awoke. That's when he realized he had slept on the deck without a shirt and in his underwear.

He looked about and then across the way where a young woman, two boats down, lived on her 36-foot Catalina. "I hope she didn't see me up here," he said out loud.

Drew went below to put on his board shorts and went for breakfast at the marina deli. He finished off the morning with a second cup of dark Jamaican coffee while seated in front of the deli, reading the local *Boater's Gazette*. Like all single young men flush with money, he couldn't wait to spend it on a new adult toy. He was drooling over an ad for a new 34-foot Hunter yacht. He even conjured up a name for it—Victory. *A little egotistical, but what the hell. A win is a win, and as long as I win, the cash comes in. Victory is the perfect name.*

To his surprise, the good looking woman walked up and asked to sit.

Oh, crap. She's got to have seen me.

"You're Drew, right? The lawyer?"

"Yes. How do you know I'm a lawyer?"

"It's a small community here at the marina. Besides, everyone has been talking about you and your trials."

"I hope it's good. And you are?"

"Oh, sorry. I'm Mia. Mia Lombardi," she said as she grasped Drew's hand in a firm grip.

"Nice to meet you, Mia."

"By the way, your yacht has an interesting name—the Artful Dodger. Are you a fan of Charles Dickens?"

"I've read the book, but a friend of mine insisted I buy the boat. She said the name fit my personality perfectly. I'm afraid she is more a fan of boat names than the functional quality of yachts."

"Is she your girlfriend?"

"Actually, a good friend. Liz is a new lawyer in my office. We've been friends since college."

"So-o-o, Liz thinks you're a cunning and clever lawyer?"

"Nah. She's never said that. But when I asked her why she thought the name fit, she just said I was good at avoiding things."

"Commitment?"

"You know, I've asked her, 'Good at avoiding what?' But she just changes the subject."

The added comment brought a smile to the young woman's face. "You're thinking of a new boat?" she asked, looking at the *Gazette* ad section Drew had open.

"Yes."

"The new Catalinas are really roomy, especially the cabin area. You should check them out."

"Is yours comfortable?"

"Sure is. A great liveaboard. Come down and see it."

"I'll take you up on that generous offer."

"Got to go. Saturday is my grocery day and the morning is fast getting away."

"Don't hesitate to holler if you ever need help," Drew offered.

"Thanks."

The restless night was finally catching up. His two cups of coffee were wearing thin. He decided to go back to the Dodger and lie down. But before he slept, Drew checked his phone. There it was, a text message from Lieutenant Maria Steele. As Drew read the long message, he wondered why she was being so conversational and friendly.

Drew slept late into the afternoon. This time his dreams were more enjoyable. When he woke, he was thinking of the woman in the boat near his. He moved into the cabin and fixed himself a Coke and Jack Daniels and prepared to go to Pat and Lauren's for dinner.

ooooo

Saturday Evening

THE BEAMER TURNED RIGHT onto Torrey Pines Road, heading north toward Nottingham Place. Drew Hawke always loved this part of La Jolla. It had a country smell to it. At Nottingham he turned right and then left onto Cliffridge Avenue. He pulled his convertible into the driveway and jumped out over the driver's door. A brisk walk and he arrived at the front door and entered without knocking.

"I'm home," he announced, as the door shut with a bang behind him.

Pat answered, "Right on time. We're in the kitchen."

There he shook De Luca's hand, patting him on the back. And held his arms wide for a big hug for Lauren, who wouldn't let go for the longest time.

"Nice to have you home, Drew," Lauren said.

"It's nice to be back."

Then her physical inspection started. "Drew are you injured? That man didn't hurt you, did he?"

"No. Just the opposite."

Pat immediately stepped in. "We're almost ready for dinner. Honey, what do you want Drew to do?"

"I know what you're doing, Pat. But, yes, you're right. Drew, would you and Pat set the table? We're having your favorite— pot roast with baked potatoes, carrots, celery, and a good mix of the vegetables you hated as a boy."

"Now, Lauren, you know I love all vegetables. It was just a phase."

Pat laughed and handed Drew some dinner plates and gestured toward the dining room.

Lauren started to hum as the two set the table. After a few minutes, Drew and Pat went back into the kitchen. "Pat, honey, please turn off the oven and put the roast into that serving bowl."

"Smells good. Just like always guys," Drew enthused as he hovered over the two, checking out his favorites. "I'm famished."

"It does smell good," Pat added. "Drew, the wine is over there." He pointed to a countertop. "I bought two new cabs for you to choose from."

At dinner, Lauren questioned Drew as she tried to catch up on his ever-changing life.

"Do you still date that judge?" she asked cautiously.

Drew paused eating, knowing she never approved of the woman. "No, I don't. Haven't seen her for a long time."

When Drew tried to change the subject, Lauren persisted. "How about that lovely Liz Bernquist?"

"We're good friends. But I'm just not ready to get serious with anybody."

"Lauren," Pat said, "I told you a young man has to feel confident in his chosen profession before he can feel confident in a serious relationship."

"Is that what you did, Pat?" asked Lauren with an obvious disapproving stare at her husband.

Drew quickly intervened. "Law is a very demanding mistress, Lauren. Frankly, my practice is totally consuming and more than a challenge at this stage of my career."

"I see. Is that why you were with that waitress from one of the bars? The young lady we met when Pat and I went sailing on your yacht? She, too, was very nice."

Pat began squirming in his seat, knowing Drew did not like the inquisition.

"Her name is Kat," Drew replied. "I thought you and Pat would find her good company."

"Oh, yes. She was quite the conversationalist. Very delightful."

Lauren obviously didn't care for Kat, either. Probably thought she dressed too sexy.

Once again Drew attempted to change the subject. But Lauren persisted.

"Have you been going to church?"

"Of course."

"Father O'Connor said he hadn't seen you in a while."

"I will go this Sunday." In desperation Drew added, "Lauren, this is a feast. It is delicious. Ah, by chance did you bake any dessert?"

"Absolutely. Apple pie. Did you leave room?"

"I'll make room. But first one more small bit of roast beef and a dab of gravy."

Lauren smiled. Her boy obviously liked the meal she had prepared. Any concerns about his fighting or his rather loose choice of women were forgotten.

"I know Pat is dying to talk to you about our trip to the East Coast. Why don't the two of you go into the living room and chat while I prepare dessert. Apple pie is at its best warm, smothered in ice cream."

"You're spoiling me."

Once in the living room, the two men huddled. In a low voice, Pat divulged, "MacNeal called this morning. When he dropped off the Pansky file to the Feds on Friday, he informed Agent Mancini the DA intended to seize the Pansky home security cameras. That's when Mancini told him they already had the security equipment."

"That's too bad. I would have loved to see who was at the home the night of the murder. Now, no telling what they might do with that surveillance footage. Not knowing what happened that night is driving me nuts."

"You may yet get to find out. MacNeal said when he told Mancini he hoped the cameras caught something, the agent told him, 'The Capitol Police had camera surveillance on the house the whole time. We know who was there and who came and left. The home security system is only additional.' "

"The Capitol Police! Why are they doing surveillance out here?"

"Apparently, they provide protection, including video security monitoring, for congressional members when they are at home."

"How can they surveil so many members? There are hundreds of them."

"You're asking the same questions I did. Mancini told Mac-Neal they don't do it for all members of Congress, just those in line of succession and certain party leaders. Senator Pansky was a high-ranking member of his party and of the Senate Foreign Relations Committee."

"Did Mancini say what the surveillance cameras showed?"

"No, but that's something you should demand to see if they arrest your client."

ooooo

Sunday, 5:20 a.m.

A SOUND ECHOED IN THE ROOM, bouncing back and forth off the walls and ceiling of the loft, as a man tried to sleep. The sound reverberated in his head, growing louder and louder. His eyes moved but remained closed. Half asleep, he rolled over on his stomach and pulled a large pillow onto his head. But even so, the words . . .

> When I do my walk, walk, (oh)
> I can guarantee your jaw will drop, drop, (oh)
> 'Cause they don't make a lot of what I got, got (ah, ah)

repeated over and over in his mind.

> When I do my walk, walk, (oh)
> I can guarantee your jaw will drop, drop, (oh)
> 'Cause they don't make a lot of what I got, got
> What . . . I got . . . got . . . got . . .

My phone . . . my phone, his mind screamed. He rolled over and reached to the side of the bed, but his grasp only caught air. Drew rose and rubbed his eyes.

"Okay. Alright. I'm up." He looked around for his iPhone. His only clue Meghan Trainor's "Made You Look" ringtone as it repeated one more time. He found the phone and answered the call.

"The Feds arrested Pansky," the voice said. "I just got a call from my PI at the Poway rental."

"Pat?"

- 67 -

"Yes . . . you awake?"

"Barely. What time is it?

"Just after five."

"In the morning?"

"What else would it be?"

"Christ, it's still dark outside. Wait . . . you said Katherine was just arrested?"

"Yes. Wake up, Drew. What do we do?"

"Can the PI follow the Feds so I can know where they're taking her?"

"He's already doing that. His name is Todd Tocksten, a college kid I hired to work the night shift." There was a moment of silence. "Hey, Drew, don't hang up. He thinks they're on the way to the FBI Sorrento Valley field office."

"As soon as he knows where they've taken her, have him call me on my cell. I'm getting dressed and will head over there."

Twenty minutes later Drew pulled up to the field office as a tall, young man ran up to him. "They took her . . . they took her to the back of the building. I couldn't follow. The back entrance is all enclosed."

"Those sons-of-bitches. They purposefully arrested her when they knew no one was awake. Now they're going to interrogate and I can't get to her."

"So, what do we do?" asked the wannabe PI.

"They screwed me. It's Todd, right?" Drew said and held out his hand.

"Nice to meet you, Mr. Hawke," Todd said as he shook hands.

"Please, call me Drew. I just hope she listened to me and refuses to say anything. Did the FBI lock the house?"

"No. A whole bunch of them were still there when I left. But it looked like they were finishing up. I didn't get close because I figured I should follow and find out where they were taking her."

"Did the Feds make you out?"

"Oh, yeah. One pulled in behind me when we turned onto the southbound Five. When we got close to here, I was blocked off by yet another of their black Chevy Suburbans. "He pointed to the Chevy parked in front of the FBI building. "He's watching us right now,"

"Okay, let's go see him."

"You're kidding."

"Nope. Come on."

The two started to walk toward the black SUV only to have it turn on its lights and drive up to the road leading into the driveway to the building's back entrance. Drew started to follow.

"No good going back there," Todd said. "It's got a ten-foot-high security fence with concertina wire and some sort of gate keypad. They got cameras everywhere."

Drew thought for a moment, rubbing his chin. "Okay, Todd, we'll call it a day. When's your relief coming on?"

"Not until eight."

"Go on back to Poway and watch the house. Take pictures and write in your logbook what has happened. Be thorough. Tell your relief to continue watching the house. Have him write down everything he sees or hears. Oh, yeah, take pictures of every car that drives by. Get the car's license number if possible."

"Will do. Sorry, man, I did everything I could think of."

"Todd, you did good. I bet it was kind of a rush."

"Ooh, yeah. This stuff can be exciting. I didn't know what those Feds would do."

Breathing hard, the college kid was obviously reliving it all.

Drew noticed the white-knuckle grip on his cell phone. *I bet no one could pry that phone from him.*

"That must have been a tight situation for you."

"Hell yes. The FBI have guns and could have forced me over. Worse yet, they could grab me and God knows what would happen. People disappear once the government gets a hold of you."

Drew smiled. "Your heart racing?"

"Yeah, just thinking about it again."

"Okay, get going. I'll wait until you leave. Don't worry, you did just great."

CHAPTER EIGHT

Monday, 4:40 p.m.

THE INTERCOM ON DREW'S DESK BUZZED.

"Yes, Debbie."

"There's an attorney, Ms. Liberty Jala, on the phone. Should I put her through?"

"Yes, please."

Drew punched the lighted button on his phone. "Good afternoon, Ms. Jala."

"Drew, I saw you called Sunday and this morning. I'm sure it was about your client. The FBI arrested her Sunday morning, and I'm calling to let you know she will be arraigned in Federal District Court tomorrow at nine a.m. Will you be there?"

"Of course, Liberty. Why didn't you call earlier?"

"Sorry, I know it looks like I was avoiding you, but I was in a meeting in Los Angeles over the weekend."

"How convenient."

"Drew, please, I don't play games like some U.S. attorneys. I really was at a meeting of agents in LA."

"Sorry," apologized Drew. "You can imagine how suspicious one would be given the circumstances—early morning raid on a day I couldn't get access to a judge. Further, I called everyone and not one return call."

"I know you called Agent Mancini and myself, but this is the first time I could respond."

"Where's my client now?"

"In the downtown federal detention facility."

"Will you oppose O.R. for Katherine?"

"Unless Agent Mancini gives me a reason against releasing her on O.R., I will recommend release but with an ankle bracelet."

"Thank you, Liberty, I appreciate the call. See you Tuesday."

○○○○○

On Tuesday morning, Drew Hawke approached the federal officers manning the security screening area in the16-story Federal Courthouse located at 333 West Broadway. The building was quite a contrast to the old federal courthouse next door. That structure was built like a fortress, a reddish-brown exterior with small, narrow windows, a tiny lobby, and dark narrow hallways.

After clearing security, Drew was greeted by local artist Robert Irwin's prized public art, the Acrylic Prism, which dominates the courthouse's atrium lobby. The art piece was a highly polished 33-foot-tall obelisk made of translucent acrylic. Drew paused for a moment to admire the bright sunlight shining through the all-glass atrium and the sudden, unpredictable changes of light transformed by the sculpture, creating a very peaceful glow amongst the many plants in the lobby.

What a stunning statement, he thought. *This whole building shines so clear and transparent. I just wish the FBI was so transparent.*

As Drew proceeded to the elevators, he wondered why the arraignment wasn't in the old building where criminal arraignments were normally held. He exited the elevator and was greeted by two federal marshals in body armor and carrying automatic rifles. They asked where he was going. After telling the marshals, he was directed to the courtroom down the hallway to the left. At the courtroom door, he was stopped again by another marshal, who checked his list, nodded, and opened the door.

Inside the courtroom, he spotted a familiar face. "Hey, Ms. Jala, why all the security?"

"This is not your normal murder case, Drew."

"I guess not. What's going on?"

Without answering his question, she said, "I have informed the court we will oppose O.R. for your client. The complaint is on the defense table and lists all the charges against her."

"Okay, but you didn't answer my question. What's going on?"

At that moment, two federal marshals brought in Mrs. Pansky, and Drew walked over to her as they seated the woman at the defense table.

"Katherine, I hope you didn't talk when they arrested you."

"No. . . . Well, after about two hours of them asking questions I did say yes when they kept saying, 'Isn't it true you told the media you caused your husband's death.' "

"No! Why, Katherine?"

"I thought I had already said that and it wouldn't hurt."

"I understand. But you didn't say anything else, right?"

"I did as you told me."

"Good."

Drew picked up the charging sheet and quickly scanned it, then paraphrased its contents for Katherine. "The U.S. Government has charged you under 18 United States Code Chapter 51, section 1111 (a) which alleges you killed, in the first degree, a member of Congress, to whit, Senator Nevan

Pansky. The punishment demanded in this complaint is . . ." Drew paused and cleared his throat. ". . . the death penalty or life in prison as stated in section 1111 (b). The complaint has additional charges of 'assault on a Congressman and kidnapping resulting in the death of a senator.' "

"Oh, God. What have I done? Lord help me," Katherine cried out and buried her head in her arms in a torrent of tears. Drew put his arm around the crying woman, whose body trembled. Drew looked over at Assistant U.S. Attorney Jala, who turned away and sat down.

In a soft, low voice, Drew said, "Katherine . . . steady now. I'm here for you. The government always throws the book at you. This is not what you will face if you were to agree to a plea bargain. Please look at me."

She lifted her head and tried to brush back her tears with both hands. Still trembling, she looked to Drew.

"Katherine, the autopsy had good findings for us. The ability of the government to convict you on murder is questionable, if not impossible. I told you to let me probe for defenses. Please get a hold of yourself so I can explain. I need your help. We have to be a team. I can't do this effectively on my own."

She turned her head toward the young lawyer.

"Come on, be strong," Drew said. "Be the woman I know you are. I need that strength I know you have."

Slowly, Katherine raised her head, wiped aside tears, and brushed her hair back from her forehead. Drew let go of his embrace.

"That's it, Katherine," he encouraged.

Drew started to read the full complaint to her but thought otherwise. "Katherine, these charges are bullshit. They really don't make sense. The government goes on to allege you tortured, murdered, and attempted to cover up the murder of your husband. These allegations don't fit with your public statement that you caused Nevan's death, nor do they match the findings of the autopsy report."

"Drew, I just wasn't expecting all this."

"These charges are the parameters within which the government intends to prove their case. My job is to tear apart their case. And, I intend to do just that. You with me?"

"Yes, I will try."

Drew handed her a box of tissues and gave her another hug. Then he looked at Ms. Jala and the court's marshal. Both were staring at Drew and his client. Liberty Jala had a drawn look to her face and appeared moved by what she saw. Drew stood and walked over to the marshal.

"We're ready whenever the magistrate is ready to come out."

A few minutes later, "Come to order," announced the marshal in a loud voice. "This United States Federal District Court is now in session, the Honorable Edwin Xavier Knox presiding. Please be seated."

The magistrate looked at Mrs. Pansky and her very apparent distraught state. He then stated, the United States of America versus Katherine Margaret Pansky. Please make your appearances."

"Assistant United States Attorney Liberty Jala."

"Andrew Jackson Hawke for the defendant, Katherine Margaret Pansky. My client is seated next to me."

"Mr. Hawke, has your client been informed of the charges against her?"

"Yes, Your Honor. At this time, she waves formal reading of the charges and is prepared to enter her plea."

"Katherine Margaret Pansky, how do you plead?" the magistrate asked.

"Your Honor she pleads not guilty to all charges and speci-fications," Drew replied.

"Very well. I will set the preliminary hearing sixty days hence and a settlement conference one month after that. Does your client waive time, Mr. Hawke?"

"No, Your Honor. And we wish to proceed to the prelimi-nary examination hearing as required by 18 USC section 3060 and the Federal Rules of Criminal Procedure 5.1, and then to trial as soon as possible."

"Mr. Hawke, to have such a hearing in two weeks as re-quired under section 3060 is inconvenient for this court. And, by the way, I have yet to see defense counsel rush to a prelimi-nary examination hearing when the discovery process hasn't even started."

"I understand, Your Honor. I would normally waive time, but to date the Federal Bureau of Investigation and Assis-tant U.S. Attorney Liberty Jala have not informed me about what evidence they have to support the charges listed in the complaint."

"Mr. Hawke, isn't that what discovery is all about?"

"I agree. But in this case, Your Honor, the evidence of this tragic affair doesn't match the alleged charges. I demand to see such evidence so I may be prepared to challenge the evi-dence during the preliminary hearing."

"Mr. Hawke, what you say doesn't make sense. You demand the prelim in two weeks without even knowing what the evi-dence is. You understand the government doesn't have to use its primary evidence at the prelim. It can use any evidence it wishes, even hearsay or other inadmissible evidence."

"That is correct, sir. But at least I can ask the witnesses, even if it is only one witness reading from a report, the source of any of conclusionary or hearsay statements."

"I see. Ms. Jala, your position?"

"Your Honor, I could provide to Mr. Hawke portions of the investigation reports, all of the arrest report, any evidence seized at Mrs. Pansky's house, and certain other evidence to-morrow so Mr. Hawke can review them. I suggest we continue this hearing to Friday morning so Mr. Hawke can review my discovery, and then we can set a date for the preliminary hearing at a time convenient for all."

"Ms. Jala's offer is fine," Drew responded, "except I will also want to see the U.S. Capitol Police surveillance video of the Pansky home—that includes two weeks prior to the senator's death and, of course, the evening and morning after his passing. I would also want any intelligence the Capitol Police, Secret Service, and FBI have regarding Mr. Pansky and any person suspected of murdering him or being a threat to the senator."

"Mr. Hawke, this is not a discovery hearing," stated the magistrate while looking sternly at Hawke.

"Your Honor . . ."

"Yes, Ms. Jala."

"May we have a recess so I can talk to Mr. Hawke about discovery?"

"I think that would be a good idea. We will recess for one hour, at which time this court will reconvene in my chambers so we can have a more relaxed discussion of Mr. Hawke's demands."

"All rise," the marshal ordered. "This court is now in recess."

As soon as the magistrate entered his chambers, Jala blurted out, "What the hell are you doing, Hawke?"

"Liberty, I might ask the same of you."

Katherine, who was watching with an expression of horror, asked, "Drew, what's happening?"

"Katherine, I'll explain in a minute."

"Liberty, can we talk in the hallway?" Drew asked as he gestured to the door.

Once out in the hallway, Jala immediately reprimanded him. "Hawke, you are poking your nose into too many agencies and their investigative work. I don't think any court will grant you the evidence you want."

"Actually, Liberty, it's my job to poke. And, what is all this security? I've never been in this courthouse or any court where officers are everywhere and armed with automatic rifles—not even for the most wanted cartel figure in the world. What is it you're not telling me?"

Assistant U.S. Attorney Jala stood looking at Hawke, seemingly frozen.

She obviously doesn't want to tell me or doesn't know if she can.

"Let me put it this way, Libby. If I may call you Libby."

She still just stared.

"Here's the thing," Drew continued. "You have to either release my client and dismiss the charges or bring me into the circle of knowledge and make me a part of whatever you are doing."

"Are you trying to blackmail me, Hawke, with this ridiculous tactic of rushing to the preliminary hearing? If you are, you're stupider than I thought."

"Then let's proceed, Ms. Jala."

"Hold on, Hawke, I'm not done. I'm just the trial attorney. The multi-agency discovery you are demanding is not a decision I can make."

She raised her hand when Drew started to argue further. She turned and walked off down the hall, paused, and returned. "How about this . . . we will tell Magistrate Knox that

Mrs. Pansky is to be transferred to one of our safehouses where she can still be protected. She will technically be under armed custodial arrest. I believe that would be agreeable to you, and I am sure she will prefer it to the detention facility. Further, you do not waive time and we set a preliminary hearing date within the fourteen-day requirement for a person who is in custody. I will talk to my superiors and get back to you at the end of this week or early next week about your demands."

"So I am sure of what you just said . . . Katherine will still be incarcerated but in a federal safehouse protected by U.S. Marshalls; the preliminary hearing will be within fourteen-days as required for a person who is in custody; and you will talk to the powers to be about letting me know what all this cloak-and-dagger shit is about?"

"Not agreeing to all your colorful deep-state imagery, yes."

"Done. But, Ms. Jala, you keep implying Mrs. Pansky may be in danger. If she is, why? If not, then why not just release her with a GPS bracelet?"

"All these guards are indeed to protect her. The government thinks she is a valuable witness, and we must make sure she doesn't face the same fate as her husband."

"Why is she such a valuable person?"

"The answer to that is above my paygrade. But believe me, the protection is necessary."

CHAPTER NINE

THE PRIVATE, SECURE PHONE on the presiding judge's rear credenza rang. Judge Brian O'Shea swiveled his chair around and read the scrolling readout on who was calling. He pressed the speaker button and answered.

"Yes, Sam, what's up?"

"Judge, I am getting all sorts of tips about Katherine Pansky being arrested by the FBI. And today I learned our grand jury issued a criminal indictment, and one of your judges has issued a warrant for her arrest. What is going on?"

"All good things, Sam. All good things. It appears the one big threat to your re-election is in a world of shit. Everything we've been talking about has erupted. Senator Pansky is dead and his vile incest has finally been exposed. The Pansky name is totally discredited!"

"I'm aware of that, Brian, but what's going on with her being prosecuted for his murder?"

"My contact in the U.S. Attorney's Office says the Feds want something else. Something more important than trying her for murder. If so, they might let our DA go after her for killing her husband. That's why the indictment and the arrest warrant were issued."

"That explains everything. But what if she gets off?"

"Sam, she won't. If the U.S. attorney backs off, Hawke and

his client will be back in my ballpark where I control how trials turn out. Believe me, by the time I am done, she will be a convicted felon and no threat to ever run against you for mayor."

"So we can stop digging for dirt? Things are getting expensive."

"Hell no, Sandleson! What is wrong with you? We continue on as planned. How do you think Chief Shaughnessy found out about Pansky's illegitimate son? I can't go around spouting off these secrets, even if I have known about them for years. The police and the DA have to uncover them. Believe me, the trial will be a juicy one. And, don't forget the more we dribble out one shocking revelation after another, the more we discredit Pansky and hopefully poison a jury against her. What better way to make you look good than to criticize an incestuous politician and his murderer."

"But, judge, shouldn't we keep our distance from this whole mess?"

"Absolutely not. Who do you think is behind all this? Hell, it's not you. I told you I would take care of things. Now, here's what's next. I'll arrange for reporters to unexpectedly corner you and ask you about the Pansky mess. That's when you say something to the effect of, 'Incest is an act against God, as is murder.' Remember that. Write it down. Say nothing more. Just leave it like that. Give them a headline and refuse to comment further because of the upcoming trial."

"Okay, Brian. If you insist."

"Sam, I insist. Don't undo my good work. I've got it all planned out. You will be re-elected next year."

CHAPTER TEN

Monday the Following Week

DREW HAWKE and Assistant U.S. Attorney Liberty Jala sat in the U.S. Department of Justice suite of offices for Oliver T. Wyland, the United States Attorney for the Southern Judicial District of California. As Drew looked around the office, he was taken aback by the eloquent and rich furnishings of the office.

My God, the federal government spares no expense in outfitting an official's digs.

At that moment the door opened and a man in a blue suit, who appeared to be in his forties, stepped out.

"Ms. Jala, Mr. Hawke, I am Assistant U.S. Attorney Steven Saven. I am the assistant to Oliver Wyland. Please follow me. The three entered yet another lavishly furnished anterior office. Saven paused and knocked softly on the far door.

"Yes, come in," a voice responded.

As Drew and Liberty entered, the young attorney noticed two men seated in the room, the older man behind a magnificently hand-crafted mahogany executive desk. The other man sat in a corner.

"Mr. Wyland, Assistant Attorney Liberty Jala, and Andrew J. Hawke," announced Steven Saven.

"Ah, yes, Ms. Jala, nice to see you again," Wyland enthused as he walked around the large desk. He stopped and shook her hand warmly.

Drew noticed the obsequious response of the woman as if she was greeting royalty.

"I keep hearing great things about you," Wyland said.

"Thank you, sir."

Wyland turned to Drew and said, "And you must be the young troublesome attorney I now have to deal with. Welcome, Mr. Hawke." There was no handshake.

"I don't know how to respond, sir, other than to say I am impressed by this whole meeting and especially how lavishly the U.S. government spends its money on offices."

"I see we already agree on something, Mr. Hawke. Please be seated."

Hawke and Jala took the two chairs in front of Wyland's desk.

"Now, my attorneys tell me you won't postpone Mrs. Katherine Pansky's legal proceedings and are attempting to force the matter to a quick trial."

Drew nodded but Wyland ignored the acknowledgement and continued on.

"To do so will probably expose my office's current investigation of an important national security matter. How can you and I come to a mutual agreement so I can do my mandated duty?"

"Sir, it is not my intent to obstruct any investigation."

"Oh, come on, Hawke, we both know you are playing an ace in order to get the most favorable outcome for your client."

"That is my *mandated* duty, sir." Drew intentionally emphasized the word mandated.

"Of course. Now let's stop posturing. I could give a rat's ass about prosecuting Mrs. Pansky for the death of her husband. I'm after the foreign agents who blackmailed Senator Pansky into passing on important security documents to the Chinese."

Drew interrupted. "Blackmailed the senator over his potentially career-ending extra-marital affairs with young interns and prostitutes you mean?"

"I see you are not as dumb as your blunt legal tactics suggest."

"I will admit, sir, I lack the sophistication of a polished man like yourself."

Jala's head swirled toward Drew in a manner that demonstrated shock, if not objection, to the young lawyer's display of contempt.

"Well said, Drew. Now that we know each other, what do you want?"

"First, why arrest Mrs. Pansky in the first place? I am puzzled."

"You tried to hide her from us, and then you instructed her not to talk to us. But more importantly, we need to see what she may know about her husband's criminal activities."

"Fair enough," replied Drew. "Here is what I would like: Let me see the U.S. Capitol Police security video which will document who entered and left the house when the senator was in San Diego. I also want to see the Pansky home security camera recordings. I believe you confiscated that, too. Both the home and Capitol Police video must be unedited and with their original time and date stamps."

"What else?"

"I also want to see any other evidence, including audio or video recordings, the government has that will exonerate my client." Drew paused for a reply.

Wyland turned to his right and looked to the stranger

seated in the corner. After a pause, Wyland looked back at Drew and continued.

"All is granted with this caveat: You can't keep any of the evidence nor have copies of them. You can view them only in one of our secured rooms. Second, you will see only the evidence we have regarding the actual murder. That will include video recordings inside and outside the house on the day and evening of the murder only. They will be unedited copies of the originals. However, you will see nothing relating to my espionage investigation, including information about the senator's nefarious activities. I don't think you know the type and extent of the damage Pansky's actions have caused this country. And, I have no intent of revealing such to you. Further, our conversation today never happened. You can never refer to it, even in your defense of Mrs. Pansky."

"So that I understand you clearly, you will exclude all of the blackmail information and any proof of the senator's sexual escapades. But, sir, I intend to show at trial, through civilian witnesses, Mr. Pansky's incestual rapes of his daughter and his many extra-marital affairs. These are key to my client's state-of-mind defense."

"As long as the evidence of his horrible acts do not come from the material we provide, I can't object. You obviously know a lot already. And, I warn you, if you somehow find out about the actual treasonous actions of Mr. Pansky or attempt to allude to them, I will step in. Further, any national secrets which Mrs. Pansky knows or any information pertaining to governmental matters my investigation deems important, you will not use."

"That is a broad area."

"Indeed, it is. But be assured, what you view will be of value to you. It will put the entire puzzle together."

"U.S. Attorney Wyland, since I don't know what you will give me and how it may affect my defense, may we talk further if I need clarification on what you provide or if I need other documents your information alludes to regarding the murder?"

"Please call me Oly. I feel we are on first-name basis. Yes, of course we can talk further. But, I can't promise we will provide anything further, given our current investigation."

"We have a deal, sir. I always take a man at his word."

"As do I. However, you and your client will have to sign a confidential agreement outlining these terms. One of the conditions of the agreement will be you and your client are sworn to secrecy, under penalty of imprisonment, about anything you may learn of our investigation, it's connection to espionage, and national security. One last thing. The agreement will not identify what evidence you will be seeing."

"Sir, if I may. Since you don't give a rat's ass about prosecuting Mrs. Pansky for the murder of her husband, I assume you will be dismissing all federal charges against her and grant her immunity from all federal prosecution, including anything her husband may have been involved in? After all, in order for a contract to be binding, there must be a quid pro quo. Or, as the law states, a bargained-for-agreement."

"Ha, I see you are quite the negotiator, Mr. Hawke. And with a sense of humor. I will be sure to remember you and your style the next time we run into each other. Yes, why not. Let the State of California prosecute her if they wish. However, she must tell us everything she knows about her husband and his traitorous dealings. Failure to do so waives any immunity we grant her."

Turning to Ms. Jala, Wyland said, "Liberty, tell Steven the terms of our agreement. I'm sure Mr. Hawke will have some suggestions. Have our legal department review it. Then get it done. And make sure everything is as I have stated. I need action immediately. I don't care if you have to work twenty-four-hours a day."

"Yes, sir."

"I hope you have been paying attention. Don't screw this up."

"I won't sir," came the reply as Jala stiffened her back as if she was about to stand.

"Mr. Hawke, any questions you may have should be directed to Ms. Jala. She will be working directly with Steven and myself. As soon as the agreement is signed, I will release your client from the safe house."

Wyland pushed his intercom button. "Steven, our guests are ready to leave."

As Steven Saven escorted Drew and Ms. Jala out of Wyland's office, Drew looked back at the man U.S. Attorney Wyland never introduced. The two were in an intense conversation.

"Him again. The Fed with no socks," Drew whispered under his breath.

CHAPTER ELEVEN

Friday, 9:45 a.m.

DREW HAWKE and a male court stenographer sat in a large conference room at the FBI's Sorento Valley office, waiting for the interview to begin. Minutes passed until an FBI agent escorted Katherine Pansky into the room, followed by Assistant U.S. Attorney Liberty Jala and Agent Kiefer Mancini, who was pulling a brief case with wheels. Katherine was seated next to Drew, and Ms. Jala and Mancini took the seats across the table from Katherine and Drew.

"Are you ready to proceed?" asked Mancini.

"Yes," answered Drew. "But I have one question. Are you or Ms. Jala asking the questions?"

"I will. Ms. Jala is observing."

"Then who is behind the two-way mirror?" asked Drew, pointing to the mirror behind Jala and Mancini.

"No one." Not waiting for further questions, Agent Mancini proceeded,

"Mr. reporter, swear the witness." Once sworn, Mancini asked, "Mrs. Pansky, as part of your agreement with the United States government, you are here today to answer questions about you and your husband, Nevan Pansky. Some of our questions may expose you to further federal prosecution,

BOOD OF THE FATHER

irrespective of the agreement you have signed. Such charges could include espionage. Do you understand what I just said?"

"Yes."

"Has your lawyer, Andrew J. Hawke, explained the consequences that may result as a result of your testimony?"

"Yes."

'Those consequences may include federal prosecution, conviction, and incarceration. Did Mr. Hawke tell you this and what possible charges may be filed against you?"

"Yes."

"Do you have any questions?"

"No."

"Mr. Hawke, do you have any questions?"

"No. The only thing I will add for the record is the United States government has specified in our confidential agreement that it will not pursue charges against my client for the death of her husband. In addition, the federal government has granted Katherine immunity from federal prosecution for the actions of her husband and any involvement she may have had if she truthfully answers all your questions. That is completely different from your interruption of the agreement."

"You are correct in your recounting of the agreement. But if she lies at any time, or withholds any information, or refuses to answer my questions, she can be prosecuted as I have described. Any other clarifications, Mr. Hawke?"

Yes. If my client lives up to her side of the bargain, Katherine's answers are to be sealed and never made public to any state prosecuting authority or any later federal government inquiries or prosecutions."

"Thank you, Mr. Hawke. It is so noted and your comments are to be part of this transcript."

"Mrs. Pansky, your husband has been a member of

Congress for twenty-nine years. At any time during your marriage, were you involved in any way in his congressional duties? For instance, his duties in Congress, the operation of his office, campaigns for election, his overseas travels and actions, or any entertainment activities?"

"Yes, sir. However, once I became pregnant with Nathan, and later with Lydia, the amount of time I was involved diminished significantly."

"By significantly, what do you mean?"

"I had a family to care for and a household to run. As both children got older I had to perform one hundred percent of the parenting duties. You know how that is, taking them to school, parenting days, tutoring, after-school activities, trips to the doctor, and everything else young children need."

"Did you ever travel with your husband on any congressional junkets or travels overseas?"

"Initially, yes. Later, very seldom."

"When you did travel with your husband, where did you go?"

"The few trips I took with Nevan were normally to visit our troops. We went to several bases in Europe, Guam, and Japan. I also accompanied my husband on official visits to Great Britain, France, Israel, Moscow, and the Vatican. I may have left something out, but that should be it."

"Did you ever travel to Hong Kong, or any part of what is currently mainland China?"

"No. His visits to Mongolia and China were done later, when I had ceased to travel with him."

"Mrs. Pansky, did you have anything to do with your husband's finances?"

"Of course. We maintained several bank accounts together and have several investment accounts with our broker R.B.C. Wealth Management."

"Yes, I've seen those accounts. Did you know your husband maintained other financial accounts in his name?"

"Yes. He has several accounts associated with his congressional office and for his re-election campaigns. I have no access to those accounts."

"No, Mrs. Pansky, I mean several personal checking and savings account only in his name."

"Are you saying Nevan has bank accounts I don't know about?"

"Yes, it would appear so.

"No, I didn't know that."

"Did you also know your husband had two bank accounts under assumed names, one in Hong Kong, the other in Bali, Indonesia?"

"I did not know that."

"Do you know your husband has three passports? One USA passport and two other country passports under assumed names?"

"Oh, no!"

"Did you know your husband and a Ms. Sykes own property in Virginia?"

"Why, no."

"Do you know a Ms. Sykes?"

"Yes. I learned of her recently."

"Then you know your husband has a son by her?"

Mrs. Pansky slumped back into her chair, her head down. After a couple of breaths, she answered, "Yes. I've met the young man. He is currently in college."

Mrs. Pansky turned to Drew. "Can we take a break?"

"Yes, of course. Kiefer?"

"Absolutely. Let me know when you're ready to resume. However, please understand, Mrs. Pansky, as part of your agreement with the government you will have to continue answering our questions no matter how personal or disturbing."

"I understand. I just need a break."

A few minutes later, the two returned and Mrs. Pansky looked somewhat pale but said she was ready to answer questions. Agent Mancini resumed questioning.

"Mrs. Pansky, where does your husband keep his important documents?"

"They would be in his den. Some are also in a wall safe."

"What wall safe?"

"The one behind the wall in the den."

"Mrs. Pansky . . ."

"Yes?" She looked at the agent, who appeared irritated.

"Mrs. Pansky, exactly where is the safe? We've gone through the house and found no safe. Further, so did the police. So, be specific. Where is it?"

"You should answer," Drew instructed. "You said, 'Behind a wall?' "

"Drew, it's behind the wood paneling, below the picture of George Washington on his inaugural barge."

"The painted wood engraving?" asked Drew.

"Yes."

"Mrs. Pansky, what is the combination to that safe?" Mancini asked.

Katherine looked at Mancini and then to Hawke. Drew nodded yes.

"It's thirty right, seventeen left, and forty right. But I have some personal family documents in there. Some I will need since I am the surviving spouse."

"The agreement you signed allows us access to all items in your house or any other place we deem necessary. To avoid disagreement over the contract's language you signed, here is a court-ordered subpoena to enter and seize any such items. We will itemize all documents found under the subpoena and return anything we feel is no of interest to us. Again, this procedure was stated in the agreement you signed."

Mrs. Pansky looked to Drew, who nodded.

"Mrs. Pansky, we wanted to question you today because there is evidence your husband has been passing government secrets to the Chinese. Payment for that information has been made by their foreign agents to his Hong Kong bank account. Mr. Pansky would then transfer money to his Bali bank account. Both accounts are under his alias names."

Katherine stared at the agent, shaking her head.

"Besides the safe, if your husband wished to hide anything in the house, where would he put it so you or possibly others wouldn't find it?"

"I don't know."

"Mrs. Pansky, I have to ask again. Where would he hide things? Remember, you lie to us or not answer our questions truthfully, we will renew our prosecution for the murder of your husband and further charges for lying."

"I don't know what to say . . ." A long pause ensued as she and Drew quietly whispered back and forth. Drew then addressed Mancini.

"My client doesn't know of any hiding place in the house other than the safe. But her husband told her to stay away from his grandfather's old desk. He even yelled at Katherine once when she opened a desk drawer. Later, when he found the housemaid dusting the desk, Nevan angrily asked what she was doing. He told her to leave the desk alone; it had important documents that shouldn't be disturbed."

"Is that true, Mrs. Pansky?"

"Yes."

Rummaging through a file folder, Mancini turned the file toward Mrs. Pansky and asked, "Would the desk in question be this one?" He pointed to a photograph.

"Yes, that's Theodore Pansky's nineteenth century mahogany desk. The one he had in the U.S. Senate."

The questioning continued for another hour and a half.

"Mrs. Pansky, that is it for today. But, as the agreement states, we can question you at any time if we desire more information. For now, however, based upon what you told us, I would like you and Mr. Hawke to accompany us to your home while we conduct a further search."

○○○○○

Mrs. Pansky and Drew followed FBI Special Agent Kiefer Mancini, his partner Agent Robert Ballard, and two FBI evidence technicians into the house and to the den. Once at the den, they found the strange man who had been in U.S. Attorney Wyland's office.

Without introducing the man, Mancini asked, pointing to a painting on the wall of Washington standing on a barge, with sailors rowing, "Is that the art?"

"Yes."

Mancini began tapping on the wall paneling. "How do you open this?" Turning to Katherine, he asked, "Where's the button or whatever to open the panel?"

Katherine pointed to the wall and said, "Take the picture off the wall hook."

Agent Mancini grabbed the picture and lifted it.

"Careful. That thing is only one of two remaining 1889 engravings of Washington's review of the fleet on his inauguration. Please give it to me."

"Now what? It's a blank wall," the agent in charge said.

- 95 -

"Rotate the picture hook one hundred eighty degrees to the right so the hook is upside down. Then pull on the hook. The panel will open."

Sure enough, the wall panel opened, exposing the wall safe. Mancini used the combination to open the safe. He pulled out two bundles of cash and a number of documents, which he quickly went through. At that time the unintroduced stranger moved closer.

Again, Agent Mancini examined each document, this time closely as he called them out one at a time. "Will, trust, power of attorney, house deed . . ." He paused. "Bank account statements, safe deposit box agreement. Nothing about a Chinese bank account or safe deposit box."

Mancini handed the safe's contents to the stranger, who looked through them and shook his head.

"Count the cash and photograph the papers and place them into an evidence bag," Mancini instructed one of the field techs. He then pointed at a desk. "Mrs. Pansky, is that your husband's desk?"

"Yes, sir."

Agent Robert Ballard began opening drawers. They were all empty due to previous police searches. But the left bottom drawer was still locked. "Kiefer, why wasn't this one pried open?"

"Good question," replied Mancini as he looked to the two FBI techs, who shook their heads.

Ballard re-examined inside and underneath the center drawer as he pulled it out. "Wait! There's something behind this drawer," he told Mancini.

Ballard reached underneath and grabbed something attached to the back of the desk where the center drawer would be flush when closed. He ripped loose a taped envelope, which he immediately opened. "There's two keys," he announced.

Mancini examined the keys as the stranger watched.

At this time, Drew looked to the stranger and demanded, "Who are you?"

Mancini answered, "Drew, this is Agent Finnigan MacIntosh."

Before Drew could question the stranger further, Mancini asked, "Mrs. Pansky, does your husband have a safe deposit box?"

"Yes, we do. It's with Bank of America."

"Only one safe deposit box?"

"Yes."

"We've already examined that box. This key looks like it's for another bank."

Holding up the larger of the two keys, Mancini looked to MacIntosh. "What have we got here?"

MacIntosh looked carefully at the larger key. "There's a key code next to the key's grip. And look at the dragon symbol on the key."

"Mrs. Pansky," asked MacIntosh, "do you know what these keys are for?"

"No. I've never seen either of those keys before."

MacIntosh handed the keys to Agent Ballard and pointed to the locked drawer. Ballard tried the small key first and it worked. The drawer had a few miscellaneous papers, which he gave to Mancini and MacIntosh, who found them of no interest. Ballard examined inside and underneath the drawer.

"Nothing . . . wait a minute," Ballard exclaimed. "The drawer's bottom seems shallow." He examined the depth of the inner bottom and felt the underside of the drawer. Ballard then knocked on its bottom. "I think there's a false bottom." He tried to pull the bottom up but couldn't.

"Break it open," Mancini ordered.

"Oh, no," exclaimed Katherine. "The desk is priceless!"

"Proceed, Robert," ordered the agent in charge.

Once the bottom was broken out, agent Ballard smiled.

"Got something." The agent pulled out a large envelope and opened it. "Bingo. There's three file folders with red borders . . . and . . . they're marked Top Secret—one SCI, another SCIF."

Drew started to step forward but Mancini put out his hand. "Sorry, Drew."

Ballard handed the files to MacIntosh, who opened each folder, examining the pages carefully. "They're all here," he announced.

MacIntosh picked up his metal briefcase, flipped the numbered combination lock to open, and placed the files inside. The agent then unwrapped a pair of handcuffs on a chain from around the case's handle, secured the case to his wrist, and left.

Agent Mancini then escorted Drew and his client out to Drew's BMW, at which time Drew turned to Mancini and demanded, "Who was that guy?"

"Agent Finnigan MacIntosh, I told you that before."

"No, I mean who is he really? He's not FBI, correct?'

"No, he's with the CIA."

"Is he a spook or a handler?" Drew said, emphasizing the word "handler."

Mancini turned with a surprise look. "How the hell did you know . . ." his voice trailing off. With a stern look, the FBI agent replied, "Sometimes, Drew, you ask too many questions. It is none of your business who or what MacIntosh is."

With that the agent turned and walked Katherine over to three U.S. marshals and instructed them to take her into protective custody. "Hawke, contact Ms. Jala to arrange the release of your client."

As Mancini headed back into the house, he yelled over his shoulder, "Now go home, Hawke."

CHAPTER TWELVE

The Following Monday, 9:10 a.m.

DREW HEARD A SOFT KNOCK at his office door.

"Come in."

Debbie entered and offered in a low voice as she closed the door behind her, "Drew, there is a reporter from the *San Diego Herald* and a pushy camera woman out here wanting to see you,"

"Is it Jack Zane?"

"I don't know. This place is like Grand Central Station with Feds, reporters, and unannounced drop-ins. How am I to keep track of their names? But one thing's for sure, that camera woman is rude. I had to stop her videoing the office and me—me no less. I told her, 'If you don't stop filming, I'll throw you out,' and I meant it."

"Now, Debbie, be nice. A little publicity never hurts."

"I don't want nobody taking my picture when I'm not ready."

"Okay, let's see what they want."

As Drew came around desk in a Levi's T-shirt and jeans, Debbie protested.

"Oh no you don't. You put on that sport coat and brush back your hair. That woman doesn't know how to make people look good."

"Yes, Debbie, of course."

As Drew put on his coat, Debbie reached up and brushed back some loose hairs.

Then, looking down at herself, she started fidgeting with her clothing. "How do I look?" she asked as she adjusted herself within her rose-colored blouse and patted down the sides of her hair.

"You're beautiful, Debbie. You ready?"

She nodded. Debbie followed as Drew stepped out and greeted the reporter.

"Hey, Jack, didn't know you had an appointment."

"I thought you said I could always drop by whenever?"

"You're right. I forgot. And who's this lovely lady?"

"One of my assistants. She also films for the *Herald* blog and our e-newspaper. Nancy Schwartz, Drew Hawke." Zane smiled and added, "Let me warn you, Nancy, there is a price to pay for any exclusive interviews Drew may give you."

"Jack, what are you doing? Ms. Schwarz, don't listen to Jack. But I have to ask you to turn off the camera. I don't want you disrupting my office and staff. I'll give you plenty of time for pictures later when we're done."

Turning to Jack Zane, he queried, "So, what's up? You here about Pansky?"

"That's right."

"In that case, let's move into the conference room where we can talk uninterrupted by phone calls."

Once all were seated, the young attorney stated, "Ask away."

"How did you get the Feds not to prosecute?"

"Wow! Who told you that?"

"Did you strike a deal?"

"Come on, Jack, those are heavy questions. Where did you get such ideas?"

Drew paused for a response. *I'm going to run this interview.*

Not Jack Zane. Drew just sat there, looking straight into Jack's eyes, waiting for an answer. Finally, the reporter broke first.

"I checked the arrest records at the federal jail. Mrs. Pansky was arrested on murder charges and then released several days later. But no one knows where she is. Plus, no criminal charges were filed against her in the Federal District Court. So-o-o, how'd you do it?"

"Did you talk to the U.S. Attorney's Office? Is that where all this is coming from?"

"So you did strike a deal," Jack repeated.

"Come on, Jack, you know how this works. The person to be asking all these questions to is the U.S. attorney in charge, not me. Those Feds choose when to prosecute and who. I have no control over such decisions. Hell, sometimes they wait for years to file a complaint."

"Is that what's happening here?"

"Jack, I have no idea. I'm just the defense attorney. I wish I could control things, especially for my client's sake, but no can do."

Zane sat in silence. Then he played his hole card.

"My sources in the DA's office told me they are going to prosecute Supervisor Pansky. Has anyone in the DA's office told you to walk Katherine in for arrest?"

"News to me, Jack, especially since the Feds have the ability to claim exclusive jurisdiction. Have you verified this?"

"I even have a copy of the grand jury indictment. Here's a copy."

Drew took it and slowly read. When done he asked, "How in the world did you get this?"

"I have my sources."

"When was this indictment issued?"

"Look at the date at the end."

"I did. The date is a week ago. When is the indictment to be executed?"

"I don't know. The DA filed it several days ago when they got Judge Brown to issue an arrest warrant for Katherine Pansky. They're looking for her right now. Here's a copy of the arrest warrant and sworn affidavit Assistant DA Jack Farrat gave to Judge Brown justifying the need for your client's arrest. Are you going to self-surrender her or continue to hide her?"

"She's not hidden, Jack. May I make a copy of these?

"Only if you answer my question."

"Jack, if I self-surrender her, I will ask you to accompany the two of us. Alright?"

"It's my exclusive, right, Hawke?"

"Of course, Jack."

ooooo

The following morning, Drew Hawke sat outside Department 9 of the Superior Court waiting for Judge Francis Brown to call him for his 8:30 a.m. emergency hearing. As promised, reporter Jack Zane and his camera woman sat alongside. Drew checked his watch for the third time: 8:40. *Frank Brown is the hardest working judge in this courthouse, but he is terrible at being on time.*

Just as Drew was about to knock again on the courtroom door, a deputy sheriff came out.

"Morning, Drew. The judge is ready to see you."

Drew and the *Herald* duo rose, but Deputy Patrick Studdard raised a hand to stop the reporter and his photographer. "Sorry, only Drew. Please wait."

As the deputy and Hawke walked back to chambers, Drew asked, "Patrick, I haven't seen you in several months."

"They temporarily assigned me to Judge Gay's department. His bailiff got sick with a flu-type thing that went into pneumonia."

At that moment Patrick knocked on the open door to Judge Brown's chambers. "Attorney Hawke, Your Honor."

The judge rose to shake Drew's hand, then turned to those already seated. "Drew, I think you know Assistant DA Jack Farrat, Chief of Police James Shaughnessy, and his lead detective, Tom Clayton." The judge returned to his seat.

"Gentlemen, I see you got my notice of this hearing," Drew stated as he took the empty chair in front of the judge. Neither of the three officials acknowledged Drew's greeting.

"Drew, your ex parte papers are really a series of motions regarding your client, Supervisor Katherine Pansky, and the indictment filed against her."

"That's correct, Your Honor."

"Drew, call me Frank, we are in chambers, off the record, and we all know each other well."

"Yes, sir. Thank you. The purpose of my ex parte papers is to allow Mrs. Pansky to self- surrender, have an immediate arraignment, and proceed as quickly as possible to trial. I also ask that Katherine be released on her own recognizance so she may assist me in her defense. I will be filing a motion challenging the grand jury indictment, and if my challenge isn't successful, I will move for a trial as soon as the law allows."

Judge Brown looked at the Assistant DA. "Jack, I see no reason why Mrs. Pansky can't self-surrender. Do you object?"

Clayton replied, "I asked you to issue a warrant for her arrest, judge, because Hawke was hiding her from us. She should be locked up."

"Judge, if I may respond briefly?" Drew asked. Brown

nodded. "Mrs. Pansky has not left the county. The reason she isn't living in her home is because that is where her husband died. I moved her to a rental so she could mourn in peace. This entire tragedy has been very stressful, especially with the paparazzi hounding her. I have reporters and photographers outside my office and the Keating Building. I am followed everywhere I go. And, I might add, also by police detectives."

Assistant DA Farrat growled, "Don't try to sugar coat your intent to keep her away from us and frustrate our investigation. I ought to arrest you . . ."

"Now, Jack," interrupted the judge. "Let's try to keep this nonconfrontational."

Drew spoke up, "Jack you know the Feds were all over the senator's death. They even told you to stay out of it and invoked federal law to purposefully exclude state involvement. And you never called me up or asked where she was. Hell, judge, even the Feds knew where she was staying and interviewed her. The DA's office nor the police ever requested an interview."

Jack Farrat appeared ill at ease as he shifted his weight in his chair.

Drew continued. "And, what does Jack do, Your Honor? He secretly gets a grand jury indictment without knowing all the facts surrounding the senator's death, and then asks you for a warrant stating the DA's office believed Katherine was a flight risk. I've attached copies of Jack's sworn affidavit stating why he needed an arrest warrant to my papers."

"Drew, I read your papers and the attached motions as well as Mrs. Pansky's sworn declaration in support of your motions, including her statement she had to surrender her passport to FBI Agent Kiefer Mancini."

Turning to ADA Farrat, the judge asked, "Jack, is it true you were told by the U.S. attorney and the FBI to stay out of their investigation?"

"Yes, sir. The Feds invoked U.S. Government code 18 U.S.C. 351 and told us they were taking over. We had to give them all our evidence."

"Then why did you go to a grand jury and then ask me for an arrest warrant?"

"The Feds sat and did nothing. They wouldn't respond to our inquires, and I felt we owed it to the public to take action. Besides, nothing in the United States Code says we can't preserve our jurisdiction by filing a complaint or indictment."

"I agree the death of Senator Pansky is of very high public concern. But I don't need the federal government coming in here and telling this court to keep our nose out of things," Brown added raising his voice. "The judges of this state don't particularly like such federal meddling. So a head's up on things would have been helpful, Jack Farrat."

Turning to Drew, Judge Brown asked, "Are you asking me to stay this case while the federal agencies proceed with their actions?"

"No, sir. However, I do feel Jack and I can inform the U.S. attorney in charge that the district attorney wants to proceed and see if the Feds object. If they don't, then let's go to trial. In the meantime, I ask you to recall my client's arrest warrant. Let her be arraigned this morning without being arrested and you decide if she can be released on O.R. That's all I want."

"Jack, unless you have a reasonable objection, I am inclined to do what Mr. Hawke wants. What do you say?"

If looks could kill, the stare at Hawke by ADA Farrat would have worked. The judge waited.

"Sir, I have no objection," Farrat finally mumbled.

"Your Honor, if I may explain further?"

"Yes, Drew."

"The Feds shouldn't object to arraigning my client on the pending charges while Jack talks to U.S. Attorney Oliver Wyland." Drew paused, but Farrat didn't speak. "I have Mrs. Pansky in the courthouse and ready to self-surrender," Hawke offered. "I should also add that Jack Zane of the *San Diego Herald* is outside. I believe he will ask to be in court for her surrender and plea."

"Very well, bring your client in. As we discussed, you and Mr. Farrat are to contact the U.S. attorney and report back to me as soon as possible. Now, I've got a nine o'clock calendar to get to. And, Hawke, no grand standing in court about anything we've discussed here in chambers. That includes any opinions you have about the grand jury indictment."

"Sir, I understand."

As Drew and ADA Farrat walked out, Farrat exploded. "You planned this whole thing, didn't you?"

"No, Jack, I did not. Now, I have the U.S. attorney on speed dial. Should we use my phone to call or do you wish to call on your own? We can easily do this after Katherine's arraignment."

There was no answer. Jack and the two police officers turned and walked away.

"Jack, see you in ten minutes?"

Again, no response.

ooooo

Forty minutes later Judge Brown paused his morning calendar. "Ladies and gentlemen, I have a special matter not on calendar. With your patience, I call the case of the People of the State of California vs. Katherine Margaret Pansky. Will counsel please make their appearances."

"Assistant District Attorney Jack Farrat for the People."

"Andrew Hawke for Katherine Pansky, who is present in court and by my side, Your Honor."

"Mr. Hawke, has your client been appraised of the charges against her?"

"Yes, sir. She has read the indictment and I have thoroughly discussed the allegations with her."

"Mrs. Pansky, is that true?"

"Yes, Your Honor," Katherine announced in a strong voice.

"Do you understand the nature of the charges against you and, if convicted, their consequences at sentencing?"

"Yes, sir."

"Then how do you plead?"

"Not guilty to all allegations, Your Honor."

"Very well. At this time I recall the arrest warrant. Mrs. Pansky, since you have voluntarily appeared here on this matter, I will now proceed to the issue of bail. ADA Farrat, do you request bail?"

"Yes, sir. The People request a bail in the amount of one million dollars."

Drew, shocked, turned his head toward Farrat. A murmur could be heard from those in attendance at such a high bail request.

"Mr. Hawke, do you wish to respond?"

"Your Honor, Katherine Pansky, upon learning of this secret indictment, immediately stepped forward and self-surrendered to this court. I don't believe requesting bail of such a person is proper. Nor would it encourage other innocent people to do the same. Katherine Pansky is a county supervisor sworn to uphold the laws of this state and the county she serves. She has suffered the terrible loss of her husband as anyone knows from reading the newspapers or viewing the news. As a longtime resident of San Diego, and given the fact her children are going to school here, and, most importantly, her desires to contest these charges and prove her innocence, I believe she is a candidate for release on her own recognizance. She so requests an O.R. release at this time. Your Honor, if I may, as her lawyer, I urge you to give Katherine such a release so I will be able to have her full assistance in preparing for her trial."

"Mrs. Pansky, the court appreciates you voluntarily stepping forward and requesting this arraignment. It speaks highly of yourself and your desire to challenge these charges." The judge then paused.

Drew held his breath. *Come on, Brown, do the right thing.*

"Mr. Farrat, why bail at all, given Mrs. Pansky initiated this morning's hearing and her appearance now?"

"Your Honor, the charges are for murder. No matter what good intentions are first shown, people panic and flee."

"Mr. Farrat, I don't see how any amount of money will stop a person who panics as you suggest. Only my denying bail will stop such an emotional reaction."

"Frankly, judge, the People prefer no bail and her confined behind bars until trial."

"I see." The judge paused again, then decided. "Mrs. Pansky, I am going to put myself out on the preverbal limb and grant you release on your own recognizance."

"Thank you, sir."

"Don't make me regret my decision."

"I won't, sir."

"The conditions of your release are as follows. You will make all court appearances. Failure to do so will result in the revocation of your O.R. release and your arrest. If you become ill or some other fate prevents you from being in court, you will immediately tell your lawyer, who will inform this court and the district attorney's office of your circumstances in a timely manner. You must waive your Fourth Amendment right and submit to all searches and, if necessary, seizures of your person and property. You will also provide to this court your current address. If you relocate your residence, you must get the court's permission first. Do you accept these terms?"

"Yes. I do so willingly. Thank you."

"To make myself clear, ma'am, you make all court-ordered appearances. For you to be excused, you will have to be near death or suffering from some deadly communicable disease. Otherwise, you will appear, if necessary, on a gurney with nurses in attendance."

"I understand, sir."

"Your Honor?"

"Yes, Mr. Hawke."

"I ask that my client's current address be put under seal for privacy purposes."

"Granted."

"Further, the defense will not waive time. And we wave the preliminary hearing and ask to proceed to trial within the time required by the law."

"Mrs. Pansky, is this what you want?"

"Yes, sir. It is what my attorney recommends."

"Hawke, are you sure this is what you want to do?"

"It is. The prosecution has no case."

"Very well. I will set the date for trial. . . . Ah, madam clerk, what's the trial calendar look like?"

"Frankly, sir, it's a mess," she said, shaking her head.

The judge motioned her to the side of his bench. They talked for several minutes. Judge Brown even looked at the trial calendars for his department and the other judges assigned criminal matters. Finally, he turned to the lawyers.

"Gentlemen, we will have a trial setting hearing for this case on this coming Thursday. Both attorneys will appear at nine a.m. Mrs. Pansky need not appear. The court will now take a fifteen-minute recess."

CHAPTER THIRTEEN

A BLACK PHONE SAT on the conference table facing Drew; Matt and Elizabeth sat to his right, and Debra to the left.

"While we wait for Pat's phone call, why don't I summarize the latest with Katherine Pansky. As you know, the Feds dropped their charges against Katherine for her providing testimony which led them to recover some top-secret documents. U.S. Attorney Wyland also agreed to allow the district attorney to proceed with their state case against Katherine for the murder of Senator Pansky."

Debbie spoke up, "So we only need to deal with the state case from here on out?"

"Correct. The Feds are out. As you know, I pled Katherine not guilty to the charges in the state case, didn't waive time, and demanded an early trial. That means we go to trial late next month. Our phone call today should tell us what Pat has learned about the senator's second family in Virginia. Do you guys have any questions?"

Matt looked around, then raised his hand.

"Yes, Matt."

"Why are we interested in the kid you fought weeks ago?"

"Somehow Chris Sykes is involved. He came up to me when I was at the Barleymash and told me Katherine didn't kill the senator. The troubling thing about this encounter is he became emotional and ran off when I asked how he knew that."

"Drew, that doesn't seem a good reason to have De Luca traveling to Virginia," stated Liz.

"Normally, I would agree. But Pat was already going to be in New Jersey investigating the C.T.I. case and its connection to Mayor Sandleson. Besides, for some reason Chief Shaughnessy has the DC police investigating the Sykeses and Nevan Pansky. So, I thought, let Pat try to find out what the police chief is looking for."

The phone rang. Debbie leaned forward and pushed the speaker button.

"Law offices, Debbie speaking."

"Hi, Debbie. It's Pat."

"We're all here, Pat," injected Drew.

"Good. Here's what I learned. Chris Sykes's mother is Ms. Yasmine Sykes. She died several years ago of stage-five cancer. As her cancer worsened, Ms. Sykes and Chris moved in with Yasmine's younger sister, Amena Gleeman, until Yasmine passed. Though Nevan Pansky had supported the family over the years, he refused to pay for her medical bills. According to Mrs. Gleeman, Nevan told Yasmine, 'I've told you a dozen times to purchase medical insurance for you and Chris. And what'd you do with my money? Spent it on silly clothes and alcohol.' "

"Do you believe the sister?"

"Yes, Drew. She seemed very believable. But here's the important part. When Yasmine died, Chris was very upset and swore he would kill Nevan for abandoning his mother. That's when he started his mixed martial arts training. Amena Gleeman told me several times Chris believed his mother would still be a live if she'd received the expensive medical care she obviously couldn't afford."

"Are you suggesting Chris might be a suspect?"

"Can't rule it out. Yasmine's death was nearly four years ago. When I asked Amena Gleeman if Chris still wanted to kill Nevan, she said, 'I don't think so.' She also said, 'The boy was only seventeen and very emotional after she died.'"

"Did you tell Mrs. Gleeman Nevan was dead?"

"No. I just told her I was hired to see how Chris was doing since his mother's death."

"I see. Did Pansky continue to support Chris after she died?"

"The sister said yes. After Yasmine's passing, Pansky arranged for Chris to go to the University of San Diego and made a significant contribution to the boy's trust so he could afford to do so. She added that Chris decided to take up the college offer about two years ago and is currently enrolled at the university."

"So, Pat, are you sure there is no indication Chris is still angry with his father?"

"Can't say for sure. Mrs. Gleeman stated when Chris left for San Diego he was excited to meet his father instead of just talking to him over the phone the few times he would call."

"How often did Mr. Pansky see his son?"

"Hardly ever. The boy was eight or ten when he last saw his father."

"What a bastard," Liz said softly.

"Yes, Liz, from everything I've learned he was a horrible father and a worse husband," answered Pat.

"Sorry, Pat," Liz apologized.

"Anything else, Pat?" Drew asked.

"That's about it, except my visit with the senator's staff confirmed Mrs. Pansky's statement that her husband was sleeping with all his young female interns, as well as many, many other East Coast women. But, no one knew if he had any other illegitimate children."

"When you talked to the senator's staff, did they mention if he had any death threats?"

"Oh, yes. Too many to count. All threats are immediately reported to the U.S. Capitol Police. That's one of the reasons a special protection squad was assigned to Nevan."

"Are there any recent threats or serious sounding ones that stand out?"

"Drew, I think the staff is so used to such threats they just pass them on to the USCP. You'll have to get that information from the lieutenant you get along with so well."

"Pat, that won't happen. Ah, regarding C.T.I., let's wait until you get to the Caymans for a report."

"Thank you. I really have to hurry; my flight leaves at one forty-five p.m."

"Travel safe, Pat."

The phone went silent.

"Any comments, guys? I think Chris Sykes is a non-suspect at this time."

"Any other evidence linking him to the murder?" asked Liz.

"None other than him telling me Katherine didn't kill her husband."

"You know, Drew," spoke up Debbie, "a son's love for his mother is very strong. If that young man wanted to kill his father, I don't think such an emotional feeling would go away quickly."

Matt injected another thought, "I know you have been

busy, boss, but the notes you took when you viewed the U.S. Capitol Police surveillance footage . . ."

"What about them?"

"You asked me to put together a timeline of who visited the house on the night of the murder. Your notes said Chris Sykes was in the house. Sounds like that is important."

"Could be, Matt."

"The timeline also shows Sykes arriving with Lydia Pansky. And, boss, the two left together a half an hour after Lydia's brother, Nathan, shows up. Mrs. Pansky enters the house hours later. She never leaves the house, but her son does. I included the times you noted in my report. It's in the pile of the stuff next to your desk that you asked me to do. Boss, could it be Sykes killed his father?"

"I didn't think so, but with this new information, it's a possibility. He certainly is physically capable of doing so. Let's see what else we come up with."

"So what's the connection between Lydia and Chris?" asked Liz.

"Don't know, guys. I'll ask Katherine. Right now, how about we meet again once we have some answers. Remember, trial is next month."

"Drew," Debbie offered, "I have this Thursday clear in the morning. Should I put us down, say eleven a.m.?"

"That works for me. How about you two?" he queried, looking to Liz and Matt.

Matt spoke up, "I'll make time."

"Me, too," added Liz.

"Drew, should I clear the calendar for the following three weeks so we can have several trial preparation meetings?"

"Thank you, Debbie, good idea. Liz, as part of the jury

selection process I need you to prepare a juror questionnaire, and specific questions I can ask jurors during voir dire."

"Alright. What type of juror do you want?"

"I think we want someone like Katherine. A woman, preferably a mother, and for male jurors, men with young daughters. The jurors should be semi-religious with daughters. I'm looking for parents with strong beliefs about what a father-daughter relationship should be."

"Okay."

"Also, prepare questions I can ask jurors about how they think a young girl would react if her father touched her in a sexual manner. For instance, would a thirteen-year-old girl be afraid to tell anyone; would a child be ashamed and even blame herself for what happened."

"You seem to be questioning jurors as if Lydia is on trial instead of Katherine."

"That is exactly right, Liz. We want prospective jurors who are receptive to the belief that a very young Lydia wouldn't know what to do when confronted by a sexual act. Even less if it is done by her father. And once attacked wouldn't know what to say and to whom."

"You're saying we have to show Nevan as a scoundrel and Lydia as an innocent child afraid to speak up."

"Correct. What's the underlying purpose of such questions? I need to determine if any juror will have a prejudice against Katherine for keeping the family together after learning of the molest. Write me questions to ask like: Should Katherine have stayed married after her sixteen-year-old daughter told her Nevan had been raping her for three years? Would you blame Katherine if Nevan tried to rape Lydia again?"

"Drew, what if a juror says Katherine should have left?"

"If a juror says she should have left, then change the

hypothetical to: What if Nevan promised never to touch Lydia again, and Katherine told her daughter what Daddy did was wrong and she should tell mommy if he tries again?

"In other words," Drew continued, "when Katherine decided to stay, she felt Lydia was old enough to know right from wrong and that her mother would protect her. That is the story we want to tell through our questioning of the jurors. We are in essence trying our case during juror selection. All these inquires build up to a final question: As a mother, would you violently defend your child if you came upon a man raping your daughter?"

"I see," answered Liz. "You're trying to convince the jury that if Katherine killed Pansky, she did it defending her daughter."

"That's right. What you must do, Liz, is frame all such questions as though we are looking for juror bias or a prior juror experience which would make the juror not have an open mind to the actions of Katherine and Lydia. It is a tightrope we must walk between seeing if a juror will accept the facts of our defense, while we appear to look for biased jurors. The judge will shut us down if we stray away from searching for bias. That's it in a nut shell. We don't want a juror that says Katherine should have divorced and gotten her children away from her husband. That is not what she did."

ooooo

Drew approached the Vista North County Executive Suites where he rented temporary space to meet North County clients. As he walked into the lobby, Tibbey, the fifty-six-year-old receptionist, smiled.

"Hi, Drew. Your conference room is ready and your people are already here."

"Thanks. How are you today?"

"I'm great," she said , "but that wretched woman with Elizabeth sure appears down and out. The poor thing. Is she homeless?"

"No. Why would you say that?"

"I don't mean to be rude, but her clothes are quite dirty and worn. Should I have the janitor clean up when you're done?"

"I doubt that will be necessary, but you are right, she's down on her luck."

Drew went through a door and entered the hallway leading to the glass-enclosed conference room. As he opened the door, he muttered to himself, "Now I know why Tibbey had questions."

"Been shopping for a new outfit?" he asked the two seated at the table.

"Goodwell rejects," responded Liz. "Doesn't Katherine look great? With the wig and all, you can barely recognize her."

"Ladies, why such an outfit?"

Katherine laughed. "Liz wouldn't let me go to Vons for groceries without this wig and our new disguise."

"And it worked," said Liz with a smile. "Nobody recognized her. I was worried, being a county supervisor, that Katherine would be easily noticed. But, dressed like this, no one recognized her."

"Are you okay with such a disguise?" Drew asked Katherine.

"It is actually fun, Drew. I even had a young boy about eight, the dear thing, ask if I was hungry and offered me a candy bar."

"His mother wasn't so generous," added Liz. "The woman quickly pulled the boy away and told him not so quietly such people have cooties."

Drew smiled and pulled out a chair, but once seated became serious. "Katherine, if your disguise is that good, continue to use it. But never go outside the house without Liz, or call me and I will have one of our bodyguards go with you. Don't need your picture plastered all over the media, especially in that outfit. Since the U.S. attorney granted you immunity and released you, we have to continue to hide you so the paparazzi don't find you. A photo of you in this outfit would be front-page news. So if you have to get some fresh air, let us go with you."

"I guess they could follow me back to the house and harass me day and night."

"That's correct. That's also why you took a leave of absence from the Board of Supervisors. There is just no way you could attend meetings and not be followed."

"I understand, Drew."

"Now, I asked to meet today so we could talk about your defense as trial is fast approaching."

"That's good news. I want to get this over with as soon as possible."

"I understand, Katherine, but I need answers to some questions. Before we go there, I want to say I think we can beat the charges or, if convicted on something, get a vastly reduced sentence. Maybe even house arrest. If that happens, you can continue on with life and be close to your children."

"Mr. Hawke, that would mean the world to me. After all this, my children need me more than ever."

"Our defense is based on forensic evidence as derived from the autopsy of Nevan. The police are basing their case on the assumption you killed your husband. I intend to prove you did not."

"How can you do that?"

"First things first. In order for us to succeed, I need straight, honest answers to my questions. Your answers will help fill in important parts of my defense theory. So please be truthful."

Katherine, with a somewhat questioning look, nodded and Drew proceeded.

"You told me the first time you met Chris Sykes was nearly two years ago. How did that happen?"

"He came to the house and asked to see Nevan. After the two talked for some time, he left. That's when I asked Nevan who the young man was. After some prodding, my husband said I would find out sooner or later that Christopher was his son. I told him there had been rumors for years about Nevan having a second family in Virginia. I demanded to know if Chris was part of that family. Nevan was shocked I knew. He begged me to understand and forgive him for his unfaithfulness."

"Did you?"

"I slapped him hard and went upstairs."

"That didn't answer my question. Did you forgive him?"

"Hell no. The son-of-a-bitch acted like I didn't know about his continuing sexual affairs with his interns and the other women in DC."

"I see. Tell me, is Chris dating Lydia?"

Katherine sat back with a questioning look on her face. "Ah . . . why do you ask?"

"They seem to be with each other a lot and very affectionate. Ma'am there is no reason to lie. As your lawyer, you should be disappointed in me if I didn't already know about them."

Katherine looked at Drew as though she had a flood of potential responses racing in her mind.

"Katherine, come clean. I can make the worst secrets look good. That is what I do."

His client just sat there. Drew persisted.

"I believe you want to be with the children so please answer the question. I don't need surprises at trial, especially one a jury could interpret as the reason you killed Nevan."

After a pause, she said, "Yes, they are dating. But no one is to know."

"The DA may already know." Drew then asked the obvious question. "Did you kill Nevan because he had a second family in Virginia, or because his Black son was dating Lydia?'

"No." The woman looked down and said nothing more.

"Katherine, why were Lydia and Chris at the house during the time Nevan was murdered?"

"That's enough, Hawke. If you persist, I will fire you and plead guilty. I've told you the children are off limits."

"They may be off limits, and I will probably never raise their relationship at trial, but if the DA does, I need to know what's going on so I can save our defense."

"Mr. Hawke, Lydia and Chris were not there when I arrived."

"Katherine, I know that. I also know that Chris and Lydia left after Nathan arrived. And I know you didn't arrive until over two hours later. I saw video of the house showing all this. Ma'am what was going on while everybody was in the house?"

"Mr. Hawke, I just can't say . . . I'm sorry."

The agitated woman burst into tears. Drew got up and walked around the room several times, waiting for composure. Finally, he leaned against a wall and stared at his still-wailing client. *What the hell went on in that house? And why won't she tell me?*

After a few more minutes of Liz trying to console the woman, Drew announced, "Katherine, I can't put you on the stand. If the DA knows about the kids being at the house and you refuse to answer questions about them, as sure as there is a hell, we will lose."

"I understand."

"Even if you insisted on testifying, the prosecutor would tear you apart. He will start with the theory you hated Nevan for fathering an illegitimate son, a Black son who is now dating Lydia. He will do this backhandedly so as to let those on the jury who are prejudiced against close siblings dating, or even those who harbor deep feelings about mixed couples, think that is why you killed him. Only God knows where things will go from there. Frankly, even if we get a good open-minded jury, Farrat's cross examination will be horrendous. I don't think you could handle it, especially every time he tries to bring Lydia into the murder."

"Then I will not testify."

"But that means, Mrs. Pansky, we are right back to square one—our forensic defense. Frankly, I think our decision to rush this case to trial appears to have been the right choice. Hopefully, Katherine . . . hopefully, the prosecutor may not have had enough time to figure out what really went on in your home that night and the children's part in this horrible affair."

The client just sat there, slumped in the chair, with Liz's arm around her.

This is going nowhere, but I have to ask, he thought as he sat down next to her. "Katherine, where were you between five p.m. and eight p.m. the night of the murder?"

"I was at . . . wait a minute . . . why?"

"All I need is an alibi that you weren't in the house when Nevan died, that's why."

"Does that mean you need witnesses who will have to come into court?"

"Yes."

"Oh, no, I'm not going to drag innocent, wonderful people into this horrible mess."

"Katherine, we're talking about your life here."

"I don't care. I've dedicated my body and soul to children,

and I will not further disgrace or drive away very important benefactors to a cause dear to me and so vitally needed by children."

"But, Katherine . . ."

"No, Hawke. I told you I came to you to plead guilty. In doing so, I also protect my children. That includes Chris—he's an innocent kid—and I will not endanger them or the causes I have dedicated my life to. It is who and what I am. You will not take them down with me. That's final. No."

"I understand, Mrs. Pansky." *Man, this lady is morally bound to her beliefs.*

"Thank you, Drew. You are a very kind person. Now what do we do? Go to the DA and strike a deal?"

"Not at all. We can always do that even in the middle of trial. I told you, if things look bleak, I would get us a deal. I still have a defense, which hopefully will raise enough reasonable doubt to convince a jury to acquit. You still trust me?"

"Yes, Drew. But keep my kids out of this, and tell me before you bring any alibi witnesses forward."

"Yes, ma'am."

CHAPTER FOURTEEN

Monday, Three Weeks Later

DREW, KATHERINE, AND LIZ stepped out of Matt's double-parked van on Union Street and walked south toward the corner of Union and C streets. The entrance to San Diego's new 369-foot-tall California Superior Courthouse stood straight ahead. The low-pitched drone of four television trucks, and their generators parked ahead of them, drowned out the sound of a morning trolley proceeding east on C street. As the trio walked past the trucks, their twenty-foot-tall satellite antennas ominously towered over them. A crowd of reporters milled about in the outside portico to the courthouse entrance.

No sooner did the three step up onto the first of fourteen steps leading to the portico than the crowd of reporters rushed down the steps, shouting a blur of questions. Drew held up both hands.

"Guys, please. One question at a time. First, Jack Zane, for the *San Diego Herald*."

"Drew, does Supervisor Pansky intend to take the stand?"

"You know better than to ask that question, Jack. Mrs. Pansky is innocent and we intend to use every option to acquit her of the charges."

"You." Drew pointed to a woman in the gathered crowd. "Yes, the reporter from CNN."

"Who do you say killed Senator Pansky?"

"That is not the defense's job. We intend to prove emphatically, however, that Katherine did not kill her husband. . . . Yes, the woman at the back. You guys should give the ladies room to get closer."

"Thank you, Mr. Hawke, but I can hold my own," the woman said.

"I believe you can," replied Drew as the group of reporters laughed.

"Mr. Hawke, if you won't say who killed the senator, please answer how he died."

"That is part of our defense. You will have to wait until our expert takes the stand to find out how the senator actually died. I'm sure ADA Farrat believes he knows the answer. But I encourage you to stand by. I think you will find our case quite interesting."

A dozen questions flew at once as the reporters tried to be heard.

"Please, please," Drew responded. "I think all your questions will be answered once the trial starts. This morning's hearing is a pretrial conference with Judge Steinman. He will tell us if we start this afternoon or tomorrow."

Dozens of hands raised as reporters shouted over one another. Again, Drew silenced the gathering.

"The only thing I ask of you is to keep an open mind until you hear our defense. So how about we go in. I have to get to the pretrial conference. I'm sure the judge doesn't want us late."

One or two reporters still tried to get an answer to their questions as their compatriots parted, opening a passage for the three to enter the courthouse's 48-foot-tall atrium and proceed to the security screening.

Once through security, the three strode to the elevators. Liz pushed the button for the Department 1505 floor and turned to Hawke.

"Drew, why did we get reassigned at the last moment to Judge Steinman? We've had Judge Gonzales-Black for pretrial and she was to handle trial. What happened?"

"Probably Presiding Judge Brian O'Shea. He's always moving cases around. I think he likes controlling cases and their outcomes."

"That doesn't sound right," responded Katherine.

"There are a lot of things in the law that aren't fair. You just have to learn how to neutralize their effects and avoid any prejudice to your client," Drew replied, a serious look on his face.

Hawke had never appeared before Judge Joel Steinman but knew of his reputation. Many attorneys called him a procedural fanatic with a fiery temper. Others viewed the 5-foot, 5-inch judge as a dominating egotist with a Napoleonic complex. Whatever others thought of the judge, Drew was confident he could get along well with the man.

Drew opened the door to Department 1505 and told Liz and Katherine to have a seat in the first row of the gallery.

Drew walked up to the barrister's rail, right behind the bailiff.

"Morning, I'm attorney Drew Hawke," and offered his hand as a greeting.

The deputy sheriff greeted the young attorney and took his hand. "Caleb Wells. Relax, the other deputies have told me about you."

Drew smiled. "I hope it's all good."

Still holding Drew's hand, the deputy pulled Drew close.

"Be careful in here. Listen to what the judge demands. Never cross him."

At that moment a loud voice echoed in the courtroom, "Hawke! Get in here."

Drew turned but couldn't see anybody.

"Deputy Wells said, "It's the judge. Say, 'Yes, sir,' and quickly."

Drew stepped to his left so he could see beyond the judge's bench. There he was—a short man wearing a white, long-sleeved, French-cuffed dress shirt, a dark-blue tie with gold stripes, and a pair of unbelievably bright-red suspenders.

"Yes, sir, but the prosecutor hasn't arrived."

"I could give a shit. Get in here."

Liz started to move toward the judge, but Drew put his hand out, stopping her. At that moment ADA Farrat walked in.

"Jack, the judge wants us in chambers."

The two started toward the judge only to have the judge stomp his foot.

"I didn't say you, Farrat. Hawke get in here."

"Sir, we can't be having ex parte talks. It's unethical."

"I determine what is ethical and unethical, Hawke, not you."

Drew stood frozen. Deputy Wells, in a low, forceful voice, said, "Go, Hawke. Get in there."

Drew just stood there. "Sir, I never refuse a judge's order, but I can't endanger my client's defense by having a conference with a trial judge without the prosecutor. Please, sir, whatever you have to say to me I'm sure can be said with Jack Farrat present."

"Then get your asses in here. Now!" shouted Judge Steinman as he whirled about and stomped into his chambers, his angry command amplified by the sound of his hard-soled elevator shoes reverberating throughout the courtroom. Drew told Liz to wait and started toward the door, with Jack Farrat following.

Once inside, the judge demanded, "Shut the damn door." Still standing, he continued, "When I say something, it is an order, not a request. You understand that?"

Both attorneys answered yes.

"Sit," he demanded, pointing to the two side chairs in front of what appeared to be a rather tall desk. The judge went behind the desk and sat in his chair.

Hawke nearly fell backward as he sat down in his chair. *What the hell? The chair's legs have been shorted.* Drew looked over to Farrat, whose knees were almost touching his chest. *Is this guy for real?*

"So, you're the infamous, Andrew J. Hawke. You're a little taller than you look on TV," snorted the judge from his highly elevated executive chair.

"Infamous, sir?"

"Don't challenge my words, Hawke. I know about your theatrics. There will be no such antics in my courtroom. Do you hear me?"

"Sir, I am not sure what you are . . ."

Looking down on Hawke, Steinman smiled. "Say, 'yes,' Hawke. A 'yes' is what you want to say. Not a blabbering ramble of excuses."

"Yes, sir."

"That's better. Now, here are the rules. No surprise witnesses. What's on this witness list are the only people who will testify in this trial," said the man as he waived about the joint witness list. "Further, no suddenly found evidence. All evidence will be disclosed in advance of trial and approved by me. Any objections to proffered evidence will be decided by me this afternoon in our pretrial conference. At the same time, I will rule on your suggested juror questionnaires. My decisions are final. Jury selection will start tomorrow. Any questions?"

Drew looked over to Jack, who stared wide-eyed straight ahead.

"One more thing, Hawke. In this courtroom I am G-o-d," he growled. "You cross me and I will make your life miserable. Be warned, I just don't fine for contempt, I put people like you in the calaboose, with a hefty fine. Not one day or two days but for w-e-e-ks," Judge Steinman slowly crowed, adding a grin.

"Now, get the hell out of my chambers."

The two lawyers walked out together. Once out of hearing, Drew whispered, "Can you believe this guy?"

"Hawke, don't look to me for help. My office knows all about this guy. You're on your own." Farrat punctuated his comment with his usual wiseass chuckle.

The ride back to the office was somewhat subdued. Every time Katherine or Liz asked what happened with the judge, Drew said they would talk about it back at the office.

Once inside the office, Drew said, "Mrs. Pansky, you may as well leave. Matt will take you to the safehouse. I will pick you up at seven-thirty tomorrow morning. The attorneys will meet with the judge this afternoon to go over trial procedures. The judge changed things slightly. I will give you a call late this afternoon with an update."

ooooo

Judge's Chambers, 1:30 p.m.

"Gentlemen . . . oh, yes, lady. I believe you are Ms. Elizabeth Bernquist?"

"Yes, sir."

"Welcome to my chambers, Ms. Bernquist. Now, the purpose of this afternoon's meeting is to determine if there are any objections to the proposed evidence and witnesses. Mr. Hawke, your witness list is extremely long. Why? If you were to call all these people, we will be here for weeks."

"Your Honor."

"Yes, ADA Farrat."

"Mr. Hawke has told me he only intends to call his client and one expert."

"Is that correct, Hawke?"

"Yes. But since I don't know what the prosecution has in mind, I have listed those witnesses I deem necessary for a proper defense."

"Oh, really. That will not be the case. Two defense witnesses it will be. Any objections to my ruling? . . . I see no hands raised. Good. That's settled."

"Drew glanced at Farrat, who refused to acknowledge his questioning look.

"Now, about your suggested juror questionnaires and possible voir dire questions. Do you have any additional questions or matters you wish to add? ADA Farrat?"

"Sir, no."

"Good. Mr. Hawke?"

"No, sir."

"I see, young man, you are getting the grasp of how things work in this department. Very well. I have decided not to use either of your suggested juror questionnaires. I will instead use the juror questionnaire in California Rules of Court, Standard 4.30.

"Your Honor . . ."

"Nuh-uh-uh, Mr. Hawke. There will be no debate. The questionnaire is done. Now, based on the responses of each juror to the court questionnaire, I will ask follow-up questions, if I see that as necessary. During my direct statements to the jurors, I intend to follow my normal course of inquiry about any physical problems they may have. Such as vision, hearing, or medical difficulties that might affect the jurors' ability to serve. I will also inform them about the length of the trial and hear any excuses that their job won't allow them to miss work."

The judge looked up from the papers he had been reading from. "Hear me clearly. I don't cater to the willy-nilly use of one's job as an excuse not to fulfil their duty as a juror. I will use my judgment on such issues on an individual basis. I will then lecture the jury panel on their civic duties as jurors, how they should be unbiased in applying their experiences to this case's facts, et cetera. I will then read the indictment, introduce the defendant, and Mr. Hawke. Thereafter, I will introduce Mr. Farrat. Now, regarding any questions you may ask the jurors . . . Yes, Mr. Hawke, your hand is raised?"

'Will you also read the list of prosecution and defense witnesses?"

"Of course. I'm no idiot. I will do everything as outlined in Rules of Court 4.30. And that will be it. Now, once I am done, I really don't see why you two will need to ask the jurors any questions. All non-qualified jurors will have been dismissed by me."

"Excuse me, sir."

"Y-e-s, Mr. Hawke," the judge said with a condescending tone of voice.

"Standard 4.30 states attorneys should be allowed to question jurors."

"Mr. Hawke, I know you like to try your defenses in the voir dire questioning of jurors. I've read transcripts of your last three voir dires. I even attended the jury selection of your last criminal trial. I find your tactics abusive of the jury system and prejudicial to justice. You will not do the same in this case."

"I'm sorry you feel that way judge, but California Code of Civil Procedure section 223 says counsel for each party 'shall have the right to examine, by oral and direct examination, any of the prospective jurors.' Are you denying me the right to question jurors for bias and suitability to serve?"

"I see you know your codes. You will indeed be a pain in the ass during this trial."

"Sir, are you denying me that right?"

"No, Mr. Hawke. You each will have ten minutes for your mining for prejudice. But I warn you, if you stray away and begin to delve into other matters, I will terminate all questioning."

"I don't mean to be rude, Your Honor . . ."

"Quite to the contrary, Hawke, you are rude by your very nature. So what is it now?"

"The code states, 'The trial judge shall not impose unreasonable or arbitrary time limits or establish an inflexible time-limit policy for questioning of jurors. Aren't you doing exactly that?"

"One might agree with such a statement, except my questioning of the jurors and my explanation of their duties as a juror are so thorough that there will be no need for your further inquiry for prejudice, which we both know is a ruse, a maneuver, a trick . . ." the judge said as he stood and slammed his fist on his desk. ". . . for you, Hawke," he continued, raising his voice even higher, "to try your defense and choose jurors that only favor your case. No, Mr. Hawke. No! You will not stray away from specific inquiries into bias that I have already covered nor raise other ridiculous issues. Is that understood?"

"I assume, sir, you will put your decisions of our meeting this afternoon on the record?"

"I see no reason to do so."

"In all due respect, sir, I would like them on the record."

"That, Mr. Hawke, will be for you to do during the actual voir dire process if for any unfathomable reason you find the need to do so. Gentlemen, we are done here. Exit now."

As the two walked out of chambers and into the court-room, Farrat spoke, "Hawke, you really know how to piss a judge off. When will you learn?"

"I know when I am being railroaded. This whole thing—the last-minute reassignment from Judge Gonzales to Steinman—is nothing but an effort to convict Mrs. Pansky. I am not going to let that happen."

"Don't ask me for any help. You're on your own."

"Jack, when have I ever asked you for anything, except to do what is right? This judge is not right. In fact, he is a mental case."

The afternoon conference with the Honorable Joel Steinman was an obvious disaster. As Liz and Drew parted ways with ADA Farrat, the angry young attorney turned to his associate.

"Elizabeth, don't say anything during this trial. Let me take the brunt of his fury. I need you out of jail so we can file emergency appeals to the appellate court. War has been declared by that lunatic. And I believe the general behind this mess is the Presiding Judge Brian O'Shea. He wants Katherine Pansky convicted for some reason."

CHAPTER FIFTEEN

TUESDAY

"Hear ye, hear ye, this court will come to order," Deputy Sheriff Caleb Wells called out as the judge, in his black robe, entered and stepped up onto the elevated bench platform. "Department 1505 is now in session, the Honorable Joel Steinman presiding. Please stand for the Pledge of Allegiance to the flag of the United States of America." In unison, Judge Steinman, in a loud, high-pitched voice, led those in attendance: "I pledge allegiance to the flag of the United States of America and to the republic for which it stands, one nation, under God, indivisible, with liberty and justice for all."

"Please be seated," Deputy Wells said.

Still standing, Judge Steinman addressed the courtroom of potential jurors, news media, and interested observers.

"I now call the case of The People of the State of California vs. Katherine Margaret Pansky. Counsel, state your appearances."

"Assistant District Attorney Jack Farrat for the People."

"Attorney Andrew J. Hawke for the defendant Katherine Pansky, who is present. Your Honor, the defense waives the formal reading of the charges and is prepared to proceed."

"Mr. Hawke, I asked you to only state your presence, not for an oration. Be more attentive to my orders."

Drew stood motionless and did not respond.

The judge continued. "The People of the State of California have charged you, Katherine Margaret Pansky, with Penal Code section 187 for the murder of your husband, United States Senator Nevan Pansky. The San Diego County Grand Jury indictment reads further that you did willfully kill Nevan Pansky in the first degree—"

Drew stood and stated, "Your Honor, Mrs. Pansky has read the indictment, had all allegations of the indictment explained to her by me, and has previously entered a plea of not guilty."

"Mr. Hawke, I am sure you don't want the very serious charges the twenty-one members of the San Diego Grand Jury have indicted your client on to be read aloud, but I feel the audience, especially the media, want to know the exact charges against the defendant."

"In all due respect, sir, I have already given the reporters and media personnel a copy of the indictment, and, if I may point out, the said indictment is automatically made a part of this trial's record. And, sir, I specifically waive formal reading of the charges so as to only expedite the jury-selection process. We have nearly forty prospective jurors to question."

"Mr. Hawke, one more interruption by you and I will hold you in contempt. Is that clear? I decide how things are done in this court, not you. Now, where was I? . . . Oh, yes . . ."

The judge, still standing so all could see him, continued to read the charges, which included manslaughter in the first degree with enhancements for each charged count, including the use of a gun. The judge even included the sentencing range for each charged offense.

Drew just shook his head as he sat down, took pen in hand, and noted on a yellow pad, "Jury contamination—reading indictment? Turn horrible alleged crimes into sympathy for client." He then flipped the sheet to a clean page and wrote, "When Steinman is done reading the charges, stand and in a strong voice . . ."

Drew paused and touched his client's arm, and scribbled some more words, showing her what he had written.

"How do you plead to the indictment, Mrs. Katherine Margaret Pansky?" the judge asked.

Holding the yellow pad in front of her, she rose. "I emphatically deny those horrible acts. I did not kill my husband!"

A murmur went up in the standing-room-only courtroom as reporters quickly took pen to pads and made notes.

"Mrs. Pansky, I just asked for your plea."

Drew immediately rose. "Your Honor, my client answered your request the only way she knew how. If you wish, I can instruct her as to how I think you want her plea entered."

"You know, Mr. Hawke, you jumping up and down is getting on my nerves. Sit down! Mrs. Pansky, do you plead guilty or not guilty?" demanded the judge.

Still standing, Drew leaned over and whispered in her ear. She looked to the judge and said, "I plead not guilty." Again she looked to Drew who whispered more to her. "I also," she paused, "deny all allegations . . . and . . . enhancements."

Steinman stared at Hawke. His face flushed red as he threw the charging sheet onto the bench, turned, and sat down. The judge shifted in his chair as he looked through the papers in front of him. Finding his yellow pad, he looked up and spoke in a loud and still high-pitched voice.

"Ladies and gentlemen, it is my duty to now conduct the search for twelve impartial jurors and two alternates who will sit in judgment on this case. Madam clerk, please call the first fourteen prospective jurors."

As each name was called, Deputy Wells directed the

potential juror where to sit. Once all were seated, the judge turned to the jury box and began to speak, this time in a calmer, controlled and somewhat deeper voice.

"Juror number one . . ." He pointed to the juror seated in the first row, next to the witness stand. ". . . the deputy has handed you a sheet with a series of questions. Please look at those questions."

While the juror looked at the sheet, Judge Steinman stepped down from the bench and stood in front of the assembled prospective jurors. When juror number one looked up, Steinman began. "Now, answer each question from the top of the sheet, starting with your name or your juror identification number."

With a look of confusion, Drew immediately looked to Farrat, who sat stoned-faced. *Judges don't question jurors by leaving the bench. What is he up to?*

Each perspective juror read from the same sheet, providing their name or juror ID number, along with their occupation and that of a significant other, if any. After the jurors finished answering the questions, the judge then asked if any of the fourteen seated jurors had ever served on a jury or grand jury. The judge then asked if any of the seated jurors knew the lawyers in the case, the defendant, or anything about the case to be tried. All of the perspective jurors raised their hands and either said they had heard of attorney Hawke, his client, or the death of Senator Pansky.

"Regardless of any preconceived thoughts or information you have about this case, Mrs. Pansky, or for that matter about Mr. Hawke, will you be able to ignore those thoughts and decide this case based upon the facts as presented in this courtroom? In short, I am asking if you can be unbiased and only make your decisions in this case based upon what you hear in the courtroom?"

What is the judge doing? All people have biases, most of which are based upon their upbringing, education, work, and life traumas, mused Drew as he scribbled more notes.

All the jurors nodded yes to the judge's question.

"Good. That is exactly what we want. Jurors who are capable of rendering findings of fact based solely on courtroom witness testimony given under oath."

That's it! My God, he is lecturing, not questioning the jurors on their prior experiences, which may affect how they interpret what they hear.

Drew began writing more extensive notes as the judge blissfully passed from one area to the next of potential prejudice toward Mrs. Pansky, the senator, and what they had heard through the newspapers and television. Drew underlined two times the words on his note pad: "This is not a voir dire for prejudice. He is just teaching the jurors to say what Steinman wants to hear."

The judge continued to lecture for a good forty-five minutes as he discussed with each juror what they knew about the case and the parties. All fourteen told the judge they would judge the case only on the facts heard in court. Several jurors spoke glowingly about Drew Hawke and how he had spectacularly proven his client's innocence in previous cases. From the judge's facial expressions, these praises appeared to irritate him.

"You understand, ladies and gentlemen, that the process of reaching a just and righteous verdict is a collaborative process steered under the astute hand of an impartial judge whose sworn duty is to render justice."

Several jurors looked confused. The judge turned and walked toward Hawke and the defense table, a contemptuous smile creasing his face. Standing in front of Drew, he scrutinized the young man, then looked back toward the jury.

"And," he continued, raising his right index finger in the air, "it is only through the process of our legal system, which includes the police, their astute investigations, the prosecutor and, on occasion, the defense attorney, can the true facts be known. That is the process that you must base your decisions on in this case. Not a personality, no matter how flamboyant the person may be. Such showmanship distorts the evidence and will keep you from a proper verdict."

For emphasis, Steinman thumped his fingers on the defense table before he went on, in a raised voice. "You must render your decision only on what the witnesses say under oath."

Many of the jurors looked at one another and then to Drew.

I hope their looks are ones of disbelief, Drew pleaded to himself as he noted on his pad, "The madman has just committed reversable error and personally attacked me in an effort to poison the jurors against my client and me."

Steinman resumed his position in front of the jury and continued asking if any juror had been a victim of a crime, knew or had contact with a police officer, or had any relative, close friend, or a relationship with anyone involved in law. This question caused several jurors to raise their hands. After two hours of questioning, in particular questions about certain jurors' answers on their questionnaires, the judge then asked if any of the fourteen could not serve on the panel because of the nature of the case, its expected seven-day length, or due to any other reason.

"Yes, juror number four."

"My work, Your Honor," answered the juror. "I can't miss any work time."

After listening to the juror's reasons, the judge looked to the juror and then addressed his remarks to the entire panel.

"Ladies and gentlemen, very little is asked of you as a citizen of this country. Yes, some of you have stood up to protect this nation and may even have been seriously wounded in battle trying to defend our country. The United States Constitution and its justice system is a vital part of the American way of life. It is the foundation of our freedoms. Now we ask for a few days of sacrifice in return so our system of justice can work. I know it is difficult, but without your participation, justice" . . . the judge paused ". . . justice as we know it cannot prevail. So we will take a recess. During that time, I want you to ask yourself, can I really not serve? If you conclude you can't serve, then call your employer and ask him if you can have the time off to do your duty. If the employer says no, I want to know his name and phone number. It is my intent to have all of you who are here today to serve, if chosen."

To say the least, the fourteen seated and the reaming perspective members of the forty-person jury panel were stunned. Deputy Wells then announced, "This court is now in recess for fifteen minutes."

ooooo

Supervisor Pansky, Liz, and Drew exited the courtroom and walked toward the north end of the courthouse, then turned left toward a secluded alcove next to two bathrooms.

As they walked, Katherine spoke softly, "Drew, I don't think the judge likes you."

"Frankly, Katherine, I don't think he likes anyone. But you are right, something is amiss here. Someone is trying to railroad you for murder. I don't know if it's Steinman or somebody else."

"If it's that bad, maybe I should try to strike a deal with the DA?"

"Be patient, Katherine. We have a strong defense planned.

The judge can only prejudice things so far. The jurors appeared to not like his personal attacks on me. That is a good sign."

"But, Drew, I don't want to risk a life sentence. I am only going along with this trial because you said I could mitigate my liability."

"You're correct, and that is what I intend to do. If I feel we need to change course, we will have a serious conversation about a plea deal. I know Jack Farrat. I can work with him. For now, let's see how things go. Okay?"

"If you say so. I trust you, Drew Hawke. My life is in your hands."

CHAPTER SIXTEEN

ONCE COURT RESUMED, the judge stepped up on the raised platform and stood next to his bench. Slowly, he looked across the gathered audience and then stared at the defense table. He turned his gaze to the jury box.

"Ladies and gentlemen, does anyone ask to be excused from their duty as a citizen of this country?" No one spoke up.

"I see no hands raised. Assistant District Attorney Farrat, you may conduct your juror inquiry. You have ten minutes," the judge stated.

Farrat rose. "Your Honor, I have no questions. Your inquiry was more than sufficient."

Still standing, a smiling Judge Steinman looked to the defense table. "Mr. Hawke, I assume you have no questions, too?"

"Thank you, sir. But I do."

Drew rose and walked up to the jury box. "Ladies and gentlemen, how many of you are familiar with Supervisor Pansky's statement to the media where she said, "I caused my husband's death? Please raise your hands if you have." All the jurors raised their hands.

"Mr. Hawke, I have already questioned the jurors about their feelings toward Mrs. Pansky," snapped the judge. "Why do you repeat the process?"

"Sir, you did not ask this specific question. I seek a specific answer not a general feeling about my client."

"Careful, Hawke, careful."

"Juror number five, you had raised your hand regarding knowing about Mrs. Pansky. Do you know what Katherine meant by the word 'caused'?"

"I assume, Mr. Hawke, she meant 'I killed my husband,' " answered the elderly woman.

"Will you keep an open mind as to her true meaning of the word 'caused' until the defense puts on its case?" asked Drew.

"I guess I can."

"Good. After all, one doesn't know if her choice of words were ones of guilt or remorse for not leaving the man who molested her daughter."

"That's enough, Hawke. No more questions."

"Your Honor, you said I have ten minutes. Have you changed your mind?"

"Enough of this line of questioning. Move on, attorney Hawke."

"Do any of you have a bias or deep-seated anger toward my client because she didn't take her children and leave once she learned of Nevan Pansky's incest? Please raise your hand if you do." No one did so.

"Juror number ten, do you think Mrs. Pansky should have left?"

"That's enough, Hawke. I said move on."

"In all due respect, sir, I do need a specific verbal response for the record."

"Ladies and gentlemen," the judge interceded, "to expedite things, if you have any such ill feelings or beliefs, please raise your hands. Seeing none raised, move on, Hawke."

"Thank you, sir. Do any of you believe in the concept of self-defense and whether one can take a life in self-defense?"

"Oh no, no, no. We are not going there. Your time is up."

"I'm sorry, sir, I have a right to see if a juror does not believe in self-defense when a person is charged with murder, especially when that person is a woman of inferior strength or is defending a member of her family."

"No. Emphatically no. You're done."

Juror number four raised his hand. "Yes, juror number four, what is it?"

"Your Honor, I believe no one can take a life even if theirs is threatened. It is against God to do so."

"Your Honor, I request a sidebar on the record?" asked Drew.

Steinman appeared near apoplexy as his face reddened and his fists clinched. "Get over here," he growled, pointing to the area farthest from the jurors, by the court clerk.

Once Drew, Farrat, and the court reporter were at the far side of the bench, the judge leaned down and demanded, "What are you trying to do, Hawke? I told you there was no need to question these jurors further."

"Apparently, sir, you missed one. We can't have anyone as a juror who is so biased against taking a life. My client has self-defense and other mitigating factors, which the law allows. Self-defense is a legitimate ground for a not guilty verdict. At the worst, it is the difference between murder and manslaughter."

"I have charged murder in the first degree, Your Honor, which does carry a potential life sentence in California. We are not talking about the chair," offered Farrat.

Drew shook his head at the ADA's nonsense statement. "That is not what I'm worried about, judge. I can't have a person with such a bias deciding self-defense or murder."

"Enough, Hawke. I will handle this. Now go sit down. Your time is up for questioning."

Drew and Farrat resumed their seats. Steinman sat hunched over deep in thought. Finally, the judge looked up and addressed the jury.

"Is there anyone else who feels the same as juror number four?" No one raised their hand.

"Juror number four, you are excused. Please go back to the jury assembly room. Madam clerk, call the next prospective juror."

Deputy Wells held the barrister gate open and directed a new prospective juror, a woman, to chair number four. Once she had taken her seat, the judge continued.

"Have you heard all my questions today?"

"Yes, Your Honor," answered the woman.

"Would you answer them the same as the other seated jurors?"

"Well, yes, except I do think self-defense of one's self or your family is proper."

"Fine. Any questions counsel?" Before Farrat or Hawke could respond, the judge declared, "We have a jury. Jurors please stand, the clerk will now give you the juror oath."

Drew looked to Jack, who just gazed straight ahead. After the jury was sworn, the judge declared that the trial would begin the next day.

As the judge rose, Deputy Wells announced, "This court is adjourned until nine a.m." He then added, "All members of the jury panel report back to the jury assembly room. The fourteen jurors just sworn in please be outside this courtroom by eight-thirty a.m. tomorrow."

ooooo

Once back at the law office Drew, Katherine, and Liz sat in the conference room.

"Katherine, we accomplished what I wanted today. I planted the idea that your statement to the press did not mean you murdered your husband and, better yet, that our jury will have to decide if Nevan was killed in cold blood or died by someone's hand defending themselves, or you defending your daughter. That is a total victory."

"If you say so. But, Drew, I'm worried. This judge is really dictatorial."

"Oh, he is that for sure. Yes, I wanted to do more, but Judge Steinman wouldn't allow any questions about the jurors' background and experiences, which is important for determining how they feel about cases like ours. I tried but he wouldn't have it. But I believe the jury recognizes he is keeping me from telling them more about the case. In my opinion, Steinman looked unreasonable as he blocked even my most innocuous questions. I'm convinced they also want to hear our side of what happened that Sunday night. Joel Steinman will not prevent the jurors from doing the right thing once they hear our story."

"I don't know, Drew, the judge seems determined to control what the jurors will hear."

"Katherine, the key to your defense is my expert medical examiner. No judge can stop an expert from saying how and when your husband died. Once the jury hears that testimony, they can't find you guilty of murder or manslaughter. Case over. You walk free."

"Sounds good. But the trial doesn't appear to be going as you originally expected. I hope you have an exit plan if things go wrong. If you don't, tell me and I will find one."

CHAPTER SEVENTEEN

Wednesday

THE JURY WAS SEATED. Prosecutor Jack Farrat and his lead San Diego Police Detective Thomas Clayton sat at the prosecution table, nearest to the jury. Drew Hawke, Katherine Pansky, and co-counsel Elizabeth Bernquist took their seats at the defense table, to the right.

"All rise, Department 1505 of the San Diego Superior Court is now in session. The Right Honorable Joel Steinman presiding," announced Deputy Caleb Wells. After the Pledge of Allegiance, Judge Steinman took the bench chair and Deputy Wells announced to the courtroom crowd, "Please be seated."

Judge Stein scanned the courtroom and smiled. "Good morning, ladies and gentlemen."

"Good morning, Your Honor," came the response from the courtroom.

"I have a few preliminary remarks before we begin. First, as the media knows, I am not a fan of live television coverage of judicial proceedings. In my opinion, they distract from the duty of finding justice. That is especially true when attorneys and even witnesses play to the camera. That will not happen in this court. Do you hear me?" roared Judge Steinman as he intentionally stared at attorney Hawke. The jurist held his stare inordinately long so all could see who he was addressing.

Looking back to the audience, he continued. "But because of the apparent overwhelming interest of the public in the death of a member of Congress, and at the insistence of the media, I have, after lengthy consultation with Presiding Judge Brian O'Shea, agreed to allow TV coverage of this trial, with the following rules.

"I have ordered a thirty-second delay in the live broadcast of proceedings. Anytime—I repeat—anytime I order the cameras off, they will go dark and broadcast will immediately cease. Failure to do so will result in the confiscation of the cameras and the arrest of the offending media personnel. Second, any playing to the cameras by the attorneys will result in their immediate reprimand and sanctioning.

"Now, ladies and gentlemen of the jury, from time to time there will be an objection by one party or the other. If I sustain the objection, you are to ignore the question and any answer you may have heard. If I overrule the objection, the question stands and the witness will be instructed to answer. Second, any comments by the attorneys, if there be any, are to be ignored.

"All objections are to be by the Evidence Code, gentlemen . . ." He again looked intently at attorney Hawke. "For instance, you will say 'objection,' 'leading,' 'hearsay,' 'argumentative,' et cetera."

"Mr. Hawke, I didn't hear your response."

"Oh . . . yes, sir," stated Hawke, rising in a sign of respect.

"Good. ADA Farrat, you may make your opening statement."

"Thank you, Your Honor," stated Farrat as he rose and walked across the well to stand in front of the jurors. "This case, my fellow citizens, is a simple one. It is one of vengeance executed in anger. An anger so intent that it resulted in the murder of Senator Nevan Pansky. Vengeance; yes, *vengeance*," he emphasized, pointing an accusing finger at Katherine Pansky. Taken out on her husband for his incestual acts with her daughter, Lydia Pansky. Sadly, this is a case of a sexual predation first inflicted upon an innocent thirteen-year-old girl. No wonder Katherine Pansky killed her husband. Wouldn't you?"

"Objection, Your Honor. There is no evidence my client killed Nevan Pansky. His statement is argumentative."

"Overruled. ADA Farrat, move along."

"Yes, sir."

Drew noted all the jurors writing in their spiral note pads.

Smiling, Farrat walked over to the defense table and faced the defendant. "The state will prove, through our experts, that on the night of the murder, gunpowder residue was found all over Mrs. Pansky, indicating she had just fired a weapon. The weapon a Glock 19 handgun. The same weapon testing proves killed her husband.

"We will also introduce video taken of Mrs. Pansky at a news conference where she admitted to knowing about her husband's incest. Incredibly, she stated, 'This Sunday . . .' the night, ladies and gentlemen of the jury, that Nevan Pansky was murdered, 'This Sunday, I caught Nevan sexually attacking my precious child. That is why he is dead.' "

ADA Farrat walked behind the accused and stated, "Mrs. Pansky continued to speak as the gathered media stood shocked."

Drew looked at his client, who had tears running down her cheeks, then stood. "Objection. Mr. Farrat is editorializing. This is improper. There is no evidence about the media's reaction in the video to be shown. Further, the prosecutor is trying to intimidate my client by standing next to her. She is in tears by his tactics."

"Overruled. Mr. Hawke, this is opening statement. Sit down."

"Thank you, Your Honor," answered Drew.

"Thank me for what, Hawke? For overruling your ridiculous objection?"

Drew smiled and sat down. *I do believe I am making the judge look cold and callous. Not my intent, but I hope the jury sees how prejudiced the judge is against me and Katherine. I pray the jury understands Farrat's hovering around Katherine is an intentional act of intimidation and is improper.*

The judge gestured with his head for the ADA to move back toward the prosecution table. As Farrat slowly walked, he said, "We will also prove that Senator Nevan Pansky had a longtime sexual relationship with a known prostitute in Virginia. A sexual relationship which produced an illegitimate son. I will let you decide if that is another reason the defendant killed the senator."

Voices could be heard as the gallery apparently reacted to the news of a second family in Virginia.

"Objection, Your Honor."

Before Hawke could state the formal objection, Steinman interrupted. "Mr. Hawke, if you stand up one more time or object I will hold you in contempt. Sit d-o-w-n!"

Once again, the jurors wrote furiously in their notepads.

God, I hope they are not writing anything critical of me.

"Quiet," the judge ordered in a shrill voice as he pounded his gavel. "Please remain silent."

Farrat stood at the prosecution table. He placed a hand on the back of his chair and finished his opening statement.

"Ladies and gentlemen, there will be much more evidence produced during this trial. But I ask you to not forget my words: 'vengeance executed in anger.' They will guide you to a verdict of guilty—a guilty judgment against Katherine Margaret Pansky . . . for the murder of her husband. Thank you."

Judge Steinman looked toward the defense table. "Mr. Hawke, I assume you waive your opening statement until it is your time to put on the defense's case?"

"No, sir," stated Drew as he rose to speak to the jurors. Standing at the edge of the defense table, he paused and made eye contact with each juror. When satisfied he had their full attention as he spoke.

"The defense will produce an expert witness who will testify as to when Nevan Pansky died and what exactly killed him. When and what," he said, pausing so his words could echo in the silent room. "Those two words, I submit to you, will be the crucial evidence in this case. When did the man die, and . . ." raising his voice for emphasis . . . "what killed him. Please don't forget those two words: *when and what*. I believe these words will be fundamental to you reaching a fair and just verdict of not guilty for my innocent client, Katherine Pansky. Thank you."

Drew turned and resumed his seat as the panel of twelve jurors and two alternates wrote furiously in their spiral notepads. A murmur once again went up in the gallery as reporters and observers look at each other and asked what exactly had the young attorney meant by his short and abrupt statement.

Judge Steinman looked at Hawke with a contemptuous if not angry sneer as the attorney resumed his seat. Once seated, Hawke looked directly back at the judge. *Object to that Steinman.*

Finally, the judge turned to Farrat and said, "Call your first witness."

"The People call to the stand San Diego County Crime Scene Investigator Evelyn Murry."

Deputy Wells walked up the main aisle through the gallery, opened the doors of the courtroom's main entrance, and called for the witness. In walked a thin, good-looking, thirty-ish woman immaculately dressed in a black business suit, her long black hair flowing about her shoulders. Without pausing for instructions, she walked directly to the barrister gate and opened it. Pausing as the gate closed behind her, she raised her right hand.

The court clerk rose and asked, "Do you solemnly state or affirm, under penalty of perjury, that the evidence you give in this trial shall be the truth, the whole truth, and nothing but the truth?"

"I do."

Again, without being prompted, Ms. Murry handed Deputy Wells a computer memory stick, then walked directly to the witness stand, seated herself, and made eye contact with the jury panel to her right.

"Ms. Murry, what is your occupation?" Farrat began.

"I am a scientist employed by the San Diego County Sheriff's Crime Laboratory. I have a bachelor's degree in criminal forensic science, a second bachelor's degree in chemistry, and a master's degree in biology with an emphasis on DNA as it relates to criminal investigations. My master's dissertation was 'Using mitochondrial and genomic DNA markers to solve a crime.' "

Same old Evelyn Murry, Drew thought as he smiled at the woman.

"The Sheriff's Laboratory . . . which agencies use its services?" Farrat asked.

"The Sheriff's Crime Lab's mission is to provide impartial, reliable, and accurate forensic science to the Sheriff's Department and the criminal-justice community."

"Does your laboratory provide forensic services to the San Diego Police Department?"

"That's correct. We also provide accurate and impartial forensic services to the criminal defense bar." Looking at Hawke, she added, "Such as attorney Andrew Hawke."

"Good morning, Ms. Murry. Nice to see you again," spoke Hawke.

She smiled back.

The judge rapped his gavel for silence. "Next question, Mr. Farrat."

"Mr. Hawke has used your services before?"

The witness nodded yes as she continued to look at Hawke. "You might say that, Mr. Farrat."

"Does that mean your testimony here today will be affected by having done work for Mr. Hawke?"

"I wouldn't say I worked for Mr. Hawke. We know each other from prior cases, and I have testified as a witness for Mr. Hawke. But," turning her gaze from Drew to the prosecutor, "I assure you my testimony will not be affected by any of my prior experiences with the man."

Drew looked down and attempted to keep from smiling. As he did, he noticed out of the corner of his eye Liz and Katherine staring at him.

"Thank you, Ms. Murry. Now to the case at hand. Were you called to investigate a crime scene at the La Jolla home of Senator Nevan Pansky?"

"Yes, around ten p.m. on a Sunday this past June, I received a call from San Diego Police Detective Thomas Clayton requesting my services regarding the death of the senator."

"What exactly did he say to you over the phone?"

"His exact words were, 'I have a dead man with a head wound. He is holding a gun in his right hand. It has been fired.'"

"Did you proceed to the residence?"

"Yes."

"As you drove to La Jolla, did you think you would be investigating a suicide?"

"I never assume anything until I have completed my investigation."

"Did you notice anything unusual once you got to the crime scene?"

"Yes, I did. I observed defendant Katherine Pansky on a gurney, about to be transported to the hospital. After learning she was present when the police arrived, I ordered the paramedics to wait while I swabbed her hands for any DNA or other evidence and tied plastic evidence bags over her hands. I also instructed one of our CSI techs to go with her to the hospital, collect her clothing, and do a thorough testing of her hands. Later, I examined the collected hand and clothing evidence."

"Did you find any gunshot powder on her hands or clothing?"

"Yes, I did."

"Would you please explain to the jury what you did find."

Looking to the jurors, Ms. Murry said, "I first test fired the Glock 19 handgun found at the crime scene."

"What did you find?"

"The test-fired bullet matched the bullet that pierced the senator's brain. And the traces of gunpowder found on the defendant's clothing and hands also matched the residue emitted by the weapon I test fired."

"Please explain how you determined the bullet which killed the senator came from the weapon you test fired?"

"Objection, lack of foundation," Drew stated. "The witness has not been qualified to render an opinion as to the cause of death."

"Yes, yes, Mr. Hawke. ADA Farrat, please lay the foundation."

"Ms. Murry, did you determine how Mr. Pansky died?"

"No, I did not. I left that determination to the San Diego County Medical Examiner. I was only asked to investigate the crime scene and determine if the Glock 19 found near the body was the weapon used to shoot Mr. Pansky in the head. In the process, I also determined that the weapon had been used by Mrs. Pansky."

"Is there any doubt in your mind that the powder residue found on the defendant's clothing and right hand came from the crime-scene weapon?"

"I have no doubt. It is my opinion the defendant fired the Glock. It is also my opinion the bullet from that weapon pierced the senator's brain."

ADA Farrat turned and looked puzzlingly at Hawke as if wondering why no objection to the damaging opinion testimony.

Yes, Jack, you have as much leeway as you need. Ask all the questions you want. I will not object, the defense attorney mused as he smiled back at Farrat.

ADA Farrat paused as if confused and then looked to the jury. "I have no further questions for Ms. Murry."

"Mr. Hawke."

"Thank you, sir." Drew rose and approached the witness.

"Ms. Murry, did I hear you say you did not determine if the shot to the brain killed the deceased?"

"Well, yes, I said that."

Before she could add to her statement Drew asked, "Then your only assigned task was to examine the crime scene, collect evidence, and determine if the bullet that pierced the senator's head came from the Glock 19 found in Mr. Pansky's den?"

"Ah, that is not a very complete summary of my work. I was there for hours. But, in fairness to your generalized question, yes."

"What specific evidence did you find about the Glock 19.

"About seven feet, ten inches from the floor I found a bullet lodged in the den's wall behind the deceased. The distance of the wall from the deceased was eight feet, three inches. I must add, I also examined the deceased, taking care not to move him."

Drew stepped toward the witness so as to get her attention. "Where did you find the deceased?" he asked.

"He was stretched on the den floor, which is located on the first floor of the home. He was on his back, about two feet from an old, ornate desk."

"Did you determine if anyone had moved the body before you arrived?"

"The police told me the paramedics moved him as they attempted to save him."

"Did the police say how many times he was moved?"

"Yes, the sergeant said Mrs. Pansky found him in a seated position on the floor with his back against the desk. The sergeant added that Mrs. Pansky moved him away from the desk so she could give her husband CPR. I don't know how the sergeant knew Mrs. Pansky moved the body."

"What else did you do?"

"I directed my assistants to measure the room, draw a complete diagram of the room and its contents as well as take photographs of everything."

"Ms. Murry, did you find any gunpowder residue on the deceased's clothing and right hand . . . the hand the police said held a gun?"

"Of course. He was covered with the residue. He had been shot at close range."

"Residue on the deceased's right hand?"

"Yes," she answered with a searching look.

"Residue on his head where the bullet entered?"

"Of course. He had been shot at an extremely close range. I would say the barrel of the gun touched or nearly touched his head when it was fired."

"Why do you say that?"

"There was powder stippling and laceration of the forehead skin from the effects of the gases that expelled the bullet."

At that moment, Mrs. Pansky let out a howl and collapsed onto the table in tears. Drew looked to his client and then to the judge.

"Your Honor, may we have a recess?"

"No. Proceed, Mr. Hawke."

"I'm only asking for a brief moment or two to talk to my client."

At that moment, Liz Bernquist spoke up. "I've got it, Drew," she said as she placed her arm around the woman and whispered in her ear.

"Proceed, Mr. Hawke. Let's wrap up your questioning of this witness. We have a schedule to keep." Seeing Drew's shocked look, the judge added, "You're the one who wanted an early trial."

Drew looked at the jury and saw several of the woman staring at Steinman and shaking their heads. "Yes, sir."

Drew shrugged emphatically and returned his attention to the witness. "Ms. Murry, did you determine if the Glock 19 went off while my client was wrestling with her husband as she attempted to keep him from shooting himself?"

"Objection," shouted Farrat as he jumped from his seat.

"Yes, Mr. Farrat?"

"Ah . . . speculation," the prosecutor finally stated.

"Sustained. The jury will ignore the question."

"Your Honor, I just asked . . ."

"Mr. Hawke, I have ruled. Next question."

All twelve jurors and the two alternates looked at the judge in apparent bewilderment.

Obviously, the jurors want to hear the answer. I'll ask the question another way.

"Ms. Murry, is there any way you can determine if the defendant got the residue on her hands and clothing by being close to the defendant while he shot himself?"

"Objection," shouted the judge. "I told you to move on, Mr. Hawke. Don't backdoor me."

"No, Mr. Hawke, I can't say how Mrs. Pansky got the powder residue on her. I was told the paramedics had to pry her off of his body when they declared him dead."

"Ms. Murry," growled the judge, shaking his head, "please wait for my rulings. Oh-h-h, never mind. The answer may stand. Mr. Hawke, proceed to your next line of questioning."

"Just so the jury understands, how did you determine the bullet that pierced Mr. Pansky's brain came from the Glock 19 found in his right hand?"

Drew paused as the muffled cries of his client once again

could be heard. Drew looked to the judge, who simply looked away.

Turning to the jury, Ms. Murry answered, "During the manufacture of a firearm, the machining process leaves unique, microscopic markings called tool marks on the barrel's inside surface. When the firearm is discharged, these tool marks are imbedded into the cartridge casing and the bullet. These tool marks are in effect a fingerprint as to which gun fired the bullet. I compared the bullet that killed Mr. Pansky with the one I test fired in my laboratory. The tool marks on the bullets were exactly the same. I have an enlarged picture showing the two bullets side by side if you wish to see it."

Drew purposefully looked to the jurors, who were nodding yes. Drew then looked to the judge, who sat stone-faced.

The witness continued. "The picture is on the memory stick I gave to the deputy when I took the stand."

"Your Honor, may we have Deputy Wells lower the viewing screen, turn down the lights, and run the memory peg?" Drew asked.

The judge gestured to his deputy and Wells lowered the screen, then dimmed the lights.

"There," the witness said as she pointed with a laser pen she had pulled from her suit pocket. "See the markings on the bullet with the name Pansky above it?" She circled the name Pansky with her red beam of light. "That bullet pierced his brain and was lodged in the wall behind him. See those markings?" She moved the red laser light over the striation marks along the length of the lethal bullet. Those are the tool markings which match the markings on the bullet to the right, my test-fired bullet. Those markings . . ." She moved the red light over the test bullet. "They exactly match the muzzle markings on the bullet that killed the deceased."

"Again, Ms. Murry, you don't know if the bullet actually killed the senator, correct?"

"Ah, well, no, but it is quite obvious he was shot in the head."

"Isn't it true people get shot in the head and some do not die?"

"Yes. You are correct. Some live."

"Now, Ms. Murry, when you took the stand you gave us a brief history of your education. I think the jury would like to know more about your experience as a forensic scientist. For instance, have you qualified as an expert witness in the Superior Courts before?"

"Yes, I have. I have been so designated by the judges of this Superior Court and the courts in Los Angeles County, Orange County—in fact all the courts in Southern California and many throughout the state."

"Are you a professor at San Diego State University teaching criminal law and criminal forensic science?"

"I am an associate professor, yes."

"I believe you have written several scientific papers and recently lectured at the Annual Conference of the American Academy of Forensic Sciences on the underlying science of firearms and tool-mark examination, correct?"

"Why, yes. I didn't know you knew about that."

"In effect, aren't you considered one of the leading forensic scientists in crime-scene investigations and, in particular, what lay people call ballistics, the science of matching fired bullets to the weapon used?"

"Yes," she answered with a somewhat embarrassed smile as she looked admiringly at Drew.

"Your Honor, I offer Ms. Murry as an expert witness on all the above-mentioned areas of her education and expertise."

"She will be so designated."

"Ms. Murry, did you find any other evidence in your examination of the murder scene which proved my client shot the deceased?"

"No, sir. We did find many of her fingerprints all over the den, but since she lived in the home, I can't say when those prints were made."

"Ms. Murry, did you learn if the home had an interior or exterior security camera system?"

"I did find an ADT security system with cameras, but the system went offline earlier in the day. ADT said the security system and cameras were turned off at the home's control panel. So there was no surveillance during the night of the murder."

"Ms. Murry, I have no further questions."

"Mr. Farrat, do you have any follow-up questions?" the judge asked.

"No, sir."

"Then this witness may be excused. Call your next witness."

Drew immediately rose and asked, "Your Honor, it is approaching ten-twenty. May we take a morning break?" As he spoke he looked to the jury and then at his still emotionally distraught client, who was seated upright in the embrace of co-counsel Elizabeth Bernquist.

At that moment, a woman juror spoke up, "Yes, judge, a break would be greatly appreciated."

Several of the other jurors nodded in agreement as they looked at Katherine and her reddened, tear-streaked face.

"Very well. We will be in recess until quarter to eleven."

"All rise. This court is now in recess," announced Deputy Wells.

CHAPTER EIGHTEEN

Court Resumes

SEATED IN THE WITNESS STAND was Aidan Cole, Farrat's next witness.

"You may proceed, Mr. Farrat," announced Judge Steinman.

"Thank you. Mr. Cole, would you state your name and occupation."

"I am Aidan Cole, San Diego County's chief medical examiner. I run the county's Medical Examiner's Department."

"In layman's terms, your facility would normally be referred to as the coroner's office?"

"That title is really inappropriate, Mr. Farrat. My department is a medically qualified facility that investigates deaths occurring under unusual or suspicious circumstances. Our team of forensic scientists conducts on-site investigations of crime scenes in conjunction with the county criminal laboratory, performs autopsies to determine the cause of death, and runs various types of laboratory work to help law enforcement understand the cause of death. We also perform postmortems and initiate inquests."

"Is your department accredited?"

"We are accredited by the American National Standards Institute and the National Accreditation Board as a testing and calibration laboratory. We also work closely with all San

Diego County health departments. We are a critical partner in the county's efforts to control communicable diseases, including zoonotic disease outbreaks."

"So I may understand what you just said, your departments does postmortem examinations to determine the deaths of individuals from diseases like HIV, hepatis, hantavirus and COVID-19?"

"Correct."

"And by Zoonotic disease, you're referring to the passing of diseases from animals to humans?"

"Yes, but to be more specific, Zoonotic diseases are caused by harmful germs like viruses, bacteria, parasites, and fungi, which can cause many types of illnesses in people and animals."

"Did you have an occasion to respond to a crime scene at Senator Nevan Pansky's La Jolla home?"

"Yes, sir."

"When did you arrive at that residence?"

"It was late Sunday evening when we got to the home. A little after eleven p.m."

"Did you examine the deceased senator?"

"Yes. I first talked with Ms. Murry from the Crime Lab, and then I did a brief physical examination of the deceased senator."

"Later, did you do an autopsy to determine the cause of death?"

"Yes, counselor. He died from blunt-force trauma."

"Can you be more specific?" asked ADA Farrat.

"In lay terms, he suffered bone-breaking blows to his face, head, chest, and the back of the neck. The cervical neck was violently twisted to the right, shattering the C-2 and C-3 vertebrae. Cervical bone splinters were imbedded in the tendons and ligaments of the neck, and in the spinal cord itself. The brain stem, however, was completely severed from the spinal cord. The vertebral arteries in the same area were also dissected, denying blood to the brain."

"Did Pansky suffer a gunshot wound?"

"Yes. A bullet entered the forehead and frontal lobe, traveled through the brain, exiting out the upper back of the brain and skull."

Low whispering could be heard in the courtroom as the violent nature of the man's death became clear.

"Quiet, please," ordered the judge.

"Dr. Cole, did you determine if Mr. Pansky died by accident?"

"Nevan Pansky was violently and intentionally murdered."

"Thank you. Your witness, Hawke," said Farrat as he walked back to the prosecution table.

Drew spoke as he rose from his chair, "Dr. Cole, to make your description of the trauma inflicted on Mr. Pansky clear to the jury, would you assist me in defining a few things?" The witness nodded.

"Good. Isn't it true the brain is a complex organ that controls thought, memory, emotion, touch, vision, motor skills, and bodily functions?"

"Yes."

"Some of the most important bodily functions are the lungs and heart, isn't that correct?"

"Yes. The lower brainstem controls breathing, regulating the inhalation and exhalation of air, and the heart's muscular contractions move oxygenated blood throughout the body, including to the brain."

"So, doctor, if the heart ceases to function, to beat and move blood through the human body, including to the brain, one dies?"

"As you simply put, yes."

"Please explain how the brain communicates with the lungs and heart."

Looking toward the jury, the doctor explained, "The brain sends signals through a neural pathway in the spinal cord to the diaphragm and other respirator muscles to inflate the lungs."

"So, if the spinal cord is severed from the brain stem, as you said occurred to Senator Pansky, he dies."

"You are correct. The brain can no longer tell the respiratory muscles to operate, causing an instantaneous arrest of respiration. Within a matter of seconds brain death ensues from lack of oxygen delivery."

"Now, a gunshot to the brain can also prevent the brain from communicating with the lungs and heart?"

"Yes, Mr. Hawke."

"You also said that a bullet went through the brain of the deceased . . ."

"No. No. Stop! I killed Nevan," shrieked a young lady as she jumped up from her front-row seat behind the defense table. "I killed him," she cried as tears ran down her contorted, anguished face.

"No, Lydia, don't," yelled Katherine as she looked behind her. "Don't, honey. Don't."

"No, Mom, you've done enough. I killed my father while he was raping me. I hit him with a heavy metal statute," she shouted over the rising voices of the gallery.

"No, Lydia, you have a life to live. Stop!" cried out Katherine as she turned and tried to go to her daughter.

Drew turned and grabbed Katherine around the waist as she reached over the barrister's rail and hugged her daughter. Over their mournful sobs, Steinman pounded his gavel and, in a high-pitched voice, demanded order. But he was ignored by all as the tragic scene unfolded.

"I said order! Silence!" To the judge's dismay, no one even looked in his direction. "Bailiff . . ." Deputy Caleb Wells stood frozen as he watched the two women. "Deputy Sheriff Wells," shouted the judge, his body shaking in anger as he bellowed.

"Yes, sir," Wells finally responded as he turned to the judge.

Over the roar of the audience and the flurry of cell phones raised to capture the moment, the judge ordered, "Arrest that woman." He pointed his gavel at Katherine and her daughter, Lydia.

"Which one, sir?"

"Dammit, man, take them both back to the holding cells."

"Yes, sir."

Drew helped Wells coax Katherine to release her grip as the deputy gently took her left arm and pulled her back. A second deputy sheriff stepped forward and grabbed Lydia.

At that moment, Drew heard Nathan, who was standing next to his sister, whisper, "Remember what I told you," as the deputy moved her through the barrister's gate and past the defense and prosecution tables.

"Quiet, quiet, quiet in the courtroom. I order you to shut up and sit down," the exasperated judge yelled as he waived his gavel about. "Dammit, Hawke. See what you have done?" The judge reached underneath his bench and an alarm went off, which only added to the confusion, raising the volume of voices as everyone wanted to know what was going on.

Within seconds, two more deputies, one with a gun drawn, rushed into the courtroom from the doorway leading to the judges' chambers.

"Arrest him. Arrest him and clear the courtroom," Steinman

ordered as he raised his gavel over his head. At that moment, the diminutive judge realized the cameras were still recording.

"Shut off those damn things," he ordered. "Cease filming."

Two additional deputies rushed through the courtroom doors from the public hallway.

"Confiscate those damn cameras," ordered the judge, pointing the gavel at the TV cameras. "Clear the courtroom. I say, clear this courtroom," he commanded as three more deputies rushed through the door from the judges' chambers area. The judge appeared totally out of control of the situation as he pointed the gavel at Drew. "Arrest that damn lawyer."

The deputies nearest to Hawke looked to the judge as if questioning the order.

"Don't stand there, arrest the son-of-a-bitch and don't be gentle."

Hawke put his hands out in front of him as if to be cuffed and said, "Take me before Steinman shoots me," he said, referring to the handgun the little man kept holstered under the top of the bench.

The deputies looked at each other as if not knowing what to do.

"Come on, Jackson," Drew said to his longtime deputy friend. "It's the only way he'll calm down."

"Okay, Drew. Let's go."

As the two headed toward the side door, Steinman shouted, "Cuff the S.O.B."

But as the judge stepped back to sit, Drew noticed him trip over his footstool, nearly losing his balance as he fell back into his elevated chair and onto his honorable butt. Drew stopped to enjoy the scene, which only aggravated the man further.

"I hope the cameras are still going," whispered Drew to Jackson, with a broad smile.

ooooo

Fifteen minutes later, Drew was in Judge Steinman's chambers, with ADA Farrat.

"Well, Hawke, you did exactly what I expected you to do. Now you are mine," crowed the judge. "Farrat, make your motion for a mistrial and I will grant it. Hawke won't be available for the retrial."

At that moment in walked District Attorney J.R. Sutherland. "Good afternoon, Joel. I see you've had a rough morning."

"J.R., I didn't know you knew about Hawke's theatrics."

"You're all over the news, Joel. Now, you just said Jack should move for a mistrial?"

"That's right. Make the motion and I will grant it."

"Mr. Sutherland," Drew entreated, "I didn't know Lydia would claim she shot the man. My client forbids me to talk to her children. But, Mrs. Pansky is innocent. I can prove it, if we could talk."

"Shut up, Hawke," commanded the judge. "I've had enough of you. By the time I am done with you, your lawyering days will be over."

"Please, J.R., just a few minutes and I can save your office an embarrassing loss," Drew pleaded.

"Hawke, I said—" the judge shrieked.

The district attorney interrupted the judge. "Joel, let me hear Drew out. I'll discuss what he has to say in the hallway, then I'll decide what my office will do." Turning to his ADA, he said, "Jack, please join us."

Steinman crossed his arms, shaking his head as the three left the room.

Once in the hallway, Drew began. "Here it is: Katherine arrived at the La Jolla home three hours after Pansky was murdered. How do I know? I saw the Capitol Police security footage showing when she left and when she got back home."

J.R. interrupted. "Jack, you advised me the Feds told you to take a hike when you asked for any surveillance video or evidence."

"Yes, sir, they did."

"Yet, Hawke got it."

Farrat did not respond.

Turning to Drew, Sutherland said, "How did you get a copy of the surveillance video?"

"I don't have a copy," Drew answered. "U.S. Attorney Oliver Wyland let me see it and take notes. I'm sure if you ask him, he will let you see it."

"Drew, I knew I should have talked you out of leaving my office for private practice. How about you come back? It sure would improve my win-loss record."

"Sorry, J.R., I'm having too much fun."

"Ha, indeed you are. Now be specific about what the Capitol Police video shows."

"Sir, the U.S. Capitol Police video shows who entered and left the house for a twenty-four-hour period before the murder and after. Further, before Lydia went ballistic in court, Medical Examiner Cole was about to tell us when the senator died. Dr. Cole agrees with my expert witness, Dr. Wu Tang, the recently retired San Diego County chief M.E. Both the new medical examiner and the retired one place the death at between five and seven p.m."

Drew continued. "But here's where it gets really interesting. The surveillance video shows Lydia entering the house at five-fifteen p.m. Lydia's brother showed up at six-oh-one p.m. Lydia leaves about twenty minutes later. Mrs. Pansky does not arrive until eight-fifty-one, well after both experts say Pansky died. The death of Mr. Pansky wasn't reported to the police until nine-eighteen. Ms. Murry and her assistants from the Crime Lab arrived at ten-twelve and M.E. Cole doesn't get there until eleven-oh-nine."

"So how does all this show who killed the man?"

"I was getting to that with M.E. Cole when Lydia's outburst sent Steinman ballistic.

"Okay. Go on."

"Both medical experts, Dr. Cole and Dr. Tang, agree the senator was already dead when my client arrived. Your case, J.R., is based on the assumption that Katherine supposedly shot her husband in the head. But you can't murder a dead man. The Capitol Police video shows the exact time Katherine arrives back at the house."

"Did you know all this, Jack?" Sutherland asked his assistant DA.

"Ah-h, not entirely, sir. Hawke rushed the case to trial. The M.E. report said he died of blunt-force trauma and lists the bullet wound as well as the other injuries. I assumed the shot to the brain killed him, as did Ms. Murry."

"You didn't investigate further?"

I only had five weeks to prepare, and the gunpowder residue evidence and Mrs. Pansky's admission seemed enough."

"Alright, Drew, what do you want?"

"I think Jack should demand the trial continue, and you then put Lydia Pansky on the stand. Right now, I don't believe she will listen to any attorney who insists she not testify. But, she must be given legal counsel before you put her on the stand. It is my opinion Lydia is determined to save her mother. So she will take the stand. Once sworn, Jack can do his normal thorough questioning and that should reveal who killed the man. From there you can decide the next step."

"Mm-hmm. I see."

"Frankly, J.R., if you don't put her on the stand, once she lawyers up and has time to calm down, I believe she will not testify. And we both know no jury will convict a woman for killing a man raping her. I can imagine all the women and fathers in the jury room yelling, 'Death deserved!'"

"Very true. And, Drew, not stated by you, is that no jury is going to convict your client with her daughter screaming she killed her father."

"I didn't want to state the obvious, sir. Given what's happened, the only way I see you solving this crime is to put the girl on the stand. At least you will look like you are trying to get to the truth. That is exactly what the voters want and the public does have a long memory."

"Ha-ha. Always the tactician. As usual, Drew, you are to the point but correct in your judgment. I do have an election coming up."

J.R.'s expression changed. "Drew, give us some room. I would like to talk things over with Jack."

After several minutes of discussion with Farrat, J.R. called Hawke over. "Here's what I'm going to do. I will ask the jury be sent home until tomorrow morning. I will also insist Lydia Pansky be provided a public defender to advise her on her right not to testify. If she still wants to testify, Jack will ask her to submit to a police interview. If she refuses, then we will proceed with the trial tomorrow and call her as a witness."

"And if she refuses to be a witness or won't be interviewed?" asked Drew.

"We proceed with the trial, and you can put on your defense."

At that point, Presiding Judge Brian O'Shea walked into the

hallway, acknowledged the district attorney, and proceeded on to Steinman's chambers.

Drew, brow furrowed, stared at O'Shea as he passed, then turned back to J.R. "What about me? Steinman is hellbent on putting me in jail, and having me disbarred, for that matter."

"I will handle Joel. As far as you being disbarred, I leave you to your cunning personality. You're too smart to let an egotistical fool like Steinman get the best of you."

The three turned and walked back to Steinman's chambers.

The district attorney offered his hand to Judge O'Shea. They shook hands as J.R. said, "Brian, I bet you saw today's explosive proceedings."

"Explosive doesn't do it justice. I hear you want to move for a mistrial?" replied O'Shea.

Once everyone was seated J.R. spoke. "Here's how I see the situation. Joel should appoint the public defender to represent the Pansky daughter. If she still wants to testify, we will call her as a witness. The trial must go on. The public deserves a resolution. Everybody is watching this case. It's all over the news. My office opposes a mistrial."

"I'm surprised, J.R. You don't know what she will say," stated the presiding judge.

"Oh, I'm sure, Brian, it will be a claim of self-defense as well as admitting to killing her father in an effort to exonerate her mother."

"That's right," spoke up Steinman in an excited voice. "It's just another planned trick by Hawke."

"Regarding Mr. Hawke," J.R. said, looking at Steinman, "it is my position that he should not be threatened or intimidated in any way. All that does is give the defendant an excuse for an appeal. What you say or do with the young man after trial is up to you. However, all contempt charges must be removed and no onus of intimidation should be seen henceforth. Mr. Hawke must feel free to present an effective defense for Supervisor Pansky. If that can't be done, I will move for a mistrial and the appointment of a new judge."

"What?" shouted the little man.

The presiding judge interjected, "You're right, J.R. If young Hawke wants to continue putting nails in his coffin, then let him do so. However, Katherine does deserve a credible defense."

"But, Brian, you said . . ." stammered Steinman.

O'Shea raised his voice, talking over the excited man. "Joel and I were just talking about the very same thing. We have a lot of jury time invested in this trial. To abandon it now would only allow Hawke or another defense attorney to draw the matter out, which will result in an aroused public wondering why the legal system can't provide swift justice. God knows we are criticized enough as it is."

"Brian, I'm glad you and Joel feel the same way. Then it's settled," Sutherland said and turned to his assistant deputy DA. "Jack, I leave it to you to shepherd this case to a just ending."

"Yes, sir."

CHAPTER NINETEEN

Thursday

JUDGE JOEL STEINMAN addressed the courtroom. "Ladies and gentlemen, I apologize for a disorderly ending to our proceedings yesterday. What occurred was completely unexpected. However, in order to clarify things, the young lady will be our next witness. In order to protect Ms. Lydia Pansky's constitutional rights, I have appointed Deputy Public Defender Mary E. Astor. She joins us and will be representing Ms. Lydia Pansky."

He pointed to the middle-aged woman seated with Lydia at a third desk, which had been added to the well of the courtroom. "Ms. Astor, would you please rise."

A tall blond woman dressed in an all-white suit rose and briefly turned back toward the gallery so the cameras could get a closeup.

"Ms. Astor, have you advised your client of the right to remain silent and not testify?"

"Yes, sir."

"And did you advise her of the potential consequences of her testifying, including possible criminal charges?"

"I have, but only a fool would dare threaten to prosecute a rape victim defending herself."

"Please, Ms. Astor, a yes or no answer is much appreciated."

The woman placed her right hand on her hip and shifted her weight as if ready to debate the issue.

What a woman, Drew said to himself. *As usual, she is ready to fight. Astor doesn't pass up any opportunity to let people know what she thinks. Really, quite the showman.*

Steinman sheepishly cleared his throat. "Ms. Astor, the district attorney and this court want your client to clarify her statements of yesterday."

"You mean testify," spoke up Astor in a challenging voice.

"Well, yes."

"I have strongly advised her not to say a thing, but she insists on taking the stand."

"Good, then we will proceed," interrupted the judge in an effort to shut her up.

"Sir, I'm not done," Astor said. "For the record, I object to her testifying, and I demand the court question her about testifying." Taking one step forward with her finger pointed at Steinman, who seemed to shrink under her forcefulness, she continued. "You need to clearly explain the dangers of her saying anything. Maybe she will listen to you."

"Thank you, Ms. Astor." Looking down at the papers in front of him, he fidgeted. Finally, he turned to the prosecutor. "Mr. Farrat, call your witness."

"Ms. Lydia Pansky."

Once sworn in, Farrat tried to start only to have Astor rise and object.

"Judge Steinman, I asked you to voir dire my client on her constitutional right not to testify."

"Yes, of course. Thank you, Ms. Astor. Ms. Pansky, your lawyer has advised us that you wish to testify?"

"That is correct. My mother didn't kill Nevan."

"I know you said that yesterday. However, your words today may be used against you at a later time. Today's words will be very powerful since you are testifying under oath. Further, everything you say will be subject to clarification through questions by trained lawyers."

Lydia was not persuaded by the judge's gentle nudging. "My brother, Nat, who is in law school, has told me all about my rights as has Ms. Astor. But I owe it to Mom to tell what happened, as the prosecutor insists on blaming her for my father's death."

Drew looked behind him and saw Nathan mouthing words to his sister. Then, seated two rows farther back, Drew spotted a face he had seen before. *Finnigan MacIntosh, CIA. What the hell is he doing here?*

Steinman once again cleared his throat. "I'm sure your brother is a very bright law student, but you should listen and do what your very experienced attorney is telling you. I ask you to change your mind. I'll recess the court so you can talk to Ms. Astor further."

Why all of a sudden is Steinman acting so unbiased and judicial, wondered Drew.

Lydia looked to her brother. Drew again glanced back as Nathan moved his head ever so slowly back and forth. *Nathan is running this whole show!*

"Sir, I wish to testify. Ms. Astor has spent over an hour with me. My mind is made up."

"I see. Very well. Mr. Farrat?"

"Drew, can't you stop this?" whispered Katherine as she gripped his right forearm.

Drew shook his head.

Farrat began. "Ms. Pansky, I wish to ask you questions

about what you said yesterday. Today you are under oath, so your answers will be very significant."

"Yes, yes. I know. Yes, I killed Nevan while he was raping me."

Farrat shrugged and looked down, then asked, "Ms. Pansky, where did this rape take place?'

"In our home," she replied, then quickly added, "The night I killed him."

"When did you first see him?"

"I came home around five p.m. He was in the den at his desk."

"What happened next?"

"He got up from the desk. That's when his robe parted and I saw he had no clothes on. I turned to leave and he said, 'Don't go.' He wanted to talk to me about school."

Katherine grabbed Drew's right hand and squeezed tightly.

Farrat continued. "What happened immediately after he said that?"

"He walked toward me and I saw he was fully erect. I said, 'I've got to go and talk to Mom,' but he grabbed my arm, turned me around, pressing me against his big thing. He said no one's here."

Farrat paused as he saw tears well up in her eyes. Speaking slowly, he continued. "Take your time. Tells us what happened next."

After a few moments, she added, "He said it had been a long time as he quickly pulled my T-shirt up and over my head. Everything is somewhat of a blur. I don't think I passed out. I just can't remember exactly what happened next. I just can't remember."

"What's the first thing you felt?"

"Oh, God," moaned Katherine as she squeezed Drew's hand with both of hers. There was complete silence as everyone in the courtroom looked at Katherine and then back to Lydia.

"I was face down on the desk with him inside of me. It was painful."

A low but noticeable cry came from Katherine as she held Drew's hand in a death grip.

Katherine's reaction caused Farrat to pause, then he asked, "Lydia, can you tell us what happened next?"

"I yelled and said, 'You're hurting me.' "

"Did your father stop?"

"He laughed, withdrew, turned me around, and pushed me back onto the desk."

"Continue."

"The bastard pulled me to the edge of the desk and forced himself on me. I remember yelling and crying. Somehow I had a metal statute in my hand. I slammed it against his neck as he lay on me. I kept hitting and hitting."

"Continue."

"Oh, God, Drew, I can't hear this anymore," cried out Katherine as she started to stand.

Liz grabbed her around the waist while Drew whispered, "You must stay. You must stay. Please try your best."

Knowing how difficult it was for Katherine to hear the details of the rape, Drew pulled her toward him as she took her seat. *I know this is torture, but the jury . . .* Drew tried to justify in his mind *. . . has to see the pain of what the bastard did. I hate putting her through this.*

The judge banged his gavel for order as the audience reacted to the emotional moment. Drew looked at the jury, who appeared shaken by the testimony and Katherine's reaction.

"I don't really remember what happened next. It is all a . . . I don't know what to say." She slumped in the witness chair in tears.

After a moment, Farrat showed a rare act of kindness. He handed Lydia a box of tissue that the court clerk had walked over to him. Then Farrat spoke softly, "Lydia, what's the next thing you remember?"

She raised her head and looked directly toward the gallery where her brother was seated. After a pause, she said, "I was standing there . . . he had slumped down to the floor. Oh-h, forgive me . . . his face was a bloody mess. There was blood all over the statute, my hand, and me."

"The statute . . . please describe it."

Lydia looked at the ADA and tried clearing her throat. In a weak voice, she said, "It was Ronald Reagan dressed as a cowboy. The cowboy hat was dripping blood. I dropped it and ran."

"How big is the statute?"

"I don't kno . . . maybe . . . maybe eighteen inches tall," she replied between sobs, adding, "I think."

"Is it heavy?"

"Yes, sir," Lydia answered and she blew her nose. "It's very heavy. I normally use two hands to pick it up."

"You remember how heavy it was when you first grabbed it . . . when he was still on you?"

"No. It is all a white hole. I mean, I just can't remember things. Just that horrible image of his face and the blood."

"What do you remember doing next?"

"I ran to my room and called Nathan, my brother. I told him what happened."

"What did he say?"

"He was on his way."

"Did Nathan indeed arrive?"

"Yes. He told me to go home and take a long warm shower. He said he would call Mother."

"Have you talked to your brother, your mother, or both about all this?"

"Of course."

"What did you tell them?"

"I don't really remember. It has taken a lot for me to be able to talk about what I just said. I really don't want to be here or tell people about it."

"Of course. I understand. But I need to know more."

"I can't. I won't. Like I said, there is this big blackout of things I don't remember. Nathan says it's part of me not wanting to remember. He keeps telling me I should see a therapist."

"Your Honor, I have no further questions," Farrat said.

"Mr. Hawke, you may now question."

"I have no questions. This is as painful for my client as it is for Lydia. I ask that the witness be subject to recall as a defense witness."

"Your motion is granted, Mr. Hawke. Ms. Pansky, you are free to go. However, you are ordered to be available to this court in case your testimony is required further. Until I specifically tell you otherwise, please remain available. Please leave your contact information with my deputy, Caleb Wells. You may watch the trial proceedings on television, but it is our normal practice not to have a witness present in court when other testimony is being given."

As the witness stepped down, the judge addressed all present. "Ladies and gentlemen, I know it is early, but we will now recess for lunch. Return to this court by one-fifteen p.m. Have a nice lunch, everyone. Counsel, please meet me in chambers."

ooooo

Chambers, Ten Minutes Later

"ADA FARRAT, you asked for this meeting?"

"Yes, sir. I have been instructed by District Attorney Sutherland to ask for a recess until Monday morning next week. The testimony presented by Ms. Pansky is a total surprise to my office. Her details about how she killed her father are so specific, we have to consult with the county medical examiner in order to determine if the senator indeed died from her blows. Her testimony goes to the heart of our case against Mrs. Katherine Pansky."

"Were you told to ask for a recess after Lydia Pansky finished testifying?"

"Yes, I was so instructed."

"Why didn't you tell me this before I told the jury to comeback this afternoon?"

"Frankly, I didn't expect you to recess early."

""I see. Mr. Hawke, any comments?"

"Your Honor, I believe the prosecution's request is a reasonable one. I have no objection. I, too, must consult with my expert, Dr. Tang."

"Oh, for cryin' out loud, you have made a mess of my trial, Hawke. I blame you entirely for all of this. Now everyone wants another continuance."

"Sir, I had nothing to do with Lydia. As I pointed out earlier, my client forbade me from talking to her children, much less call them as witnesses. I had no idea what the children knew about the murder."

"Bullshit. This fiasco is nothing but another one of your antics. You even listed the children on your witness list."

"Sir, not to have done so would have been malpractice on my part. Every possible person that could possibly have something to do with this case is listed."

"Damn you, Hawke, you walk a thin line." He paused, then added, "Alright, when the jury gets back, I'll send them home until Monday morning. But no more delays. I don't care what you discover from here on out. That includes you, Farrat. Now get out of here."

CHAPTER TWENTY

Law Office, 3:15 p.m.

"CONGRATULATIONS," oozed Debbie as Drew, Liz, and Pat arrived at the law office.

"Thanks, Debbie, but Liz has been absolutely invaluable. Thank you, Liz."

Liz smiled and nodded.

"Drew, where is Katherine?" inquired Debbie.

"Matt drove her to Poway."

"Drew, should she be alone after this morning?"

"Matt will stay with her until Liz can go up and check on her."

Debbie shook her head as if not approving. In an effort to change the topic, Drew moved on.

"Okay, now the bad news. Guys, sometimes I don't know who is running our defense. I think the brother Nathan is behind this whole thing."

"Why's that?" asked Pat.

"He's been reminding his mother what to say and is constantly trying to be in on our client conferences. I even found him mouthing answers to Lydia while she was on the stand."

"You mean the law student?" Liz asked.

"Yes."

"I wondered why you kept looking back at the gallery."

"Pat, what's the name of that college kid you used to surveil our hideout for Katherine?"

"You mean Todd Tocksten?"

"Yes. Do you think he could act as a transfer student for the coming semester?"

"Sure. What do you have in mind?"

"Good. Here's what I want him to do.

Drew explained that his college fraternity, Lamba Chi Alpha, had a chapter at the University of San Diego. The fraternity rented a beach house year-round right on Mission Beach, with the ocean no more than seventy feet away.

"Have him hangout on the beach in front of the house. The brothers will see him and approach. Tell him to act like he will be rushing in the coming fall semester. Once they befriend him, tell him to casually, and I mean really subtly, say something to the effect of, 'Hey, someone said the dead senator's son and daughter go to the university.' "

Drew went on to say that Todd should mention Nathan's name and see if the guys know him. From there, he would be tasked with finding out as much as possible about Nathan. The attorney concluded by saying, "Also tell him to hang out at the university and see if any of the students spending the summer on campus know Nathan."

"You really seem convinced Nathan is part of the murder."

"Pat, he either murdered his father or is part of a family conspiracy to cover up who did."

"Okay, I'll talk to Todd and get back to you."

"Also, I'm particularly interested in any martial arts training Nathan may have taken. You know, hand-to-hand combat, even how to kill a man with your hands. We already know about Chris Sykes and what he's capable of, but not Nathan."

Liz interrupted. "Drew do you think Nathan—or Chris, for that matter—is involved in the killing of his father?"

"I don't know, but Nathan is all over this case. Pat, why don't we talk in my office after we're done here." Pat acknowledged with a nod. "Now, about Lydia's testimony. Debbie, ask Dr. Tang to come to the office first thing tomorrow morning."

At that moment Matt walked in.

"Matt, I thought you were with Katherine?"

"Yes, boss, but she insisted I leave. She wanted to be alone. Said she was going to take a shower and go to sleep."

"Liz, you better head on up there and make sure she doesn't talk to the kids or does something foolish."

"Okay. Call if you need me for anything," Liz replied as she turned to leave.

Drew nodded and addressed his file clerk. "Matt, I want you to do a summary of the daughter's testimony today. I hope you recorded her testimony on your computer?"

"Yes, boss. I also took notes."

"I need that summary before you go home this afternoon."

"Will do."

Drew turned to his office manager. "Debbie, once I approve the summary of Lydia's testimony, send it to Dr. Tang." He paused, looking at each of his colleagues. "I want to thank all of you for your support on this case and putting in the extra hours. What a wild ride, right?" Everyone laughed. "We wouldn't be on the verge of victory without you. Pat, let's talk."

With that the meeting broke up. Drew and Pat went to Drew's office, where he closed the door and motioned for his detective to sit.

"Pat, you've been in court and, when not, I hope you have been able to watch on TV. Who do you think killed the man?"

BOOD OF THE FATHER

"Right now it looks like the daughter, but you're right, Dr. Tang is the key."

"I agree. But Nathan's too involved. I know he is trying to protect his mother, but this mess seems too well choreographed."

"How about Sykes, the illegitimate kid?"

"That's another thing. Lydia didn't say she arrived with him, even though the video shows the two arriving and leaving together. Her testimony is too well polished. She purposely left out several things and appeared anxious to say or insisted on not saying certain things. And how could Sykes not hear her being raped? The den is on the first floor."

"So he could have easily come to the defense of Lydia and killed him in the process."

"Correct. What a mess. I have a client charged with murder and no one to point the finger at as the real killer."

"Do the Panskys know you saw the Capitol Police surveillance video?"

"No. I intentionally didn't tell anyone. I didn't even mention the video to the district attorney until Lydia wanted to testify. Even then I only verbally outlined a timeline as to who came and went, specifically leaving out Sykes."

"Tell you what, Drew, let me do some digging into the pasts of Nathan and Lydia. That's something I haven't done. Things just moved too fast while I was back east and then the quick trial date."

"Pat, it's not you. I just haven't got a handle on this case. Every time I want to take the defense one way, Mrs. Pansky refuses to allow me. I really need to know what the kids know or did. That specifically includes Chris."

"Drew, I did some checking, but I haven't been able to find out where Katherine was the day of the murder. Her secretary wouldn't tell me anything."

A soft knock came at the door. "Yes, Debbie."

The woman opened the door partially, "Drew, the district attorney is on the phone."

"Okay, put him through."

"Drew," she continued. "It is five of four. Don't forget Matt needs you to review his summary of Lydia's testimony and to add to it before I send it to Dr. Tang."

"I haven't forgotten, Debbie. If I have time, I will review it and make changes. If not, send it to Wu before you go home. There is just too much all at once right now."

"Okay."

"I've got to take this call. Pat, listen in." Drew placed the call on speaker.

"Mr. District Attorney, you're on the speaker. I'm on the floor with all the exhibits. What's up."

"I called Wyland. He refused to let my office see the Capitol Police surveillance."

"He was that way with me, too, J.R. You got to be persistent."

"Wyland did answer some questions though."

"Sir, what question?"

"Ah, piqued your interest did I, young man? You've got the video don't you?"

"No, sir. Just doing my job. Can you tell me what Wyland did tell you?"

"Sure. I asked him when did your client first leave the house on Sunday, the day of the murder. He said at nine-thirty a.m. I asked him when did she return. He said eight-fifty-one p.m. I asked him when did Lydia first arrive at the home. He said the same time you told me. In fact, he verified everything you told me yesterday."

"So where are we now, J.R.?"

"I will not dismiss the charges based on you having seen

the video. You will have to put your case on. I suggest we take your M.E. expert out of order. I'll talk with M.E. Cole and see if he agrees with what Dr. Wu Tang says. Then Jack will put on Cole and rest our case. After that it's up to the jury."

"Yes, sir. I'd sure would like to show the surveillance video to the jury. I was hoping you could get it."

"Drew, there is more going on with the Feds than what appears. I've never had them deny any evidence to me. This isn't the end of this. I intend to find out why they will not cooperate."

"Mr. Sutherland, I hope it will not be too late for Katherine."

"I will attend Monday's hearing. Good luck, Drew."

"Thank you, sir," the attorney said and disconnected.

"That is one interesting conversation, Drew," Pat commented.

"Yes, Pat. Sutherland is an honest district attorney. He's not in it for the glory. One day he will make a great governor. But still I am left with the whole case resting on my expert Wu Tang. I hate such close cases."

"Drew, calm down. You always take on the tough ones. This one is no different. Let's change subjects. How about what you want me to do?"

"Yes, see what MacNeal knows. Lydia's testimony should have the police in a panic, with Farrat demanding all sorts of things."

"Good idea, and I will look further into the three kids. Oh, I guess I shouldn't even ask, but here it goes—do we have time to discuss my trip to New Jersey and the Caymans?"

"I don't think so. I've read your reports and this corruption matter isn't going to change soon. So let's wait. Plus, I have to see what Matt has written about Lydia's testimony. After the verdict, okay?"

"I'll be in court Monday, and I'll call you over the weekend if I find out anything about the kids. Good luck, Drew."

CHAPTER TWENTY-ONE

Monday, 9:00 a.m., Trial Resumes

As suggested by District Attorney J.R. Sutherland, the prosecution allowed Drew to interrupt their case and proceed with defense expert Dr. Wu Tang. The courtroom was silent as Drew approached his medical expert, who had just been sworn in.

"Dr. Tang would you be kind enough to tell us about your medical background."

"Yes, of course. I graduated from Harvard Medical School, spent my residency at the UCLA Medical Center and a year residence at the San Diego County Medical Examiner's Office, where I worked for twenty-three years until I retired."

"Isn't it true you were the chief medical examiner of San Diego County for the last twelve years?"

"That is correct."

"Do you know Dr. Aidan Cole?"

"Oh, yes, Aidan and I are good friends. I had the honor of working with him for the last nine years when I ran the examiner's office."

"I believe you also recommended him to replace you as the chief medical examiner when you decided to retire."

"I did. He is a very qualified medical examiner, and he was a good choice to replace me."

Did you and Dr. Cole examine the deceased Nevan Pansky?"

"Yes, we did. Dr. Cole was good enough to allow me to view his examination."

"I think you did more than just view the autopsy, doctor. Didn't you assist?"

"Ah, yes. But Aidan is the chief medical examiner for the county, and it is his final opinion that represents the findings of the county medical examiner's office."

"Doctor, did you and Dr. Cole discuss the results of the autopsy of the senator?"

"Why, yes, we did."

"What conclusions did you come to after assisting in that autopsy?"

"Senator Pansky was murdered."

All jurors immediately made notes in their spiral notepads as voices rose amongst the gallery.

Judge Steinman gave a stern look to those talking as his deputy whispered for silence.

"How did he die?"

"He was killed by blunt-force trauma."

"Do you and Dr. Cole agree in that finding?"

Turning to the jury, Dr. Tang responded, "Yes, we agreed on all of the autopsy's findings."

"We hear and read about people suffering injury and even death by blunt-force trauma. Dr. Tang what is blunt-force trauma?"

Again looking at the jury as if teaching a class at medical school, he answered, "Blunt force trauma is a physical trauma caused to a human body part, either by impact, injury, or physical attack."

So the witness could continue to answer questions while looking at the jury, Drew walked over and stood at the end of the jury panel, next to the door to the judges' chambers. Standing to the left of juror number one, he asked, "Could you be more specific for the jury, doctor? For instance, could a broken bone be caused by blunt-force trauma?"

"The answer to your question is yes. Blunt-force trauma many times does cause damage to bones and the body's internal organs. By way of example, a blow to the head causing a severe concussion could lead to a brain hemorrhage or even death. But to be more specific, a blunt-force wound is any nonpenetrating injury. In the senator's case, his death was not caused by a knife or any other object penetrating his body."

"I see. How did Nevan Pansky die?"

"That is a fascinating question, Mr. Hawke. He suffered many blunt-force blows to his body. But the simplest answer is that he died at the hands of another human being."

"Can you be more specific? You just said the man suffered many blows to his body. So which blows to his body actually killed him? The autopsy report by Dr. Cole only says death by blunt-force trauma, and it then described those blows. What, exactly, killed him?"

Again facing the panel of jurors, Dr. Tang said, "Well, first, autopsies usually don't get into how each traumatic injury damaged the body and how it specifically contributed to death when the deceased suffered multiple blunt-force traumas. In California, the law only requires a medical examiner to state if the death was by natural causes or by a non-natural cause, and, if so, how. In the case of Mr. Pansky, it was by blunt-force trauma, and done in such a way as to constitute intentional murder. He did not die of natural causes."

Man, this is like pulling teeth. Wu is trying to be too impartial.

"Did you discuss with Dr. Cole which blunt force trauma killed Mr. Pansky?"

"Yes, I did. We both concluded he died of a broken neck, which severed the spinal cord, causing an instantaneous cardio-respiratory arrest, depriving the brain of vital oxygenated blood."

A moan came from Katherine as she grabbed Liz's left hand and leaned her head on Liz's shoulder. Drew looked at the jury and then to his client, who appeared to be having difficulty breathing. Again the audience reacted.

"Your Honor, may my client be excused for this portion of Dr. Tang's testimony? It is by necessity quite graphic."

Before the judge could respond, ADA Farrat rose. "Sir, the People have no objection to Mrs. Pansky being excused. I'm sure there are many in this courtroom who would also like to leave at this time. Autopsy testimony can be very graphic, as Mr. Hawke stated."

"Oh, very well. Mrs. Pansky, do you wish to be excused during the medical examiner's testimony?"

"Yes, sir. Please."

"Fine. We will pause while Mrs. Pansky is escorted out of the courtroom."

Two deputies had to assist the woman as she appeared near collapse. Drew noticed the intent way the jury followed her leaving. *I hope they believe her grief and emotion are real. It sure looks like it.*

"Alright, Mr. Hawke, proceed," the judge ordered.

"Dr. Tang, please correct me if I am wrong. What you are saying is once the spinal cord was severed, the brain could no longer instruct the heart and lungs to circulate life-carrying blood to the brain and other areas of the body. Correct?"

"In medical terms, the upper cervical spinal cord regulates blood flow, heart rate, blood pressure, breathing, and other tasks necessary to live. Without the delivery of oxygenated blood to the brain, life-performing functions cease. Thus, the brain dies, as does the rest of your body."

"Would it be fair to say the brain is like a computer that controls the body's functions, and the nervous system is the network that relays messages to the different parts of the body?"

"Yes, simply put."

"What were the other blunt-force traumas you observed?"

"Before we get to the other injuries, I would like to expand on what Dr. Cole testified to. May I?"

"Yes, of course."

"Besides the spinal cord rupture, Dr. Cole also stated the vertebral arteries were completely severed. This is significant."

"How so, doctor?"

"First there is the medulla oblongata, or commonly referred to as the medulla. The medulla is the bottom-most part of your brain and the connecting point of the brain to the spinal cord and the body's nervous system. It controls basic bodily functions, like breathing and maintenance of blood pressure. The medulla requires a constant blood supply, which is from the vertebral arteries which travel through the spinal column and connect to the basilar artery, which supplies blood to the brainstem. Those two vital arteries were severed, thus depriving the brain of blood. With both the blood supply and nerve connections severed, there was almost immediate respiratory arrest and circulatory collapse, resulting in the instant death of the senator."

"I see. Thank you for clarifying how the senator died. Now, what of the other blows to his body?"

"The senator was brutally battered in several places to his head, the right shoulder, and the back of his neck. To be specific, the left eye socket was shattered, the left jawbone at the temporomandibular joint was shattered. The facial bone above the right eye was severely cracked, as was his left ac-romioclavicular joint where the acromion meets part of the scapula and the collarbone."

"In lay terms, what do you mean by 'where the acromion meets part of the scapula and the collarbone'?"

"Sorry. I was describing where the shoulder blade and the collarbone meet. In addition, his left glenohumeral joint was not cracked but was dislocated. By glenohumeral joint, I mean he suffered a dislocated left shoulder."

"Sir, did the blow to the back of the neck sever the spinal cord from the brain stem?"

"Very good question. Normally, it is very difficult to totally rupture the spinal cord and its vertebral arteries, resulting in a quick death. What is depicted in war movies just doesn't happen that way."

"To be more specific, doctor, did a metal object sever the spinal cord?"

"I don't think so. Mr. Pansky suffered an almost horizontal tear or complete rupture of the spinal cord and its blood supply between cervical-1 and cervical-2." Looking to the jury, he explained, "C-1 and C-2 are part of the vertebral column or spine that connects to the head."

"Doctor, would you be more specific how the cervical part of the spine connects to the skull?"

"Mr. Hawke, we could spend an hour discussing how the head attaches to the body."

"I understand, sir, but maybe in a very elementary way."

"Yes, of course." The doctor turned, looked at the jury, and explained that the spinal column and the skull are held togeth-er by ligaments, tendons, and muscles. Ligaments are fibrous bands that connect two or more bones together. Tendons, also fibrous bands, attach muscle to bones. These connections help stabilize and connect joints together. This is how the vertebral portion of the spinal column, in particular C-1 through C-7, connects to the base of the head while allowing the head to move and turn. The spinal cord runs within the skeletal column and connects to the head's brainstem. If the head is turned too far to the right or left, or too far forward or backward, the spinal cord can be disconnected from the head's brain stem.

Dr. Tang concluded his description, saying, "This is how people become paralyzed in automobile accidents and from falls or any other type of trauma to the head and body. My apologies for the simplicity."

"Now again, how did Mr. Pansky die?"

It is my opinion, Nevan Pansky's neck was forcibly, intentionally, and I must emphasize, violently snapped to the right, severing the spinal cord."

"Who would be capable of doing this?"

"A man of strength and one that has been trained to execute such a maneuver."

"Would a young, strong man who is trained in the martial arts be able to do what you describe?"

"I doubt it. It would depend on the young man's strength and, most important, his training. For such a life-ending technique to be successful the man would have to be specifically trained in hand-to-hand combat and how to execute such a death act."

"Would a woman, say five feet, eight to ten inches tall, and the age of Mrs. Pansky be able to perform such a life-ending maneuver?"

"We discussed that question after the autopsy."

"A-n-d . . . your conclusion, sir?"

"Extremely unlikely, if not impossible. Nevan Pansky was a big-boned man with a muscular body. It would require great strength to break C-1 from C-2 of the cervical column and at the same time produce a complete severing of the spinal cord. More importantly, it would require a skilled person trained in such a life-ending technique. I've only seen such a complete tear one time before, and it was done by a very strong thirty-year-old Navy SEAL who was well trained in hand-to-hand combat. As he explained in his video confession, you need not only strength but more importantly you need to know how to twist the neck. His exact words were, 'It's a learned technique. You have to accelerate the head into a very fast snapping motion. That way death is assured.' I'll never forget his words."

The courtroom again reacted to the testimony, but the judge just asked Mr. Hawke to continue.

"As to whether Mrs. Pansky could execute such a maneuver . . ."

"Sorry for deviating," interrupted Dr. Tang. "I don't believe Mrs. Pansky or any woman her size and age would be able to violently sever a man's spinal cord by hand the way her husband's was done."

"Being very specific, doctor, could blows to the back of the neck, say at C-1, C-2, or C-3, with an eighteen-inch, heavy metal statue sever the spinal cord the way Mr. Pansky's was torn?"

"No. Such blows would only break or possibly shatter a cervical joint but not tear horizontally the spinal cord. The senator's cord was completely severed horizontally, almost cleanly cut through and through."

Drew glanced at the jury. "Sorry, ladies and gentlemen, but this question is important." Looking back to the witness, he continued his questioning. "Are you saying, doctor, Mr. Pansky's neck was severed in the same way a guillotine or machete severs a head from the rest of the body?"

"Oh, no. This was a tearing rupture—a twisting, ripping motion. A sharp blade like a machete would cut straight across in a clean line. No, this was an uneven twisting-tearing rupture, though horizontally. The difference is that a twisting action stretches and tears the tendons, ligaments, muscles at points differently—a more ragged but horizontal tear as the head was rotated. No, this was a quick but violent twisting action."

"Could a kick to the head cause such a tearing action?"

"Possibly, yes. But to be sure I would need to know the circumstances of how and who kicked Nevan Pansky in the head. Remember, to tear the spinal cord, the way the senator's life was ended, the shoulders had to be held as stationary as possible while the head is twisted in a swift, accelerated manner, ending in a powerful snapping action. A kick to the head would normally cause the entire body to move in the direction of force created by the kick. In my opinion, this did not happen to Mr. Pansky."

"Did you examine a heavy statue found at the murder scene?"

"A statue of Ronald Reagan was tested as a potential weapon used in the murder. Mr. Pansky's blood was on the statue. Smudged fingerprints were also seen, but someone cleaned the bottom portion of the statue. Chemicals were used, so there was no way to retrieve a useable finger print much less DNA."

"Could this weapon have severed the spinal cord?"

"No. Most likely the statute was used to bludgeon his head,

upper body, and possibly the back of the neck. The statue could not have dissected the spinal cord. Severing of the spinal cord came from a violent twisting separation, as I have stated."

"So in sum, Dr. Tang, is it fair to say this is how . . . I repeat, how . . ." Drew raised his voice as he turned to the jury . . . "this is *how* my client's husband died?"

"Yes."

"He died by a violent twisting of the head, resulting in massive trauma of the spinal cord at its junction with the medulla oblongata," Drew repeated.

"Yes, Mr. Hawke. Everything else was just a brutal battering of his body. Why, I can't say."

"I believe Mr. Pansky was also shot in the head, is that true?"

"Well, yes. A bullet did penetrate the forehead, traverse the brain, and exit out the upper back of the head."

"Did that kill him?"

"No, he was already dead when shot in the head."

A distinct murmur went up in the courtroom following the answer.

"Quiet, please. Quiet," ordered the judge.

"I guess, doctor, I should then ask you when did the senator die. So . . ." turning again to the jury and raising his voice, Drew repeated, "*when* did Nevan Pansky die?"

"The man died between five p.m. and seven p.m. The gunshot wound occurred several hours later."

"How did you determine when the senator died?"

"There were several important factors that helped determine the time of death. The first two were the temperature that early evening and the position the body was found in. Weather reports said that Sunday evening was extremely hot. Temperatures during the day reached an unusual ninety-eight degrees by one-thirty p.m. in the village of La Jolla and at the

Marine Corps Air Station at Miramar. It was a very hot day for June. The temperature in the house shortly after the county's chief crime scene investigator arrived at nine-eighteen p.m. was eighty-nine degrees."

"My apologies for interrupting, Dr. Tang. You are talking about Ms. Evelyn Murry?"

"Oh, yes. You are correct. Not only did Ms. Murry collect evidence and document the entire murder scene, but she also created a chart of the hourly temperature readings she made while in the house. Her work was very helpful. As stated in Ms. Murry's report, she also briefed Chief Medical Examiner Aidan Cole when he arrived at the house shortly after eleven p.m."

"Why is the temperature in the house so important?"

"The hotter the environment after death, the sooner the body displays rigor."

"Please explain how the position of the body helped you determine when Mr. Pansky died."

"Yes, yes. When the heart stops pumping, blood will seek the lowest point in the body. Since he was in a seated position when he died, the blood flowed to his lower extremities. The lack of blood in the upper parts of his body advanced the rigor mortis process. Ms. Murry and Dr. Cole both observed the beginnings of rigor in his eyes, eyelids, jaw, and neck. These particular areas of rigor start within one hour after death. The two also detected pallor mortis, which is paling of the skin. Pallor mortis is a lighter-than-normal skin color of a deceased. The pallor described by Ms. Murry and Dr. Cole was very distinct. Pallor is important since it starts two to six hours after death. As it was a hot Sunday evening. He died sometime before seven p.m."

"Did Dr. Cole agree with the five to seven p.m. time assessment?"

"Yes. We thoroughly discussed the conditions of rigor he observed and came to this conclusion," replied Wu while looking directly at Aidan Cole, who was seated in the front row of the gallery next to District Attorney Sutherland.

"Order please," gaveled the judge as everyone, including TV cameras, focused on Cole, who acknowledged Dr. Tang with a nod.

Drew continued. "How do you know Mr. Pansky was dead when he was shot in the head?"

"When the bullet exited the back of his head, there was minimal blood spatter. But small pieces of brain tissue were found as part of the blood spatter. Ms. Murry and M.E. Cole thought the tissue showed decomposition. Later, microscopic examination of the tissue confirmed its decayed state. I looked at the tissue slides and agreed the tissue showed significant deterioration from deprivation of oxygen to the brain cells."

"Sorry to interrupt, sir, but what do you mean by decomposition?"

"The brain rapidly dissolves after death. This is due to the breakdown of proteins and putrefaction."

Drew immediately followed up. "By putrefaction do you mean the process of decay—the rotting of the body following death?"

The witness turned to the jury, some of whom appeared distressed by the attorney's attempt to clarify.

"I'm sorry, ladies and gentlemen, some of what I must describe is rather disturbing." Looking back to the man in front of him, he went on. "Yes, Mr. Hawke, you are correct. Certain parts of the body do start the process of decay almost immediately. This is how we determine when death occurred. Decomposition of the brain often occurs within minutes after death because it is eighty percent water."

"Doctor, again referring to brain tissue found at or near the deceased, how did its decomposition help you in ruling out death by gunshot?"

"The brain tissue collected by Ms. Murry showed putrefaction, indicating Nevan Pansky was dead prior to being shot. There is no question about the timing of death and when he was shot."

"You've testified you saw the body before it was dissected for an internal examination by Dr. Cole."

"Yes. You contacted me Monday morning, the day following his death. You told me you would seek a court order allowing me to attend the autopsy. I immediately contacted Aidan and he agreed to wait for the court order before proceeding with the internal examination. He had already performed the autopsy's external examination of the body and noted all the injuries. All that remained was a dissection of the body and an examination of its tissue, organs, and structures, followed by laboratory results."

"You did in fact attend the internal examination?"

"Yes. But before beginning the dissection, I reviewed all of the reports by the crime-scene staff and the notes of Dr. Cole. We even discussed his preliminary findings."

"The opinions you express here today, are they in agreement with Dr. Cole's opinion?"

"Yes, we are in mutual agreement." Again looking at Aidan Cole, he said, "It was an enjoyable, collaborative effort."

Dr. Cole smiled back. A fact that the jury noticed and noted in their trial notepads.

Drew turned to walk back to the defense table, paused, and stepped back toward the witness. "I do have one more question. Did any of the police reports indicate when the gun had been fired?"

"Yes. The sergeant who arrived with the first responding officers noted in his report the gun had been recently fired. He could smell the odor of fresh gunpowder in the den and on the handgun."

Drew again looked at the jury. They were busy writing.

"Ah, Mr. Hawke."

"Yes, doctor?"

"There is one more important thing."

"What is that?"

"As I said earlier, Dr. Cole did the dissection. His examination of the brain—and, more importantly, the inner area where the bullet traversed through the brain tissue—showed the same decomposition."

"I thought you said, Dr. Tang, you didn't do the internal examination until after the court order was issued. That part of the autopsy was several days after he died. Wouldn't decomposition continue, especially in the brain?"

"You are correct, sir. But our refrigeration of the body drastically slows the rate of rigor mortis. Most important, as the bullet pierced the membrane of the brain, it seared in place the brain tissue it tore through. That tissue showed the same amount of decay as the piece of issue collected with the blood spatter. I saw this with my own eyes when I examined the collected tissues under a microscope. It is my professional opinion that these findings confirm Mr. Pansky was deceased when shot."

"Sir . . . thank you." Looking at DA Sutherland, Drew added, "Your Honor, I have no further questions."

Turning to the jury, Steinman stated, "We will now take our morning recess. We went longer than I anticipated, but there were many technical questions that had to be explained. See you in twenty minutes."

Drew turned to Pat and Liz. "We need to talk."

The three followed the last of the crowd out into the hall-way where television reporters were already recording their updates for the noon news. Several reporters rushed to Drew for comments, but he brushed them aside, saying, "I need time alone," as he and his defense team headed to their secluded spot at the north end of the hallway.

As the three walked, Drew unloaded his fears. "Pat, this was a disastrous direct with Wu," the lawyer whispered. "I was all over the place and followed no logical order the jurors could easily follow."

Liz tried to reassure the troubled young man.

"Drew, I thought you did a great job; I believe the jurors understood it all."

"No, no. If it becomes known the examination of the bul-let path through the brain was not part of my planned direct, people will say I was ill prepared." Drew hung his head low, shaking it as they walked.

Pat placed his hand on Hawke's shoulder. "Actually, Drew, I thought it added drama to the whole thing. Your clarification about refrigeration made the testimony that more important and believable."

"Pat's right, Drew," supported Liz. "You know, sometimes you are needlessly your worst critic," she added with a smile.

The attempt at humor provoked no reaction. She tried again.

"Besides, Wu's testimony about the bullet piercing dead tis-sue is now indelibly etched into their minds. Farrat will have to show the microscopic evidence is wrong. That appears im-possible. I don't see how the jury can come up with any other conclusion other than Pansky was dead when shot."

"Liz is right," surmised Pat. "Dr. Tang just destroyed the

entire prosecution case, which was based on Katherine shooting Nevan in the head. That was their only theory."

Once at their secluded spot, Drew began to pace back and forth while Liz and Pat sat. "You know, guys, any preparation I had for this case never matches what has come out in testimony. Every time I think I know where the case is headed, then it changes. Like Lydia's outburst and now Tang's opinion a woman couldn't execute Nevan by hand. I had expected just a no answer, not an illustration on how to kill by a Navy SEAL. Hell, Tang never even told me his examination specifically showed the bullet seared in place dead brain tissue. He just told me the tissue showed the brain was dead when shot. Now, thanks to Tang, neither Lydia nor Katherine could have killed him. Until Wu took the stand, I could have pointed the finger at Lydia and said she killed her father as he tried to rape her. Not now. I am just not the one running the defense. That scares me."

"One thing is for sure," spoke Pat, "the jury right now has to be wondering who killed the man. If not Katherine or Lydia, then who?"

Drew looked at his two compatriots. "Should I put Katherine on the stand?" he asked. "I need to show she wasn't in the house until well after her husband died."

Liz was the first to speak. "Katherine is an emotional mess. I don't know what she will say on the stand. Frankly, I believe Farrat would tear her apart."

"Liz is correct," spoke Pat. "She is full of remorse and will probably end up convicting herself. Besides, we know she will say anything to protect Lydia."

"Yeah, you're right. But I need to have someone say where Katherine was prior to returning home."

"How about Detective Thomas Clayton? In his report, he

said Katherine was at a Society for Children event until eight-twenty p.m."

"That's true. But, Pat, Clayton never verified that by talking to anyone who was there. I also never had you look into that as a possible alibi. More malpractice on my part."

Drew began to walk back and forth for the next few minutes, then sat with his head bowed. Pat and Liz said nothing.

Drew rose and looked at his two friends. "No, guys, you are correct. The only alternative is to remind the jury during argument what the prosecution theory was and how it has been proven completely wrong."

"You're right, Drew," added Liz. "There is no evidence saying she killed Nevan."

"I know. But, Liz, we are right back to her supposed confession at the news conference. 'I *caused* my husband's death.' Damn. I told her she would seal her own fate by talking to the media."

"Look . . ." Liz rose so she could be more assertive and make good eye contact with Hawke. "The ball is now in the prosecution's court. What is Farrat to do? He can't put Cole on. Cole will say that Nevan was dead when shot. All Cole will do is emphasize the testimony of Tang. Jack Farrat can't even ask the jury to believe Katherine broke her husband's neck. What's the proof? Only Cole could take the stand and dispute Wu Tang's opinions. That's not going to happen. I bet Farrat rests his case."

"Hm-mm. If he does rest, I could move for a directed verdict. Nah . . . nah, Steinman will never grant such a motion. He and O'Shea are in cahoots. For some reason O'Shea wants her convicted."

'What are you going to do, Drew?" asked Pat.

The young attorney just shook his head. "I don't know. I just don't know. I've got no one who can testify about the surveillance video. I don't have a witness who can say where Katherine was before eight-fifty-one. I can't put her on the stand. I have no witness to say Lydia left before Katherine arrived. The only person I know for sure was in that house when Nevan died is Nathan . . . and I don't know what he will say. I just don't trust him. He seems to have his own agenda. Besides, Katherine won't let me talk or call her children as witnesses. Frankly, I think Nathan planned Lydia's outburst. He certainly conducted her testimony."

Drew looked at his Apple watch. "Guys, we have to go."

On the way back, Pat whispered, "Drew, I will check with my budding PI, Todd Tocksten, and see how his investigation is going."

Drew did not respond.

CHAPTER TWENTY-TWO

Court Resumes

ONCE BACK AT THE TRIAL department's doors, Drew knocked. Deputy Wells opened the door slightly. Recognizing Hawke, he gestured for him to come in.

At that moment, Matt came running down the hallway, yelling, "Boss, boss!"

At the door, the young clerk handed a large manila envelope to Drew, who asked, "What's this?"

"Katherine's phone records, boss. You know, her cell phone. The ones we subpoenaed five weeks ago. They just arrived at the office."

"Thanks. Wait outside."

Drew took the envelope, stepped in, and immediately saw J.R. Sutherland in an intense conversation with his assistant attorney Jack Farrat. They were seated at the prosecution table with their backs to the courtroom doors. Drew stopped and motioned for Pat and Liz to stop.

"Guys," he whispered, "we'll sit in the back row." He pointed to his right. Once seated, he continued. "Don't say anything. Let's see what they do."

Jack Farrat sat back, shaking his head.

Drew opened the envelope and began flipping pages, stopping at Sunday. There he closely examined the cell-phone calls for the evening of the murder.

J.R., seeing Drew, called out, "Hawke, join us."

Once at the prosecution table, J.R. started. "I'm sure you will move for a directed verdict once we rest, am I correct?"

"Yes, sir."

"We will oppose your motion."

"Expected, sir. Besides, I doubt Steinman will grant it."

"So it goes to the jury then."

"Maybe not, J.R. Look at this," Drew said and handed the phone-call records to the district attorney. "The Verizon records show Katherine received a call at eight-twenty-two p.m. The records show the nearest cell tower to her phone was in Westfield Mission Valley mall. If these phone records are correct, Katherine was nowhere near her La Jolla home when her husband was shot in the head. Detective Clayton mentions in his report someone told him Katherine was at a meeting sometime that afternoon or evening. Also, look where the call came from—La Jolla—and the cell phone that made the call is owned by Nathan Pansky, her son."

Sutherland read the records and looked up.

Drew continued. "I think, J.R., a smart prosecutor would want to verify what the records say. Maybe call a Verizon records keeper to the stand. You could even have one of the people at the meeting with Katherine document when the meeting occurred. I certainly intend to call such witnesses."

"Are you suggesting a compromise to keep this mess from going to the jury?"

"I'm suggesting, if all this plays out, you could move for a directed verdict of acquittal. After all, you are the chief law enforcement officer of the county and are sworn to protect the innocent and convict the guilty."

"Your boldness, Drew, is amazing."

Drew turned and walked back to his defense team and sat while Sutherland and Farrat closely examined the records. Both approached Hawke, who immediately rose to meet them.

"Okay, Drew, we'll move for a continuance until Friday after lunch," Sutherland said. "You get the witnesses to verify where Katherine was and Jack will produce the Verizon expert."

"And, sir, you will then move for a directed verdict?"

"No. We will jointly make a motion for a mistrial, if and only if it all plays out as you suggest."

"Sir, I don't know if I can do that."

"One step at a time, Drew. First the continuance, witnesses, and we go from there."

"I will think it over."

"Think fast, young man. It's your responsibility to find credible witnesses who will say your client was at a meeting and not in La Jolla," J.R. Sutherland forcibly added with a look seeming to indicate he wouldn't go along with any further continuances that would harm the prosecution's case.

Drew said nothing in response but whispered to Liz and Pat. The three then went to the defense table.

District Attorney Sutherland called Deputy Wells over. "Caleb, tell the judge I wish to talk to him in chambers before we begin."

ooooo

Once in chambers with attorney Hawke, Sutherland announced, "Judge, my office moves for a continuance until this Friday at one-thirty p.m. It has come to my attention that further evidence is needed before this trial can go to the jury."

"Again?" Steinman said, raising his voice.

"Yes, Joel. My intent is to bring this matter to a just

conclusion whether that be a conviction or a not-guilty verdict."

"Is this Hawke's doing?"

"It is my decision and I make the motion. Hawke may even oppose it."

"I see. Hawke, do you oppose J.R. Sutherland's motion to recess until Friday?"

"I would prefer we proceed with the trial, but I understand the district attorney's desire to do what is right. So, no, sir, I do not oppose the motion."

"My God, another continuance. You two are making a mockery of my courtroom. Hawke, I know you are behind this and you will pay dearly."

J.R. spoke up. "Judge Steinman, I must object. I am making the motion on behalf of the people of this county. It is my decision. I warned Judge O'Shea I will not put up with prejudicial statements against A.J. Hawke. Statements that may endanger a guilty verdict. Mr. Hawke must be free to defend his client to the upmost of his ability."

A long pause followed. Finally Steinman stood.

"J.R., you must understand my intent. I do not want the jurors or the public to think this court can't run an efficient and orderly trial. The public already holds contempt for the court system, which they believe can't arrive at swift and just decisions. It's one of their biggest complaints about us."

"That is exactly why I am making the motion, Joel. I want a fair but final verdict which will not be overturned on appeal."

"Very well. When court resumes, I will announce your request was granted. Deputy Wells," the judge called out, "is Supervisor Pansky still in a holding cell?"

Stepping to the door, Wells replied, "Yes, sir. She has calmed down."

"Bring the defendant back into court, seat the jury, and let the audience in."

"Yes, sir."

Moments later, to the surprise of everyone, Deputy Wells quieted the courtroom and informed all present the trial would not resume until Friday at one-thirty p.m. due to a request by the district attorney's office.

Drew looked over at Sutherland. *The judge didn't even allow the DA the opportunity to make a statement that might justify such a recess. Man, Steinman is one mean asshole.*

Drew turned to Liz. "Take Katherine home."

Touching Katherine's arm, Drew instructed, "Do not talk to Lydia or Nathan about what is happening. The DA could say you are tampering with witnesses or orchestrating false testimony if you do. Remember, your phone is probably tapped." Drew, seeing Katherine somewhat confused, added, "I don't believe Lydia or you are going to be convicted for the murder of Nevan. So now is the time to be very cautious."

He turned to Liz. "Have Matt pick you two up at the back entrance. Pat and I will go out the front and distract the media."

As soon as Drew and Pat stepped out into the hallway, cameras came on and a deluge of questions followed.

"Please, guys, one question at a time. He pointed to the nearest TV reporter and said, "Go ahead."

"Mr. Hawke, why did the district attorney move for a continuance?"

"I'm afraid you will have to ask him. But bear in mind the defense has established the true cause of death, the forceful twisting of the senator's neck, resulting in severance of the spinal cord and subsequent death. He was not killed by a bullet to the head. Thus, we have proven Katherine's husband was already dead when shot. They can't say you murdered someone if the person is already dead. Two, Katherine's hands and body were all over her husband as she tried to save him. Thus, the presence of gunpowder residue on her. Three, Dr. Wu Tang stated it would take a man of considerable strength and special training to rip apart a spinal cord by hand. Dr. Tang specifically stated he did not think Mrs. Pansky could do that. In sum, the prosecution based its entire case on the belief that Katherine Pansky killed her husband with a shot to the head. I await their response to our expert testimony."

"Is the prosecution trying to find contradictory evidence to your stated testimony?" shouted another reporter.

"Again, I have no idea what they are doing. Jack Zane," Drew said, pointing to the *San Diego Herald* reporter.

"Drew, don't you have to prove your client wasn't present when the senator was killed?"

"Jack, we don't have to prove where Katherine was. We've already proved she did not kill her husband as the prosecution alleges. He was already dead when shot. And, the only evidence she shot him is circumstantial—the gunshot residue. Nor does she have the physical strength to sever his spinal cord. But, if there is anyone out there who can specifically say where Katherine was between five to eight p.m., please call me."

"But, Drew," followed up Jack Zane, "don't you have to prove she wasn't present when her husband died?"

"Jack, you of all reporters should know better. It is the burden of the prosecution to prove my client killed Nevan Pansky. They have utterly failed to do so. Why does the public always feel an accused must absolutely prove beyond a reasonable doubt their innocence? All the defense has to do is show the prosecution has no case. This I have done. Don't you think, if the prosecution can prove she was present at the murder scene when her husband died, they would do so? Quote me carefully, Jack. This was a hasty arrest and an ill-advised prosecution based solely on a news conference and her poor choice of words."

With those words Drew turned and walked off with Pat De Luca.

"Pat, where are you in your investigation of the kids?"

"We're working on it."

"I think Wu's testimony eliminates the idea Chris could snap Nevan's head with a kick. But Sykes is an MMA fighter. He is trained on how to use head submission holds and could have easily used one to kill Pansky. What bothers me most is what Chris said to me at the Barleymash. How did he know Nevan Pansky was murdered? Such a comment, followed by him running away, seems very suspicious, the more I think about it."

"Chris is on the top of the list, Drew. I'll also talk to Todd and see how he's doing on finding information about Nathan and Chris."

CHAPTER TWENTY-THREE

The Following Morning

DREW SAT ENSCONCED in his office going over transcripts from the trial when Debbie gave her normal soft knock at the door.

"Yes, Debbie."

"Drew, there are three ladies outside insisting on talking to you. I think one of them is the wife of Justice Conner Sashin."

"Our fourth appellate court justice?"

"At least that's how she introduced herself."

"Do you have any idea why they're here?"

"No."

"Please have them take a seat in the conference room."

Drew purposefully waited for the three to be seated, then joined them.

"Good morning, ladies, I'm Andrew Hawke. How can I help you?"

"Mr. Hawke, I am Mrs. Malorie Sashin. This is Mrs. Marta Romero and Mrs. Lindsey Worley," pointing to the women to her right. Please be seated, Mr. Hawke," Mrs. Sashin instructed.

Drew sat as directed. "Now, what may I do for you ladies?"

"Mr. Hawke, we three are part of the steering committee for the Society for Children. Mrs. Pansky is our chairperson.

We are here because you asked for someone who could say where Katherine was the evening her husband was murdered."

"Yes."

"Mrs. Pansky was with us and other members of our society preparing for the honors gala which she presided over."

"I see. Did Katherine ever leave at any time between the hours of five to eight o'clock?"

"Mr. Hawke, I said she was with us all evening," responded Mrs. Sashin.

"Well, not exactly," corrected Mrs. Romero. "Remember, Malorie, Katherine left after she received a phone call."

"Oh, yes. That's when Katherine asked me to take over the ceremonies. I guess I should have been more specific, Mr. Hawke. Katherine was there during the time that your M.E. expert said the murder occurred."

"We already know Mrs. Pansky received a phone call from her son. Do you know if she got any other calls or if Katherine made any calls while she was with you?"

"The only call we saw, Mr. Hawke," replied Mrs. Worley, "was the one she received in the middle of her announcing the awards. That's when Katherine told myself and Malorie she had to take the call. Later, she came back, very upset by the way, apologized for the interruption, and told the gathering there was an emergency at home and asked Malorie to take over."

"Can you folks estimate what time she asked Mrs. Sashin to take over?"

"It was some time after eight p.m.," replied Mrs. Romero.

"That's correct, Marta," stated Mrs. Sashin. "I remember looking at my watch and then the agenda to see if I could finish the awards ceremony before nine. We try to complete things on time."

"That's how we do things," added Mrs. Romero and Mrs. Worley.

"Would either or all of you be willing to testify in court about what you just told me?"

"Of course," all three said at once.

"Well, I do have a problem with that."

"What?" demanded Mrs. Sashin.

"You see, Katherine has given me specific instructions that I cannot call any of her friends. She threatened to fire me if I did. Her exact words were, 'I will not drag wonderful people into this horrible mess.'"

"That sounds just like Katherine," said Mrs. Sashin.

"She is such a wonderful woman," added Mrs. Romero.

Mrs. Worley nodded in agreement.

"I'm afraid Mrs. Pansky is adamant," Drew continued. "She also said she will not destroy a cause she has given her body and soul to, nor drive away important benefactors to a cause vitally needed by children. So I just don't know how I can use your great testimony."

The three woman whispered between themselves. Finally, Mrs. Sashin asked, "Could we sign an affidavit?"

"We could try, but the problem is District Attorney Sutherland may object to the admittance of such written testimony."

"J.R. is the problem?' asked Mrs. Sashin.

"In a sense," Drew answered. "But I think any judge would be reluctant to allow witness testimony whether in person or by affidavits without allowing attorneys to ask the witness questions. Anyway, my client is adamant she does not want me to embarrass you and apparently somehow endanger the Society for Children's project. So there is no way I can call you to the stand. She already threatened to fire me when I wanted to know where she was that evening."

"Mr. Hawke, we are not welting flowers," forcefully stated Mrs. Worley.

"That is absolutely correct," added the other two ladies.

"Mr. Hawke, may I make a call?" Mrs. Sashin asked, pointing to the conference room phone.

"Yes, of course." Drew walked over to the credenza and picked up the phone, and placed it in front of the woman. "Mrs. Sashin, you have to dial eight to get an outside line. May I ask who you are calling?"

"J.R."

Drew stepped back and watched in amazement.

"Good morning, this is Mrs. Malorie Sashin calling for J.R. Would you tell him this is important?"

After a short pause, she continued. "J.R., this is Malorie. Yes, I will tell my husband hello. Now, here's why I am calling. You are prosecuting Katherine Pansky, and I think we need some flexibility from you regarding testimony by myself and about a dozen other women who want to give an alibi for Katherine. She was with us when her husband was murdered."

She listened to the district attorney's reply.

"That's correct. She was with us from late in the afternoon until shortly after eight p.m. We worked together preparing and then leading the Society for Children's awards banquet. And that's another thing—why weren't you there? We had to give your award to one of your underlings. That idiot had nothing to say about your new Post-Conviction Justice team. He just accepted the award for you. How can we publicize your new program to examine potential miscarriages of justice, especially for juveniles, if you aren't there to explain the program?"

Drew listened intently as the woman dressed down the DA.

"Yes, yes, I understand. We did receive your generous

contribution, and you and Judith have been great contributors of your time. That's why I had an award for you."

She paused again before adding, "Next time, J.R., at least send your wife. Judith is such a great conversationalist and would have added to the enjoyment of the evening."

Finally, Mrs. Sashin asked, "Now, J.R., what are you going to do about Katherine? She was chairperson of the evening's proceedings on that Sunday. . . . Yes, we are at Mr. Hawke's office."

She turned to Drew. "Mr. Hawke, how do we put this phone on speaker? He wants to talk to you."

Drew reached over and pushed the conference-call button. "Just hang up, Mrs. Sashin. . . . Hello, Mr. Sutherland. This is Andrew Hawke with Mrs. Sashin, Mrs. Romero, and Mrs. Worley."

"I take it these ladies wish to testify?" the DA said.

"Yes, sir. But if I call them to the stand, my client will fire me. I am under specific instructions not to involve the Society for Children and its patrons. I guess that would include anyone from your office, since you are a member of the society."

"Now, J.R. . . ," broke in Mrs. Sashin, "how can we prove Katherine was not in the house when the murder occurred without getting this wonderful attorney fired?"

"Katherine is a very stubborn woman, and if she says she will fire Hawke, she will do exactly that," added Mrs. Romero.

"Hawke, when will the ladies say she was at the dinner?" J.R. asked.

Mrs. Sashin responded. "J.R., I just told you she was with the three of us from late in the afternoon until shortly after eight p.m. Now, why can't you do the right thing and dismiss those ridiculous charges?"

"Hawke, pick up the phone."

"Yes, sir," Drew said and did as ordered.

"What the hell are you doing?" the district attorney asked.

"J.R., they just showed up at my office. When I told them Katherine will not allow me to call them as witnesses, they decided to call you."

"That's correct," the three ladies shouted at the phone.

"Sir, my client believes she has already gravely damaged the society's cause by being prosecuted for her husband's death."

Drew listened to J.R.'s response, then said, "Ladies, Mr. Sutherland wants to talk to you. I'll put the phone back on conference call." He punched the button.

"Mr. Sutherland, can you hear us?" asked Mrs. Sashin.

"Yes. Thank you, ladies, for stepping forward and doing the right thing. I will discuss this matter with Mr. Hawke over lunch tomorrow, and we will figure out a way to get the alibi testimony to court."

"Wonderful, J.R. I knew you would do something."

"Hawke."

"Yes, sir?"

"Pick up the phone."

"Yes, sir." Drew did so and listened intently to the district attorney. "Yes, sir, I will meet you at the University Club at noon today," he replied. The phone went dead. "Ladies, I will call you after I meet with Mr. Sutherland."

"Call me, Mr. Hawke," instructed Mrs. Sashin, "I will tell the ladies what you two have decided."

"What do you think he will do?" asked Mrs. Worley.

"Ma'am," replied Drew in a very respectful way, "I really have no idea what he has planned."

"Thank you, Mr. Hawke," the ladies said as they each shook his hand and walked out.

CHAPTER TWENTY- FOUR

The University Club

DREW STOOD WAITING by the maître d' stand. A tall thin man in a black business suit, white French-cuffed shirt, and a perfectly shaped, hand-tied black bowtie saw Drew and made his way between tables toward him. As the man got closer, Drew found himself closely examining the man's perfectly combed black hair and his narrow face, which sported an extra-long nose. The man projected a unique but commanding presence.

Everything is impeccable about this guy, all the way down to his shirt's cuffs, which extended exactly an inch below the coat sleeves. A perfect gentleman.

"Do you have a reservation?" the man asked.

Finding himself still captivated by the man's countenance, Drew quickly regained his composure. "My name is Andrew Hawke."

"Are you a member of the University Club?"

"No, I am the guest of District Attorney Sutherland."

"Oh, yes. He is expecting you. This way."

As Drew followed the maître d' through the crowded room toward a window table, all heads turned. A gray-haired man in a wheelchair gestured for Drew to come to his table.

"Yes, Justice Price?"

"Drew, let me introduce my colleagues," he said, pointing to his right. "This is Justice Todd Olerud, Justice Mark Kotsay, and Justice Connor Sashin." The latter two were seated across the table from Drew. "I believe you have already met Justice Sashin's wife." The comment caused the four elderly men to smile broadly.

"Your Honors, it is a pleasure," Drew responded.

"I see, young man, you are giving J.R. hell," said Justice Kotsay." Mark Kotsay was a rather large man with a friendly twinkle to his eyes, but one Drew sensed was taking the measure of him.

"Sirs, that is not my intent, believe me."

"Nonsense. That's your job," spoke Justice Sashin. "How else can the justice system reach a valid result?"

"Drew, you are putting on quite an interesting defense. I particularly liked your opening statement and how it tied in with the testimony of Wu Tang," Justice Olerud offered. While he spoke, the rather short, thin man extended his hand. Drew grabbed it. Not letting go, the justice encouraged Drew. "Keep up the good work."

"Excellent job so far Drew," added Justice Price.

"You are all very kind. But I'm afraid I am in a dogfight."

"Ah, yes. The fun of practicing criminal law. You remind me of my early days. Regrettably I was not as brilliant as you."

"I doubt that, Justice Price."

"I see DA Sutherland is watching. I hear you're his guest today."

"Yes, Justice Sashin."

"That's what Malorie told me. She's been all over me about Sutherland blocking my wife and her friends from providing evidence."

"Sir, I didn't tell them Sutherland was obstructing their testimony. In fact, Mr. Sutherland invited me here to discuss their testimony.

"Oh, yes," spoke up Justice Price. "Beware, Drew, of the enemy offering peace talks."

All four of the justices laughed out loud. Drew blushed as he saw everyone in the room looking at him and who he was talking to. That included J.R. Sutherland.

"Don't mean to embarrass you, Hawke," said Justice Kotsay with a smile. "Go on over to J.R. We're all wondering what magic you will pull off this noon."

The maître d', who had stood by patiently, quickly led Drew to Sutherland's window table. The private University Club sits atop the 34-story Symphony Towers. Its view of downtown San Diego captivated diners. Drew tried not to take in the view when he greeted the district attorney. The maître d' pulled out Drew's chair, then, after Drew took his seat, unfolded the napkin and laid it across Drew's lap.

"I see you are friends with the justices," the district attorney stated.

"No, sir. They just introduced themselves to me."

"I see. Young man, you do have to come back and work for me. You are wasting your talents. It's places like the University Club where you should socialize and make powerful friends."

"I'm afraid, sir, I couldn't afford membership."

"Nonsense. The University Club is where all the power brokers of San Diego gather. It's been that way since 1909. Here is where your future will be made."

Drew didn't know what to say as the district attorney looked at him with a smile the young lawyer couldn't read. *Is he telling me I should go along with what he wants?*

The maître d' stood silently as if not hearing a thing.

"Fullerton, what do you recommend for lunch?" the DA asked.

The maître d' quickly handed each a menu. "Sir, I think you would enjoy the beet-cured smoked salmon with potato pancakes and a medley of vegetables. The pancakes are very light and seasoned to complement the salmon."

"Great, I'll have that," replied J.R. "Drew, your choice?"

"Sir, I will have something small. How about the Red Taco dish?"

"Very good choice, sir," the maître d' replied. "The birria tacos are a savory Mexican-style beef, slow-cooked until the meat is so tender it falls apart with a juicy explosion of tastes you will enjoy. It comes with a chili dip. Would you like wheat or corn tortillas?"

"Corn please."

"Fullerton, bring us a nice glass of wine. One you recommend to go with the salmon. Drew do you want some wine or a beer to go with your tacos?"

"A glass of beer would be great. It might calm down the chili dip."

"Sir, would you like a local beer? One the young folks rave about?"

"Whatever beer you think will go with the tacos, Fullerton. If I may call you Fullerton?" Drew added, not knowing why he just said what he said.

"Very good, sir," the maître d' replied and hurried away.

"Now, Hawke, how did you get Justice Sashin's wife and her cadre of women all riled up?"

"Sir, I did nothing. Out of the blue they came to my office. I've never met any of them before."

"Ha, welcome to the politics of justice, young man. When

I came in, Connor Sashin and company pulled me aside and wished me good luck with the female brigade you have aligned against me."

"Please understand, I had nothing to do with them. They are a force unto themselves. The three literally took over my office. I had no choice but to talk to them."

"That part I believe."

After some small talk, a waiter arrived with their lunch and beverages. *Thank God the food has arrived,* thought the thoroughly nervous Hawke. The young lawyer immediately bit into one of the rather large corn tacos.

"Drew, how are they?"

"Extremely tasty. Fullerton did not exaggerate," Drew replied with a full mouth. He had barely finished his first taco when Sutherland put down his fork.

"Okay, down to business. You got your witnesses as I demanded. But you can't use them, if I remember what you told me?"

"Yes, sir."

"So what are you going to do?"

"I got the witnesses. They are unimpeachable. I think the ball is in your court, J.R."

"Oh my, Drew, you are a ballsy player!"

"Not trying to be sarcastic, sir. I got the witnesses who say where Katherine was when her husband was killed. I'm hoping you will help with the rest. I just want to do what is right."

The two continued to eat while the DA changed topics and focused on the Padres baseball roster.

"Yes, sir, I agree. The Padres may have what history will refer to as the second 'Murderers' Row.' "

"Ah, yes, Manny Machado, Juan Soto, Xander Bogaerts, and Fernando Tatis, Jr. Quite the challenge for any pitcher," agreed Sutherland. "With that lineup, and a potentially winning group of pitchers, we may have a World Series contender."

"I think you're right, J.R. If the pitching holds up, the Padres will be hard to beat. But how do the two of us hit a home run in the Pansky trial?"

The DA smiled. "Okay, Drew. Back to business. Does your client know the women came to you?"

"No, sir."

"Then I will call them to the stand. She can't fire you for something I do. Besides, another trial will just end up as a losing case as far as I can see. Jack Farrat has no answers for what you have done. Aiden Cole is in complete agreement with Wu Tang."

"Sir, I think that is a smart move on your part. It's a no-lose proposition for your office. You end up doing the right thing, which turns a potentially disastrous trial into a triumph."

The district attorney shook his head. "Somehow, young man, you make eating crow seem like one of Fullerton's filet mignon steaks."

"That's not how I would phrase my suggestion, Mr. Sutherland."

"I know, Drew. You are just trying to do the right thing."

"Yes, sir."

"I suggest you not tell your client about my intentions until I call Mrs. Sashin to the stand. That way you don't get fired, and I won't have to deal with a new defense attorney hell bent on tearing me a new one."

"You aren't talking about Mary E. Astor are you?"

"Thank God, no. That can't happen since she already represents the daughter. No, I'm sure it will be another firebrand woman Astor will get to represent Mrs. Pansky. I just don't need a bigger mess on my hands than you have created."

ooooo

Drew was at his loft humming along to 'Ode for Elijah' by his favorite country heritage performer, L.E. Friar and the Man Cave Band, when the phone rang.

"Tami, who is it?"

"It's Pat."

"Put him on the speaker phone."

"Turning on the speaker phone."

"Hey, Pat. Wait a second. . . . Tami, turn down the music. . . . What's up, Pat?"

"You still having fun with your computer girlfriend?"

"Yes. Isn't Tami great? I can run the entire house by voice command. She will even engage in lengthy conversations with me."

"I wouldn't let anyone known you have an intimate relationship with a female computer."

"Okay, I guess I deserve that one. What have you got?"

"Just a bunch of information on Nathan, Lydia, and Chris."

"Any of it good?"

"Doubtful. Basically, it fills in background information on what we already know. All three have had a stressful life. However, nothing says they would want to kill Nevan."

"You mean they have made no specific threats against Nevan?"

"Correct. They just appear to be traumatized children. Chris, even Nathan, had some training in hand-to-hand combat. Both trained with local teachers."

"Hmm, that is interesting, but kids today take a lot of martial arts training. Tell you what, Pat, I will make a few calls."

"Drew, there is one thing. It appears Nevan did molest his son. No official reports, but after Nathan's freshman year at high school, he was suddenly sent off by his mother to a private all-boys Catholic academy. It's strange because Nathan got all A's in his freshman year at his La Jolla high school."

"Anything else?"

"Yes. Somebody left an envelope at my home. It was stuck under the front door mat. The envelope contained Nathan's admission records to Saint Michaels College Preparatory School. That's where he was sent. In the records, the mother instructed the school not to let her husband see her son and requested the school give Nathan special counseling for emotional trauma."

"Damn, it sure raises a lot of questions about Nevan and what type of sex fiend he was."

"I also learned Lydia received psychiatric counseling when she was sixteen."

"How about Chris?"

"I found two additional emails from Chris to his mother while she was dying. He expresses anger about Nevan not helping financially with his mother's medical treatment. But after she died, I found nothing more."

"Sounds like a good amount of background info but no smoking gun—not to make a bad joke."

"Understood. I agree; nothing concrete."

"What about your budding PI, Todd? Did he find anything out about Nathan and Lydia?"

"Nothing yet. Not many students on campus during the summer."

"I understand."

"I'll drop off my report to your loft tomorrow."

"Thanks."

CHAPTER TWENTY-FIVE

Trial Resumes

"ADA Farrat, call your next witness."

"The People call to the stand Mrs. Malorie Sashin."

Katherine immediately grabbed Drew's right arm, "I told you, Drew, not to involve any of my friends and supporters. You're fired."

Liz, who was to the right of the woman, touched her and pleaded, "Don't, Katherine."

"Katherine, I can't control the district attorney," Drew stated. "I warned you the prosecution probably knew more than they have disclosed to us, but you wouldn't allow me to find out. Why didn't you forewarn me about this potential defense-killing maneuver by the district attorney?"

"Oh, God, what am I going to do?"

"Katherine, calm down. She's here now. Let's see what she has to say."

Katherine punched Drew hard in the right shoulder and out loud said, "I should never have allowed you to take this to trial."

Liz tried to put her arm around the upset woman, but Katherine just pulled away.

After taking the oath, Mrs. Sashin took the stand.

Farrat approached. "Mrs. Sashin, do you know the defendant?"

"Yes, I know Supervisor Pansky," she said, pointing to the defense table. "Hi, Katherine."

Mrs. Pansky didn't acknowledge her greeting. Instead, she just looked down with a shameful expression.

"On the Sunday evening, the night Senator Pansky was killed, do you know where Katherine Pansky was?" Farrat asked his witness.

"Yes. She was with me and about a dozen other members of the Society for Children. We were preparing the hall for our annual awards dinner."

"The time frame I am referring to, Mrs. Sashin, is between the hours of say five to nine p.m. on that Sunday."

"We started arriving at the Scottish Rite Center around four p.m. When I arrived, Katherine was already there. She was busy putting out name tags where our patrons and guests were to be seated. She asked me and Mrs. Romero, who arrived right behind me, to rearrange the flower center pieces for each of the nineteen tables and put out small thank you gifts for each of the attendees who would be at the gala. Six people were seated at each table."

Before Farrat could ask another question, the woman continued. "At the front of the hall was a long head table where Katherine, I, and the other Society officers were seated."

"Thank you, Mrs. Sashin for setting the scene at the awards dinner for us. Now, do you know when Mrs. Pansky left the awards dinner?"

"Yes. She got an emergency call from someone at her home and asked me to take over as she rushed out."

"What time was that?"

"It was about fifteen or twenty minutes past eight. I distinctly remember the time because I looked at my watch. We try to finish these ceremonies by nine. I was hoping I had enough time to do so. We are always very punctual on matters such as this. We're no Academy Awards outfit."

A chuckle rose from the gallery, but the judge remained silent.

"Yes, thank you. So the time Mrs. Pansky left was between eight-fifteen to eight-twenty p.m., correct?"

"Yes," she answered again in a raised voice.

"Do you know where Mrs. Pansky went?"

"Her exact words were, 'I have an emergency at home.' "

"Your Honor, I have no further questions."

"Mr. Hawke, you may question," the judge said.

"We have no questions for the witness."

"I would like to say something else . . ." Mrs. Sashin began, but Judge Steinman interrupted.

"Thank you, Mrs. Sashin. You may step down."

"Excuse me, Joel, but I wish to add that Katherine would never harm an individual. I've known her for twenty-eight years. She is the kindest and most loving woman I know. She even loved that horrible husband of hers."

"Do either attorney wish to strike the last statement by this witness?" asked Judge Joel Steinman. "There was no question pending,"

"Well, I never," spoke Mrs. Sashin.

"Drew rose. "No, Your Honor. I'm sure the reference to my client's character is the witness's sincere belief. I doubt the wife of an appellate court justice would lie or intentionally mislead this court."

"That's enough, Hawke. I hereby strike the witness's last sentences and that of the defense counsel. Ladies and gentlemen, you will ignore these unsolicited comments. They are gratuitous."

Mrs. Sashin appeared ready to explode. But ADA Farrat briskly walked toward the witness with his hand extended to help her step from the witness chair.

"Your next witness, Mr. Farrat," stated the judge in a loud voice.

Once back at the defense table, Farrat announced, "The People call to the stand Mrs. Linsey Worley."

Once the witness was sworn in and seated, Farrat approached.

"Mrs. Worley, do you know the defendant, Mrs. Katherine Pansky?"

"Yes, I know Supervisor Pansky."

"Where was Mrs. Pansky on the night her husband was killed?"

Mrs. Worley confirmed everything Mrs. Sashin had previously testified to, and Farrat thanked her.

"May I add one more thing?" she asked.

"Yes, Mrs. Worley."

"She was very upset by the phone call. I would say she was near tears as she ran out."

"Have you told anyone else about the testimony you have just given?"

"Yes. I discussed what happened at the awards dinner with Mrs. Sashin and Mrs. Romero, who by the way is outside, and about a dozen other people who were at the awards dinner. We all agreed we would approach District Attorney Sutherland and tell him what we knew. He asked us to testify here today."

"Thank you, Mrs. Worley. No further questions."

"Mr. Hawke, you may question," the judge said.

"Mrs. Worley," Drew stated as he walked up to the witness. "You understand you are under oath?"

"Yes."

"I believe you have known my client for many years?"

"Oh, yes."

"I don't wish to insult you, but I have to ask this question. The fact that you know Mrs. Pansky, even worked with her on projects for children, would those facts influence your testimony?"

"Absolutely not."

"Do you believe other members of your society would be influenced by the fact that they know Mrs. Pansky? Let's say Mrs. Sashin."

"Oh, no. If you don't believe Mrs. Sashin and myself, you can talk to the other judges and justices who were present at the dinner. I've talked to them, and they also remember Katherine was at the dinner."

"Gentlemen, is there an objection to the last hearsay statement," asked Steinman. Drew stood and said nothing. Farrat sat in silence. In an exasperated voice, the judge added, "Very well, the statement may stand. Any other questions, Mr. Hawke?"

"No, Your Honor."

As Mrs. Worley walked out, the judge stated, "Yes, Mr. Farrat? You are standing."

"The People call to the stand Mrs. Marta Romero."

"ADA Farrat, how many more witnesses do you intend to call. Will they be saying the same thing?" asked the judge.

Drew rose. "Your Honor, I propose the following, that the district attorney and I stipulate a member of the district attorney's office and over one hundred other persons were at the awards dinner and, if called, all these people would say Mrs. Pansky was at the dinner when her husband was killed."

Farrat added, "Your Honor, the People will agree to the

following: The prosecution hereby stipulates the defendant was not at her home between the hours of five to eight p.m. on the night Senator Pansky was murdered."

"The defense accepts that stipulation," Drew said, "but I ask the ADA to change the time as follows: Mrs. Pansky was at the Scottish Rite Center between four p.m. to eight-twenty p.m."

"The People agree. The defendant was at the Scottish Rite Center between four p.m. to eight-twenty p.m."

The judge turned toward the jury box. "Ladies and gentlemen of the jury. The prosecution and defense have stipulated that the defendant Katherine Pansky was at the Scottish Rite Center between four p.m. to eight p.m. What this means is that you must accept the stipulated time and place as a fact, which you will use when considering all the other evidence in your deliberations. . . . Proceed, Mr. Farrat."

"The People rest."

"Mr. Hawk?."

"The defense rests."

"The testimony phase of this trial is over," the judge stated. "Yes, Mr. Hawke, you are once again standing. What is it now?"

"Your Honor, the defense moves for a directed verdict of not guilty."

"Mr. Hawke, you try my patience." The judge appeared to catch himself. He paused. After collecting his thoughts, he spoke. "Ladies and gentlemen, I do not like granting directed verdicts. I leave all verdicts to the jury. Motion denied. We will now take a recess. This court will reconvene in thirty minutes. Counsel will join me in chambers."

The courtroom burst into applause as the judge left the bench. All cameras were on the defendant and Drew as he hugged his client.

CHAPTER TWENTY-SIX

Chambers

DREW AND JACK FARRAT sat in front of Steinman as he flipped through the jury instruction book. Finally the judge spoke.

"I've marked all the standard jury instructions which I will give. Do you have any questions?"

"Sir," spoke up Drew, "will you give the normal instruction on party stipulations?"

"Yes. Anything else?"

"Would you tell us what instructions you intend to give along with the stipulation instruction?"

"Why should I? I've chosen all the instruction I intend to give. Do you have any special instruction you desire?"

"I just want to know which instructions you will use, that's all."

"Hawke, I'm done with you. It's over. I'm the top banana, not you. So be quiet."

"Sir, I wish to put my objections on the record."

"You can do what you want when we are back in court."

"You want me to object in front of the jury and the packed courtroom, cameras and all?"

"No. You will do it after I send the jury to deliberate. I don't want to hear anything further from you. I'm done with you. You hear me?"

Drew immediately rose and walked out without waiting for permission to leave.

"Did you see that? Did you see that?" shouted the little man. "He just walked out on me. I oughta hold him in contempt."

Farrat remained silent for a moment, then he asked permission to leave.

"Yes, get out of here."

ooooo

The Jury

ADA FARRAT rose to give his closing argument. As he slowly walked toward the fourteen seated jurors he began.

"Ladies and gentlemen, I am a deputy district attorney. As such, I am sworn to uphold the United States and the California constitutions. Since the San Diego District Attorney is the chief law enforcement officer of this county, I, as his deputy, also swear to an additional, more specific ethical standard...."

Where is Farrat going with this? I should object, but if I do, Steinman will overrule me. Maybe Farrat will open the door to an objection by appearing to testify.

"That standard is equal protection under the law," Farrat continued. "I swore to convict the guilty and to exonerate the innocent. Thus, as soon as witnesses came forward with a possible alibi for the defendant, I put them on the stand. I did so as to provide all known evidence to you, the trier of fact. It is now your decision as to whether you find this new testimony sufficient to let the accused go."

Drew sat back and pondered, *What is he up to?*

"My fellow citizens, I think not. Here is why. The words of the defendant say otherwise."

Drew clinched his fists, ready to object about Katherine not testifying.

"During voir dire questioning, all of you said, 'I saw the news video of the supervisor saying she caused her husband's death.' A very damning statement against herself. I will leave it to you if she ever held another news conference where she clarified how she caused his death."

Drew looked to Steinman who only smiled and looked away.

"Did she shoot him? Did she strike him in the face and neck with a heavy statue? Did she somehow grab his neck and yank it? Did she do so with the same force that also dislocated his shoulder in a continuing rage against the man who violated her daughter? And don't tell me a woman doesn't possess superior strength. We've all heard of a mother picking up the end of a car to free her child pinned underneath. Cars that would take two or more men to lift when coming to assist."

You walk a thin line, Farrat.

"Science. Let's talk about science. Retired Wu Tang took the stand and testified as a hired witness for the defense. I wonder how much he makes a year as a hired gun?"

"Objection, Your Honor. The prosecutor had plenty of time to ask such a question to Dr. Tang."

"Over ruled, Hawke. Sit down and stay down. This is closing argument. . . . I see you are still standing young man. Care to dig a deeper hole?"

Drew sat down in disgust over the obvious bias of the judge.

Farrat continued his closing argument. "Did any of you wonder why Dr. Tang didn't explain in greater detail how he came to the conclusions he did? Where are the photographs of those slides he found so important to his conclusions about the brain tissue and the body's lack of blood in the upper extremities? Why were you deprived of such important evidence which you could have seen and decided for yourself. Evidence that the defense will soon raise and say ruled out the possibility that the defendant killed her husband. Did she, in fact, kill him once she got home from the banquet? And don't say that was my job to point this out during my cross-examination. Wu Tang was the defense alibi witness, not mine."

Drew looked to the jury, who were fast writing in their notepads.

"Motive. Motive. Motive," Farrat said as he walked slowly along the jury box. All the jurors stopped writing and looked at him.

"Yes, motive. Who had the motive to kill the bastard," Farrat raged as he looked at each juror, his eyes wide with conviction.

"She did," he shouted, turning quickly and pointing to the defendant. "Who felt the greatest guilt for not leaving the sexual predator? She did. Who would have the greatest shame for failing to protect her children? She did. Who would, therefore, have the selfish need to seek revenge and vindicate her years of looking the other way? She did," he added, turning again and pointing to Katherine.

Farrat stepped back and stood in front of the witness stand. As he did, all the jurors looked at Katherine. Not one writing anything down. Walking back in front of them, Farrat finished.

"Ladies and gentlemen, the prosecution has provided the motive for the defendant to kill. The defendant had the opportunity to kill once she arrived at home. And," he paused, "the defendant made a damning statement of guilt for the murder. Further, through the testimony of Dr. Cole and even Dr. Tang, we know how Nevan Pansky died. He died in a vicious, violent attack. Every possible thing was done to kill the man. The only thing missing was him being butchered with a knife."

Farrat stood in silence as his words spread throughout the

quiet room. Slowly, the man turned and walked back to his table. Once there, he continued in a slow but very audible voice.

"Ladies and gentlemen, doesn't the horrible murder of Senator Nevan Pansky fit a murderer hell bent on seeking vengeance? A murderer venting years of shame and pent-up anger? I submit to you the evidence points to no one else but the defendant, Katherine Margaret Pansky," he added, raising his voice. "Your verdict must be—guilty."

With that flourish of drama Jack Farrat sat down.

"Your turn, Hawke," the judge said.

"Thank you, sir,"

Drew stood about four feet in front of the jury of fourteen.

"Folks, the prosecution just asked a lot of pointed questions, which supposedly meant my client is guilty. However, he never backed those cloaked accusations with sworn witnesses or factual evidence. Jack Farrat had all the time and power to bring any witnesses who could support his theory Katherine killed her husband. He could have even called Medical Examiner Cole to refute the testimony of Dr. Wu Tang. He did not."

Drew paused for a moment before continuing.

"When I was a teenage boy and my mother asked me a question I didn't want to answer, I would instead ask her questions as if I didn't understand what she was talking about. My mother would always reply, 'Quit looking for a way out and answer the question.' Not finding a way out, I always had to face the music.

"Now I see that ADA Farrat resorts to questions in an effort to avoid the issue before this court. Why? Because he has no factual evidence to rebut the defense's case. Questions are not facts, and it is not the defense's duty to answer such speculative questions. Where is the prosecution's evidence that Katherine killed her husband? There is none. All factual evidence the prosecution presented that Katherine killed her husband has been refuted with evidence given under oath. He didn't die by gunshot to the head. He was already dead when shot. And where did the gun residue on her clothing come from? It got on her as she tried to save her husband. How did this shameful man die? Not by a simple snapping of the neck by a woman in a rage of anger, but by a learned technique executed in such a manner as to produce a complete horizontal dissecting of the spinal cord. A maneuver which required the holding of the body motionless while the neck was snapped horizontally to the right. Such a maneuver required a well-trained man of strength."

Drew walked slightly toward the jury and paused as two jurors made notes.

"I told you in the beginning, ask yourself, 'How and when was the senator killed?' We now know how. We also know when. He was killed when Katherine was at an awards banquet for benefactors of her charity for children."

Walking back to the defense table, his words still echoing in the silent courtroom, Drew stood behind his client.

"Folks, one can find any number of reasons why Nevan Pansky deserved to die. But this fact is sure: The prosecution has completely failed to prove his wife rendered death to this disgraced man. I implore you to find Katherine not guilty. It is my opinion this is the only verdict you can arrive at under the law. My client and I pray that you do your duty."

"Mr. Farrat, your rebuttal argument?"

"Your Honor, the People have said all that is necessary. We rest."

"Very well."

A cavalcade of voices rose in the courtroom. Judge

Steinman gaveled order. Turning to the jury, the judge opened his jury instruction book and began reading. Steinman spent nearly forty minutes slowly instructing the jurors on the law and how they were to deliberate. Finally, he ordered Deputy Wells to escort the twelve who would deliberate the case to the jury room.

Once the twelve jurors were out of the courtroom, Steinman turned to the two alternates.

"Thank you for being so attentive during the trial. Before you go, please verify with my clerk your cell-phone numbers and where you will be for the next several days. If you are needed to replace one of the twelve deliberating jurors, we will call you. So stay close, as we will need you to come quickly. Again, I thank you for your service."

With that, Steinman gaveled court adjourned. Drew rose to put on the record his objections, but Judge Steinman walked off the bench without recognizing him. Drew turned to the court reporter.

"Laura, I want to make a statement on the record," he said in a low confidential voice.

"Mr. Hawke, I can't do that without the judge's permission," she whispered, leaning forward.

"Laura, he doesn't want me to object to anything. Please help?"

Looking around as the courtroom emptied, she softly said, "I'll turn on the recorder. You whisper your objections. Don't touch the recorder. I'll discover it later. Call my answering machine and leave a message saying you want a copy of the recording along with your usual unofficial written transcript. There is no need to make a request to the judge. He knows you get a daily transcript anyway."

"Thanks, Laura." The young woman got up and left.

In a low voice, Drew made his objection about the judge not allowing the defense a review of the instructions before Steinman instructed the jury, adding, "Judge Steinman has intentionally obstructed at every chance my efforts to provide my client an effective defense."

Once finished, the young man felt a great release of the tension in the muscles of his back and neck. *Finally, I've said it. I've told someone what that little shit has done to me and my client.* He turned and walked back to the defense table, where he noticed Nathan standing next to his mom. Even seeing Nathan didn't lessen his feeling of relief.

"Katherine, I believe we got in a solid defense. Your friends provided the alibi testimony we needed without involving your children, as I promised."

"I don't know if you arranged their testimony, Hawke, but I am devastated by this trial. It's a public humiliation."

"Katherine," Drew said as he sat down next to her, "any humiliation started and ended when you made that terrible statement to the press against my wishes. Now at least you have a chance to be vindicated for the murder of your husband."

Leaning close he whispered, "Ma'am, there is no way the authorities will prosecute your daughter for the death of Nevan. Her testimony was not just a solid statement of self-defense but also a plea for help as she struggles with post-traumatic stress from the rapes and her finally fighting back."

Nathan leaned over and consoled his mother. "Hawke is right, Mom. You couldn't have had things work out better. It is just as I planned."

Drew stared at the young man, obviously furious with the want-to-be lawyer.

"Liz, after I walk out, wait a few minutes and then escort

Katherine and Nathan down to the cafeteria. Keep the reporters away. Nathan, don't say anything to anyone. You hear me? No reporters. No one."

"Yes, sir."

With that, Drew got up and walked out.

CHAPTER TWENTY-SEVEN

The Verdict

Two REPORTERS and their cameramen immediately rushed to Drew as he exited the courtroom. Drew waved them off as he walked briskly down the hallway toward his hideaway at the north end of the courthouse. Once there his phone buzzed.

"Yes? Oh, hi, Nick. How's the dojo these days?" Drew stopped and listened. "Thanks, Nick. Tell your brother I say hi." The phone went dead. Drew sat down on a bench in deep thought. After about fifty minutes a voice echoed in the hallway.

"Hawke, Drew Hawke. We have a verdict."

The attorney looked up to see Deputy Caleb Wells coming around the corner to where Drew was seated.

"Do you know what the verdict says?"

"No, Drew. But when they rang the bell and I opened the jury room door, they said there was a verdict. The judge wants you inside now."

The two walked back to the courtroom, observing reporters and cameramen running into court.

I guess it's true. A quick verdict. I don't know what to make of this. Drew started to perspire. His armpits itched as his nerves took over. *There's nothing worse than a quick verdict. It could go either way.*

Katherine was already seated at the defense table. Nathan was standing behind her and Elizabeth was seated to Katherine's right. The nervous attorney took his seat.

"Can I sit with my mother?" asked Nathan.

"No. Sit in the first row," came Drew's sharp reply.

Time ticked by slowly, adding to the tension of the moment. Finally, Judge Steinman took the bench.

"Quiet in court," ordered Deputy Wells.

"Deputy Wells, please escort the jury in."

"Yes, sir."

A few moments later, the jury filed into court, but instead of entering through the door next to the jury box, the twelve deciding judges-of-the-facts came through the door behind the court clerk.

Why? Drew asked himself. *Jurors always enter from the door closest to where they sit.*

The jurors one by one walked in front of the defense table toward the prosecution and the jury box. Drew noticed each of the jurors look at Katherine and then at him. Several jurors even smiled.

Have they voted not guilty? Are the jurors signaling their verdict?

Once the twelve were seated, Deputy Wells asked for quiet.

"Ladies and gentlemen of the jury, who is your foreperson?" asked the judge.

Juror number seven rose. "I am, sir."

"Mr. Foreman, do you have a verdict?"

"Yes, sir."

"Would you please hand that verdict to the court clerk."

Once the clerk received the verdict, she walked back to her desk and handed it to Steinman. He showed no emotion as he read the form. After handing the verdict back to his clerk, Steinman gave Drew a sullen look.

"Madam clerk, please announce the verdict."

Drew touched Katherine's arm, signaling for her to rise as Drew and Liz also stood for the verdict.

"In the case of the People of the State of California versus Mrs. Katherine Margaret Pansky, we the jury find the defendant not guilty on all charged counts."

A cheer went up in the courtroom. Katherine leaned against Drew, who had wrapped his arm around the trembling woman. The judge sat stone faced. Deputy Wells demanded silence.

"Your Honor, do you want me to read how the jury voted on each count and their enhancements?" asked the clerk.

"No." Turning to the jury, the judge asked, "Is this your verdict one and all?"

The jury answered in unison, "Yes."

"Very well." Turning to the ADA, he asked, "Mr. Farrat, do you wish the jury polled?"

"No, sir," came the reply.

In a loud voice the judge announced, "Mrs. Katherine Pansky, the jury has spoken. You are free to go. This court is now adjourned," the little man announced as he stood and went toward his chambers.

The audience went wild. Nathan jumped the barrister's rail so he could hug his mother, who was in tears.

Drew looked to Liz. "Elizabeth, escort Katherine out to Matt's van. I'll call him to meet you at the back entrance." Turning to Deputy Wells, Drew asked, "Caleb would you allow Mrs. Pansky to exit again via the chambers hallway and down to the private courthouse back door? That way they will avoid the media."

"Sure thing, Drew."

Drew gently pushed Nathan back and whispered in his client's ear. "Go with Liz and Deputy Wells to the back door. Matt will be waiting. I don't want anything said to the press." Looking at Nathan, he said, "You go with your mother. It is best nothing is said to the media. Do you understand?"

"But why?"

"I'll explain everything when we meet back at the office. Believe me, it is important you and your mother say nothing."

Drew then pulled Liz close. "Have Katherine call Lydia and Chris. Make sure they come to the office immediately. Also, call Debbie and tell her to order sandwiches for everyone, including you and Matt. It's time we celebrate."

With that, Drew turned and grabbed Farrat by the arm. "Let's face the glory together, Jack. I'll compliment you on the firm grip you have on the scales of justice, and how you acted swiftly to do the right thing once the surprise witnesses came forward."

Farrat stared to pull away only to have Drew say, "Oh no you don't, Jack. This is exactly what J.R. wants. Believe me," Drew emphasized as he tightened his grip on Jack's arm.

The two walked outside to the blare of lights and a flurry of questions. Drew quieted the crowd.

"Thank you, members of the press and media, for your astute coverage of the trial."

"Hawke, how did you find the witnesses?" shouted one reporter, who was followed by several others. "Yeah, Hawke how'd you do that?"

"Come on, guys, one at a time. You did it, not me," he said, pointing to all the reporters. "Your close following of this case allowed the public to know exactly what happened on that fateful Sunday evening. Due to your reporting efforts, witnesses stepped forward to tell what they knew. To the public, and in particular to those brave witnesses who were willing to testify, I say thank you. To District Attorney J.R. Sutherland and his extremely hard-working assistant attorney . . ." He pointed to Jack Farrat. "I say thank you for protecting the innocent while you aggressively pursue the guilty. This city, indeed this county, is safer because of you, Jack Farrat, and your boss, J.R. Sutherland. Now, ladies and gentlemen, I have a very relieved client but more importantly an exhausted and traumatized woman whom I must attend to. Jack will answer all your questions. Thank you." Drew pulled Farrat forward and in a low voice said, "Jack, the stage is yours."

With that, Drew turned and walked toward the elevators and his exit from the courthouse.

CHAPTER TWENTY-EIGHT

Confrontation

DREW WALKED TO HIS OFFICE. The fresh air and noise of the city allowed him to clear his mind. Occasionally, a passerby would approach and shake his hand, complimenting him.

"I've never seen a trial like that before," one man said, apparently enjoying a morning break from his office grind.

A young man shouted from across the street, "Congratulations, Drew. If I ever need a lawyer, may I call you?"

"Of course," Drew yelled back.

Others just stared admiringly and told their friends, "That's him. That's A.J. Hawke."

Standing in front of his office at the George J. Keating Building, Drew decided not to go in, not yet.

I'm going to have a drink.

"That's right," he said out loud as he entered the Tipsy Crow, which was across from the Keating Building. As he entered, Drew noticed the two downstairs TVs had the news on.

"Congratulations, Drew," offered Jack Thorn, the prematurely graying bartender.

"Thank you, Jack. I'll have a bourbon. Do you have Widow Jane's ten-year?"

"Sure do. Neat?"

"Why not. It was a tense and hard-fought trial."

"Celebrating your win?"

"You might say that. Or getting ready for the next round."

Both men laughed.

"Here you go. No need to reach for the wallet, Drew. It's on the house. Great piece of lawyering. We need lawyers like you."

"Thank you, Jack. Really nice of you to say that. Oh, yes, here's a tip for being the best bartender in town." The young lawyer smiled as he handed his friend a fiver.

Drew went upstairs and sat in a dark corner. He slowly sipped his bourbon as he mapped out how he would expose the killer.

After a few minutes, Drew checked his watch. It was almost noon. Time to go. He downed the last sip of the brown gold and walked out.

Sure enough, as he entered the office, there sat the four: Katherine, Lydia, Chris, and Nathan. Liz, Matt, and Debbie were in the conference room setting up lunch.

"Please join me in my office," Drew said as he gestured to the four to follow. Once all were seated, Katherine and Nathan in the two chairs in front of his desk, and Lydia and Chris on the couch to Drew's the left.

"Lunch should be ready soon. I thought it would be appropriate for the four of you, my staff, and I to have a celebratory meal together before we all go our separate ways."

Drew started to say how everyone had suffered because of their tragedy and the trial when Drew saw Nathan staring at the autographed baseball on his credenza, underneath a picture signed by Trevor Hoffman.

Drew swiveled his chair to the right and picked up the ball. He flipped it to Nathan, who eagerly caught it with his right hand.

"Trevor gave that to me after one of his great saves for the Padres."

Drew watched as the young law student slowly turned the baseball in an admiring way.

"Someday, I will have things like this," he said.

Drew held up his hand for Nathan to toss it back. Nathan flipped the ball up in the air in a playful manner. Drew smiled as he caught it.

"Great catch, Drew. I bet you've played ball."

"High school and stuff. But Hoffman gave me the baseball because he was friends with my investigator, Pat De Luca. After a pause, Drew's demeanor changed.

"I know this has been very trying for all of you." He looked first to Katherine and nodded with a look of reassurance. He then did the same with Lydia.

"But, folks, it's over. You may never be able to go back to your normal lives, and some of you will have haunting memories for years to come. But let me say this much, the public is very forgiving. They may never forget about the murder, but this trial showed them you were as much victims as you were participants in a series of events which led to a tragic night."

Tears began to well up in Katherine's eyes. Drew immediately looked intently at her.

"Katherine, it is not your fault. You did what was best for the children. Children without a father to help them attend the best universities and make sure they lacked for nothing is a vital part of a parent's duty. Whatever Nevan did that tarnished any love he showed to the children, you made up by your singular devotion and the love you gave Nathan and Lydia, day in and day out."

"I made the wrong choices, Drew. The price has been too high. It is my fault."

Drew started to shake his head, but Katherine would have no part of his attempt to support her decisions.

"No, Drew, I stayed for selfish reasons. I actually enjoyed being the wife of a powerful senator. It opened doors otherwise closed to me. A social level I could never achieve on my own. Being his wife actually allowed me to find myself. To develop a purpose in my life other than raising children and taking care of a house."

"No, Mom," yelled Lydia. "We love you. You sacrificed so much for us. Dad was a worthless, selfish monster. He thought only of himself."

"Lydia is right," spoke up Nathan. "You were our lives. You always put us first. We have a family because of you."

"Nathan is right," added Chris. "You took me in when you didn't have to."

"Children, I should have done the right thing. Instead I took the easy way. Now all of us must live with what we have done," she said, looking to Drew.

"Katherine, I know what happened and how the four of you closed ranks as the tragedy unfolded."

"I know you do, Drew. That's why we trust you."

The room had reached a very emotional point, with Lydia hugging her mother as Chris wiped tears from his eyes. Only Nathan looked at Drew, his gaze questioning.

"Your father was evil," Drew said, looking at Nathan, then Lydia, and finally at Chris, where he held his gaze. "Sometimes one must do evil to end evil."

He could see that his words struck a sensitive nerve in all four.

"That doesn't mean it is right to commit murder against an evil man. 'Death deserved' is no defense in the law. Worse, it carries with it a guilt which no matter what you do will be with you until you die."

"What are you going to do, Drew?" asked Katherine as she sat erect in her seat and in total control of her emotions.

"I used to think, Katherine, the law is black and white. You do wrong, you pay. That's the definition of justice. But this case has shown me justice comes in different forms and not always the most humane. I've always known it is human to act out of emotion. A human without emotion is a lifeless ameba, just a thing. Each of you acted emotionally and to some degree for different reasons. Some in fear, some in anger, some with revenge, and some with love. How am I to judge which emotion should pay and which should be forgiven? I have not lived your individual lives. I wasn't at the house that Sunday evening."

"I understand, Drew. Thanks," Katherine said with a sigh of relief.

"Shall we have lunch, folks?" Drew offered in order to break the tension.

But before anyone could rise, Katherine stood and pulled two envelopes from her suitcoat.

"This is probably the wrong time to raise another problem, but my children and I need your help."

"How so?"

"Two young adults, a thirty-year-old man and a younger woman, claim to be children of Nevan. I need you to handle these claims. I just don't think they're real. Chris is Nevan's son, and he is now part of my family. But these two intruders are making bogus claims."

"Why do you say that?"

"Nevan was never in New York or anywhere near the

thirty-year-old man's mother when they supposedly had sex," Katherine said as she handed the envelopes to Drew. "These are their letters. Each tells a separate story of how and when Nevan was with their mothers."

"I see," replied Drew.

"I know the man is a fake because Nevan never left my side in the early days of our marriage. He was just planning his first campaign for congress and never left the state. We couldn't afford to travel, and we had no reason to go east."

"And the woman?"

"She bears no resemblance to Nevan, Nevan's mother, or grandmother. An investigative reporter tripped her up on the dates she claimed her mother lived in Washington, DC. The woman couldn't even remember what she told another reporter about the time frame of when her mother lived on the East Coast. That same reporter did some research and found the woman's mother hadn't left Nebraska for the five years before and five years after the young woman was born. The birth certificate also listed another man. They're both frauds."

"I see. But frankly I don't think I am the lawyer for this. You retained Randy Wright to represent the children. Either he or an estate attorney would be the best attorney for you."

"Nonsense. You're the only lawyer I will trust to clear up these claims. Regrettably, I think there will be others in the future."

Drew thought for a moment.

But before he could say anything, Katherine added, "Drew, I don't want anyone to raise doubts about Chris. He is a fine young man and doesn't deserve anyone throwing about nasty gossip about him because of those two imposters. You know what I mean. He is Nevan's son."

Drew nodded, indicating he understood. "Alright, I will help. But things like this don't go away quickly."

"I have plenty of money, Drew. How about a retainer of fifty thousand?"

"That's not necessary. Let's talk about this later."

At that moment there came a knock at the door.

"Yes, Debbie?"

"Lunch is served. Everything is set up in the conference room."

"Great, we'll be right out," he said, then looked to the family members. "Guys, we have to lighten things up and do a little celebrating to an end of a very terrible period in your lives. Chris, I know things haven't been easy for you. But you have a new family, one that is supportive of you and you of them. Congratulations."

"Thank you, sir."

Everyone rose and started to go to the conference room. Drew paused, throwing the baseball back and forth between his hands.

"Katherine, if you don't mind, I'd like to talk with Nathan for a few minutes about the trial and his future in law."

"I think that is a good thing. Thank you, Drew."

The young lawyer walked over to the door and shut it as he motioned for Nathan to take a seat—then dropped his bombshell.

"Nathan, I know you killed your father."

"What!"

"Yes, you killed Nevan. No reason to deny it."

"Why in the world would you say that?"

"You killed Nevan with a quick twisting action to his neck. You see, Chris is left handed. In executing that type of death maneuver, he would have twisted the neck to the left. You are right handed," Drew said as he walked back to his desk. "Should I toss the baseball to you again?"

"You've got no evidence to support such a speculative claim, Hawke. My being right handed is not proof," Nathan said excitedly.

"Oh, but I do have evidence. You see, the Capitol Police provided Nevan and Katherine with twenty-four-hour protection, which included video surveillance. I've viewed the film. It shows exactly when Lydia and Chris showed up and when they left after you arrived. I have also seen cell-phone records where you called your mother about Nevan's death. You even called nine-one-one to report a shot in the Pansky home."

"But my mom shot him . . . Nathan's voice trailed off as he remembered Wu's testimony.

"That's right, Nathan. He died by a forced twisting rupture of the spinal cord. He did not die by a shot to the head. I've even listened to the surveillance's audio. You shooting the man is clearly heard. This was after Lydia and Chris had left and before Katherine arrived."

The young man rose and began walking wildly around the room, rubbing his hands together. Sweat dripped from his face. He suddenly stopped and looked at Drew with the tense expression of a man cornered. Nathan clenched his fists.

This is it. Is he going to confess? Or will he see through my bluff?

"Relax, Nathan. I won't turn you in."

"Where's the surveillance video?" he demanded.

"I only viewed the film. The U.S. attorney has it. They wouldn't even give a copy to me or to the district attorney."

"Has the DA seen the video?"

"No. The Feds wouldn't let them see it."

"You planned all this, didn't you, Hawke?"

"No. You're the planner. The problem is, no matter how much planning you do, the actual death blows are very traumatic to the murderer. One who kills invariably make mistakes. In your case, you didn't even have time to plan the murder. The opportunity just suddenly presented itself and you acted. But after you killed your father, you did take your time to plan the coverup. Somewhat creatively, I might add. Your plan selfishly evolved into making your mother the scapegoat. You knew Katherine would gladly take the fall in order to protect Lydia. Then you talked your sister into saying she killed Nevan when she fought back his attack. Thus, providing a defense for your mom. Very diabolical, Nat."

"Don't call me Nat."

"As you wish."

"What do you want, Hawke?"

"Good question. But let me finish. I know your father violated you when you were fourteen years old. You never told your mother because you were too ashamed to tell her. A normal reaction for a young man. But she put two and two together. That's why she sent you to Saint Michaels."

"You trying to counsel me about what my father did?"

"No."

"Who told you all this, Mom?"

"Just listen. You also took a very expensive course in hand-to-hand combat with a famous retired SEAL and his martial-arts partner."

"How do you know all this?"

"You forget I have many contacts in the mixed martial arts. The point is this: They taught you how to do the move you used to kill your father. Fraternity brothers at your university had to stop you from using that very same neck snap while you were in a rage against another brother who called you a poofer."

Nathan began to cry.

"Sit down, Nathan. S-i-t," Drew demanded.

The young man finally sat down.

"Being gay is nothing to be ashamed of. Many of my clients are gay. Your brothers at the fraternity have suspected you are gay for years. Your mother will tell you she's known for years if you would only come out to her."

"What do you want, Hawke? What do-o-o you want?" he cried out as tears ran down his face.

"Get treatment, Nathan. Get counseling about your sexuality and any anger you have about your father raping you. That's what I'm suggesting. The longer you wait, the worse it will be for you. If you put off talking to someone, you may never do it. Not confronting the evils within you now will doom you to a life of lies, anger, and maybe even more violence."

"What about the Feds?"

"They have another agenda. The government isn't interested in you or prosecuting you for killing your father. Just get your head right. That, in my opinion, will be the best way to help you, Lydia, and your mother to get over the murder."

"The fool still loves him. If she only knew what he did to me and Lydia."

"She knows, Nathan."

"No, she doesn't. The pain, the shame. Now, because of this trial, Lydia and I won't be able to go anywhere. I can't go back to school. They will laugh at me, saying he raped me, too."

There was a soft knock at the door.

"Yes?"

Debbie stepped in. "Drew, everyone is wondering when you and Nathan will join us in the conference room."

"Tell them Nathan and I are having a deep conversation about law school and how to handle the stress of studying after all that's happened. Tell Katherine it is very important to let us talk. She and the children should go home when finished with lunch. I will bring Nathan to his apartment later."

The door closed.

EPILOGUE

Saturday Evening

Saint Joseph Cathedral was dimly lit as parishioners waited for confession. A young man stepped into the lofty basilica, characterized by its ornate, vaulted ceiling and colorful stained-glass windows. He proceeded through the nave and between the many rows of pews. The man stopped and knelt before the altar, blessed himself, and stood for a moment. Then he walked over to the shallow transept and knelt at the altar of the Blessed Virgin Mary holding baby Jesus. There he lit a candle amongst the rows of small red-glass holders, adding to the flickering glow bathing the loving mother and child. After a few minutes, he walked to a row of pews and sat, head bowed.

Soon a disheveled man in a pair of dingy old blue jeans and a gray hoodie walked up and sat behind the meditating man, who turned.

"Finnigan, what are you doing here?"

"Sheesh, Hawke look straight ahead."

"Hell no," came the reply as Hawke moved to his left so he could look at the man.

"What are you doing in here?" he asked again.

"I'm Irish, can't I pray?"

Drew almost laughed out loud. "The only thing Catholic about you is your Irish name. I'm surprised the walls of the cathedral haven't started to crumble."

"Humorous, Hawke. We need to talk."

"Call my office for an appointment."

"You know I don't operate that way."

"Yeah, yeah. Only in the shadows," Drew responded in a raised voice.

"Jesus, man, your voice echoes in this place. Speak softly," Finnigan whispered. "I know you hate me. You never hide your feelings. It's all over your face. But for cryin' out loud, hear me out. You may not like what I do, but every day I risk my life for our country. So please, I need your help."

"Finnigan, no. I want nothing to do with you."

"Drew, your country needs you."

"Finnigan, no 'country' shit. All you do is violate this country's laws and get people killed. I played along with you for Katherine's sake only. We're done, so bug off," Drew stated in an angry, almost hostile tone.

In a steady but soft voice Finnigan said, "That's all the gratitude I get for letting De Luca and his college friend find out about Nathan?"

"What!"

"Yes, that was me."

"I suspected you were playing with me when Wyland said I could view the surveillance video. And then later, out of nowhere, Nathan's Saint Michael's records show up at Pat's home."

"You're good at what you do, Hawke, but we need Katherine, and I wasn't sure if you would succeed. Listen up. Katherine has agreed to finish Nevan's work for us. There's one problem. She won't do it without you."

"You're shittin' me."

"No."

"Why would she do that? Wait a minute. Is Nathan involved in this?"

"Yes, I'm surprised you would say that. Nathan demanded we grant his mom, Lydia, and him immunity and destroy the Capitol Police films of the night of the murder."

I knew it. That kid is again manipulating Katherine. He is dangerous."

"Yes, he is," the agent said, leaning forward as he whispered, "Nathan is the blood of his father, a manipulating man who understands power, especially the power of sex and how to leverage it to get what he wants—from men and from women."

"I guess you would know, being Nevan's handler and all."

"Yes, Hawke, Nevan was a double agent and had been for many years. But the work he started must be completed. The documents we retrieved have to be turned over to his Chinese contacts."

"And how in the world do you think Katherine can do that?"

"She's the natural replacement. You showed she didn't kill her husband. All we have to do is let it be known she knew about the Chinese and was helping Nevan to pass secrets to them. A little chatter by us on known secure channels they monitor and the game is in play."

"This is not a game, Finnigan. You're playing with lives, Katherine's life."

"She'll be protected by me and my men the whole time."

"In that case, you're playing with my life."

"Hawke, you are too valuable to us. We would never throw you away."

"That is reassuring. But Finnigan, no! This is Nathan's plan to get rid of me while saving his own ass. If I agree, I sign my own death warrant. The kid wants me dead. I know too much."

"Yes, you do know everything about him. You exposed him and everything he has done in your office this week. Shook him to the core. Scared the shit out of him, frankly."

"So you know why I . . . wait a minute. You've been bugging my office?"

"Drew, we don't plant bugs anymore."

"You had me wavering for a time. But now I know I don't want anything to do with you. Ah, here's an idea—send the kid."

"No, he's totally unreliable. Besides, Nathan's too impulsive."

"That's your problem."

"Drew, you will never be out of our sight. Here's the plan. You will meet Katherine in Thailand. She will be on a vacation to get away from San Diego and all the publicity. You are there to visit your sensei. Once in Asia, you two hookup and give the appearance of two lovers sneaking away for alone time."

"Man, do you know what you sound like?"

"Drew, it will work. The Chinese believe Americans are obsessed with sex. You have the reputation of a womanizer, and it is not unusual for female clients to become emotionally attached to their lawyers. We just have to have you and Katherine be seen together around town before the two of you leave."

"No. How many times do I have to say no?"

"Drew, the documents you and Katherine will pass are vital to stalling the Chinese from invading Taiwan. They have already flexed their military muscle by firing their new long-range, land-based cruise missiles over Taiwan. Those missiles will force us to move the Seventh Fleet away from Taiwan. Too far east in the Pacific for us to respond quickly in support of Taiwan. It's either that or we suffer catastrophic losses to the Seventh Fleet. Either way, the island will probably fall. If

Taiwan does fall to the Chinese, the United States will no lon-ger be a credible ally in the Pacific."

"Dicey stuff, Finnigan. Why tell me all this? You know I want nothing to do with you, the CIA, or the U.S. Attorney's Office."

"I wouldn't tell you anything, except what we ask is ex-tremely vital to the United States. Ukraine may collapse if American public support waivers. And if we let Taiwan go, American credibility as a world power willing to fight totali-tarianism will be totally discredited. Tokyo will go nuclear and arm to the teeth, as well as Europe and us. All nuclear arms treaties will be out the window."

"That's quite a tale you spin. Where's the leprechaun and the pot of gold?"

"Hawke, the United States can't fight two major powers at once without the support of Europe and Japan. We are in a new era of warfare based on technology and low-yield nuclear weaponry. For the third time in one hundred years the world powers are dividing into two large military camps. One based on totalitarianism and the other on semi-capitalist democracies.

"The difference this time is the proliferation of nuclear weapons and the devastating effects of climate change on the production of food. Agriculture will soon be used as a weapon to elicit third-world countries to provide valuable minerals in exchange for food as climate change dries up traditional crops. The nearly eight billion world population will more and more look to war in order to feed itself. World instability plays into the hands of totalitarianism."

"I think you're reaching a bit, Finnigan."

"Think of it this way: Digital-age technology is changing

rapidly. The United States can no longer rely on the barriers of two oceans. Our fleets and airpower will be limited in its ability to protect this country. Autonomous-controlled aircraft, submarines, and communication systems will be needed to decide when this country is under nuclear attack and how to respond.

Finnigan explained that Russia is arming its cruisers, frigates, and submarines with 3M22 Zircon missiles—commonly known as the 'Dagger.' Many of these hypersonic missiles will be nuclear tipped. The Chinese will follow. Low-yield nuclear weapons make their use on the battlefield a reality. Super-fast hypersonic weapons reduce the lead time for us to respond. The military will not have enough time to verify a threat, contact the president, brief him, and communicate his orders.

"We are in perilous times," he concluded.

"Even if your tale is true, why do you involve Katherine and me?" Drew asked.

"Disinformation."

"You want us to deliver disinformation?"

"I've said enough. Are you in or out?"

Drew sat back in the pew, looking at Jesus bleeding on the cross.

"What you are asking is ridiculously dangerous. Why can't you disseminate this information another way, say through semi-secure government communiques? You know what I mean."

"Pansky was high enough in government and had access to top-secret briefings. We spent years sending through him piecemeal information, which they could verify and use. They trusted him. Now the information they will get through you two will scare them to death. It's based on digital electronic masking that is better than our stealth radar-avoiding science. You add to this hypersonic propulsion and both China and Russia will have to re-evaluate their military capabilities against us."

"I see."

"Drew, your country really does need you. You can buy us at least five to ten years, the time we need to finalize new technologies. During that time we can catch up and surpass the Russians and Chinese in hypersonic technology. More important, we will be able to equip the next generation of navy ships with impenetrable electronic warfare defenses, including new long-range, anti-aircraft, and anti-missile laser defenses. If we buy enough time, this will make our naval deterrence effective for another twenty-five years. What you do will prevent the fall of Taiwan and war with China."

Silence followed as neither man spoke. Finally, Drew looked at the agent. "Finn, come sit next to me."

A surprised Finnigan got up, walked around to the next row, and sat.

"Look," Drew said, "when my mother first told me she would die of cancer, I was fourteen and didn't know what to think, especially when she said I would have to become a man sooner than I should. But after she was gone, I soon learned I had to make certain choices about my life. Choices only I could make. My first big decision was whether to join the military or aim for college. Pat De Luca, my father, introduced me to a retired admiral who counseled me and spoke to a U.S. senator, who nominated me to attend Annapolis."

Finnigan's entire demeanor changed as Drew spoke softly. The Irishman seemed to understand the young man was opening up to him. The agent's shoulders relaxed and his facial expression softened as he leaned closer to listen.

"In the following year, I visited several colleges just to make sure a military career was the way to go. After a lot of thought,

I decided to attend Santa Clara University, a private Catholic school in Northern California. There I learned how to fulfill the promise I made to my dying mother: To serve my fellow man and treat all people equally, with competence and compassion. I chose the law as my vehicle to help those in need. Thus, Finnigan, I have to decline your offer. I am a lawyer and I will stay a lawyer. I leave your type of service, though necessary for mankind, to people like you."

"Drew, you said Pat De Luca was your father. You know that isn't true. Your real father didn't die as your mother said. He is alive. Do you want to know where he is right now?"

"Wow, wait a minute. How in the world can I trust anything you say, especially about this? You've played me this whole time."

"Hawke, I'm being truthful."

A long pause followed as Drew stared at Finnigan, looking for some sign the man was telling the truth. Drew was the first to speak, but somewhat haltingly.

"Assuming . . . you are right . . ." Drew cleared his throat. ". . . about what you say, you wouldn't tell me this if you didn't want something."

"Obviously, I need you to help Katherine."

Drew's face flushed as he clenched his fists. "I thought so. Shit, man," the young lawyer yelled. "You are one mean son-of-a-bitch. No. No." Drew shook his head, obviously disturbed. Then he seemed to regain control.

"Good try. But Pat has always been the father figure in my life. As far back as I can remember he has been there for me. Most important, Pat has shown me, through the way he lives, what a man should be. No, Finn, a father is more than a sexual act that helps create you. He's the man who is always there when you need him. That living example of what you can be and should be. So, Agent MacIntosh, your ploy won't work. Pat De Luca is my father and always will be. No deal. Get someone else to help you and Katherine."

Finnigan rose and reached into his pocket, then extended his hand. "Here . . . this is a special battery extender for your phone. If you insert it into the charging port on the bottom of your cell phone, you will not only have more battery life, but it allows you to call me anywhere in the world."

"Why do I need this?"

"It's not a ploy, Drew. It makes your phone a non-traceable cell phone. Push the star key and it will automatically dial my phone wherever I may be. It's my way of saying thank you for opening up to me. I respect that. If you ever need my help, call. Especially if you change your mind and want to meet your biological father. There will never be any strings attached."

Drew took the extender from the man. He squeezed it tightly. After Finnigan left, he set the device on the pew and started to go to confession, then he paused and went back. He looked at the device, shook his head, and picked it up.

No one waited to enter the confessional, although it was occupied. As he walked toward the door, his thoughts turned to his need to confess how wrong his decision was to not report Nathan Pansky for murdering his father and rejecting Finnigan's plea for help. A cold chill came over him. *Was I being truthful with the agent? Or did a streak of cowardice rise up within me?*

The door to the confessional opened and a woman exited. Drew stepped in, closed the door behind him, and knelt. A small panel door slid back, exposing a vague, dimly lit image of Father Joseph O'Connor.

"Bless me, Father, for I have sinned. I may have gone against the word of God. I think I broke my promise to him."

"And how is that?"

"I know a young man who killed, and I decided not to report him to the police."

"And why did he kill?"

"He killed the man who raped him and later was raping his younger sister."

"I see. Murder is a horrible crime and against the laws of man and God."

"Yes, Father, no matter how justified such a killing may be."

"To many, Drew, human law means revenge: an eye for an eye. So, if you kill you must receive some sort of severe punishment no matter why a life was taken."

"Yes, sir. Otherwise, vigilante justice will prevail. As a lawyer I swore to uphold our system of laws, a system that seeks to prevent an individual's emotional act of revenge. I failed my duty to the law when I decided not to report the man."

"Why did you hesitate?"

"I don't know exactly. But I think I might have acted the same as he did if it was my sister being raped."

"And how did you break God's law?"

"Thou shall not kill, Father. By my not reporting him, I assist the young man in his horrible deed of revenge."

"Drew, man's law is similar to God's. But in many instances God's teachings are far more forgiving." A silence followed as Drew bowed his head in thought. Then Father O'Connor continued.

"Remember Apostle Matthew's recanting in his Sermon on the Mount where he talked about Jesus's teachings to the gathered faithful?"

"Yes, sir."

"Christ said, 'Do not think that I have come to abolish the law or the Prophets. I have come to fulfill them.' Jesus went on

to say, 'You have heard of an 'Eye for eye, and tooth for tooth.' '"
But without hesitation, he quickly added, 'Love your enemies
and pray for those who persecute you for God causes his sun
to rise on the evil and the good, and sends rain on the righteous and the unrighteous."

"Father, I don't understand."

"Drew, Jesus died on the cross for our sins. His Holy Church
hears confessions and grants communion to sinners every
day. And, like God, the Church recognizes humans are frail
and act out of emotion, many times to the detriment of others
and themselves. Your job is not to sit in judgment. The Lord
will do this. Your task is to use the law to fulfill your promise
to make sure all people are treated equally."

A. J. Hawke Returns

Look for the next challenge A.J. Hawke faces as he comes to grips with the revelation that his father is still alive and the turbulent emotions this brings to his efforts in his pursuit of justice.

ABOUT THE AUTHOR

Donald E. McInnis is a California litigation attorney and the author of the fictional legal thriller series A.J. Hawke, Attorney at Law. Hawke is a young defense attorney practicing law in the Gaslamp Quarter of San Diego, California, where he finds himself embroiled in cases involving murder and power politics.

Early in his career, Mr. McInnis served as a Research Attorney for the California Superior Courts. Later he became a Deputy District Attorney for two different counties in Northern California and a Deputy Public Defender in San Diego County.

He has also served as a Superior Court Judge Pro Tem, has been an arbitrator for the American Arbitration Association, and a referee/arbitrator for the California Superior Courts.

BOOKS

- *She's So Cold: The Stephanie Crowe Murder Case—A Defense Attorney's Inside Story,* Second Edition (true crime)
- *The Sphynx Murder Case—*A. J. Hawke, Attorney at Law (fiction)
- *Return of the Sphynx—*An A. J. Hawke Legal Thriller (fiction)
- *Blood of the Father—*An A. J. Hawke Legal Thriller (fiction)

LEGAL TREATISES:

The Initiative Process:

Money & Politics, Citizens Initiative: Who Shall Govern, Santa Clara University Law Review, Volume 59, Issue 1, Fall Edition (2019). Also available at:

https://digitalcommons.law.scu.edu/cgi/viewcontent.cgi?article=2868&context=lawreview

Criminal Law:

The Evolution of Juvenile Justice, From the Book of Leviticus to Parens Patriae: The Next Step After In re Gault, Loyola Law Review, Volume 53, Number 3, Spring Edition (2020). Also available at: https://digitalcommons.lmu.edu/llr/vol53/iss3/1/

Children and the Law: Time to Fulfill the Promises of Miranda and Gault, The Dartmouth Law Journal, Volume 19, Issue 1, Spring Edition (2021). Also available at:

https://dartmouthlawjournal.org/article/28217-children-and-the-law-time-to-fulfill-the-promises-of-miranda-and-gault

Website: https://donaldmcinnis.com